The Place Where We Belong

The Place Where We Belong

R. K. MAYER

To my parents

Who can always see what is already there

Prologue

One of my earliest memories is from third grade. We are at the playground. Dana and I are skipping rope. Her red pigtails bounce as she jumps up and down. We take turns with the rope. She is so small and skinny that when it is her turn, she has to bunch up the rope so that she doesn't trip all over it. Mattie and Josh are waiting impatiently for us to finish jumping. We have promised that in the second half of recess, we will play catch with them. Seven and a half precious minutes of running all over the playground.

"Hey ginger mouse." Two kids march up to Dana, and intercept the rope. "Hey Dana mouse." They grab the rope and rip it away from her. Dana has a look of fear on her face. This is not her first encounter with these kids.

I indignantly march up to the bigger of the two boys: he is a tall blonde boy with flashing brown eyes. "If she is a mouse, you and your friend are both mouse shit," I say to the kids, right in their face, not caring that I am not considerably bigger than Dana, and that I am certainly outnumbered by the two formidable boys. "Is she your body guard, Dana mouse?" asks the other boy, and he shakes his skinny long fingers at my quivering friend. "Grab her," he says to his friend. The other one grabs me by the arms. "Let me go, you bully," I say. "Run Dana, run . . ."

"You can't get away, Tamara" says the one locking my hands behind my back, "not this time."

"You don't have to hit me," I tell him defiantly. "I will faint because you stink so badly."

"You little bitch," he says and grabs me even harder. "Hit her," he calls to his friend. It is only a matter of time before some part of me will be bruised or bleeding. But I don't care. I continue to struggle to resist and to get free. I close my eyes tightly and brace myself for the blow, but it doesn't come. I hear shouting and sounds of struggle, some of them my own.

I can hear scuffling and movement. But I can't hear Dana. I hope she has run away to get a teacher. I am still struggling to break free, until suddenly, I can feel that no one is gripping me anymore. "Tamara, it's OK. You can open your eyes now. They are gone." I slowly open them. Josh and Dana are standing next to me. Dana puts her hand on my shoulder. She stands on her tiptoes and whispers in my ear, "Thanks, Tamara." The two bullies are running off towards the other end of the playground. Mattie shouts after them: "Pick on someone your own size." He turns to me. His pants have a rip in them and his arm is grazed. He grins. "Well, what are you waiting for?" he asks. "Catch me if you can . . ." and he turns to run. Josh, Dana and I laugh and go off in hot pursuit.

Chapter 1

I don't care how old you are, where you are from, or what your profession is, I think humans have one thing in common: the need to belong. I am no different. It's not so much a dependency; it's more like an instinct. Despite human evolution over the past million years, we still remain pretty tribal. With me, the need to belong conflicts with the fact that – as my friends say – I am "all angles and edges." I don't fit in anywhere very easily. I don't try to be this way; I just am. I think this was what David initially found so attractive. He was so trapped in making people like him, being acceptable and acquiescent, that for him, I was a breath of fresh air. I was someone who could tell the electrician not to bother to come inside since he was late, or someone who was not scared to tell his parents that *no thank you very much, but we will not be coming to dinner.* In many ways, I was able to say and do things that he couldn't. He allowed me to become his mouthpiece, at first in situations of conflict and then in uncomfortable places, and then more or less all the time. Suddenly he realized that he had lost his voice all together. I guess that over time, my directness became less and less charming for him and more of a burden – a reminder that his own voice was sublimated. Until one day, it wasn't anymore.

So at the age of twenty-eight, I found myself newly divorced and wondering what to do next. I don't know if there is a code book for the newly divorced, but the gravitation to the tribe was stronger than anything that I can remember. To not be alone. To be out on the market. Single again is like having the scarlet letter "A" branded on your forehead: Alone, Anguished, Awkward . . . not belonging to the tribe, on the outskirts of civilization. So I grew out my pixie short hair, bought a few new pairs of jeans and tops to herald in a new era, and went to live in that infamous city of singles: Tel Aviv.

It is the usual crowd at Josh and Karina's. They are of my original tribe, sometimes more family than my own. My angles and edges fit perfectly within our intimate little circle. Josh, Mattie, Dana and I go back all the way to elementary school. Then we all went and grew up and life just happened, as it is wont to do. Josh met Karina in the army and they got married and already have a couple of kids. Mattie was almost married, but didn't go through with it. His fiancé was part of the group for a while, as was my David. David and I divorced around the time that Mattie didn't tie the knot.

David and I met at the university, in the first lesson of the first semester. We became inseparable from that moment. Mostly it was just the two of us, but sometimes, we made a formidable triple with Iris, another fellow student with whom we bonded. She was at least ten years older than we were. Already divorced once, with a young child and husband number two in tow, who looked like he was about to become history. She was totally badass and cool. She was more sophisticated and experienced than either of us. David and I were wowed and somewhat in awe of her. She spoke about sex like she knew what she was talking about and had a way of making people shift a bit uncomfortably in their seats.

David was the Boy Scout, the golden boy whom everyone loved. I was the mirror, the one who reflected what she saw without filters and without sugar coating, the one whom you kind of wanted to avoid. Iris was the beast, with no inhibitions and no concerns about improprieties. We called ourselves "the Good, the Bad and the Ugly," in that exact order: David – the Good, me – the Bad, and Iris – the Ugly. When David and I divorced, it was clear that he wanted to relieve himself of being quiet and acquiescent and *good*. He felt that the only way he could do that was to shed himself of our threesome and of the extended group of friends that he had inherited when he married me. He needed to find a new crowd, people who would not know him as David – the Good. It was a relief actually, having things back to how they used to be – almost.

Iris and I have remained close all these years, and I brought her into my little intimate circle of friends. She hit it off with everyone, including my best friend since forever: Dana.

Tonight, Dana has come alone, just like me. She is technically not married, but that is only because gay marriage isn't legal in the state of Israel. Dana has been with Aviva for longer than any of us can remember. They met in the scouts. Aviva was Dana's scout troop leader and what began as a beautiful friendship developed quite a few years later into a serious relationship with kids, a home in the suburbs of North Tel Aviv, one dog and three cats. Aviva is an honorary member of the group, but she is way too busy for our social gatherings. She is a hi-tech executive who travels all over the world selling something to do with bio-med, not sure what, just that it is likely to save mankind from some type of global medical catastrophe. She visits customers in medical facilities, labs and hospitals all over the world, and when she comes back, she always brings us weird, wonderful and exotic treats: chocolate-covered wasabi from Japan, cheese with worms growing inside of it from Italy, alcohol made from beets from Slovakia – the stranger, the better.

It is Friday night. We are sitting around the table. Karina and Josh are up and down all the time, between the kids' room and the kitchen, but the rest of us are used to this and are enjoying ourselves. Iris is entertaining us with her latest adventure. "So I was sitting in this meeting with a colleague of a colleague. He's a new guy in the office. I was supposed to be giving him training, explaining to him all the ins and outs of our infrastructure, so that he could be given his first assignment. And, as I was standing at the white board, sketching him an architectural diagram, all I could think about was what it would be like to sit on his lap. He looked so strapping, like he could bench press me," says Iris.

"Tell me that you didn't act on that," laughs Mattie.

"OK, that is what I will tell *you*," says Iris, "but to the others, I will say something completely different."

"No," says Dana.

"No way," I gasp. "You sat on his lap? Iris, you are a monster."

"My dear child, since when do I *only* sit on someone's lap?" retorts Iris with a snort.

"Where do you find these people?" asks Dana with a shudder.

"What are you talking about, Dana? Iris *is* 'these people'," laughs Josh.

"You are incorrigible!" I say.

"Not incorrigible, not at all. And take a lesson from me: it's time that you started to sit on a few laps as well," she tells me. I shrink lower in my chair. Here it comes. The usual diatribe about not being alone. Even from within my intimate group of friends. I know Iris is talking about a hook-up and not a long-term relationship, but still, I roll my eyes and glare at her. "She isn't ready," says Mattie. "She will do it when she's ready." He is sitting next to me and he squeezes my shoulder.

"Who are you to talk?" Iris says with a laugh. "When is the last time we heard something from your neck of the woods? Are you even dating?"

"I date," says Mattie defensively, "I just don't spill my guts to everyone like you all do."

"All of us? Nothing to spill here." says Dana. Josh calls out from the passageway, "Nothing to report."

"Zero from me," says Karina, from the kitchen.

"No lap sitting with the baby?" says Iris to Josh and Karina.

"Yeah, I remember those days." Dana nods nostalgically.

"That's not what we said!" says Karina stepping out of the kitchen. There's plenty of that and then some," and she blows a kiss to Josh.

"All of you are hopeless," says Iris, gesturing to Dana, Josh and Karina. "You are all suffering from a terminal case of chronic fidelity. Makes me sick." We all laugh.

"You, on the other hand, my babies," she says, gesturing to me and Matt, "I can still save the both of you. I can help you find what you are looking for." Mattie and I look at each other, eyes open wide. "Yikes," I say, "the monster has awakened."

"Oh boy," he says with a laugh.

"Don't worry," I say, "I will protect you." Mattie puts his hand on my leg and squeezes hard.

I am about to leave. I give Josh and Karina a big hug and say thanks. The others are still lounging about lazily and chatting, but I have had my dose of company for the evening.

"Bye guys, I got to go," I call out to the others.

"What's your hurry?" asks Dana. "Tomorrow's Saturday. Don't tell me that you're working."

"No way. No work. I just need a break from you lot. That's all." I say.

"Aaaah, always so delicate and refined, our Tamara," says Iris.

"That's me. Too much socializing. Must. Go. Sit. In. The. Dark."

"But I haven't given you a lap to sit on yet," says Iris. "My little black book is full."

"Next time," I say and slip out. I need to get out. I need some air. Even if it is the stifling air of a hot Tel Aviv evening.

I start to walk down the street. The air is so muggy that my clothes stick to me. I can't wait for this heat to let up.

"Tamara, wait up." I turn around. It is Dana.

"Hey Dana."

"I know you would like some alone time, but I need to get some stuff from that market next to you anyway, before I head home. Are you OK that we be alone together?" She gives me a shy smile.

"Sure," I say and I mean it. Dana and I go way back to kindergarten. She is someone that I can be quiet with. We proceed into the silent buzz of the night.

We walk three blocks down the boulevard from Josh and Karina's place towards the edge of the city, where I live. The streets are by no means quiet. They are choc-a-bloc action and activity. But we just walk quietly, each with her own thoughts. "What do you need at the market?" I ask her as we approach the entrance.

"Well, Aviva wants some of those dried mangoes and kiwi that you brought her the last time you came to us."

"I could have bought that for you, silly." I said.

"I know. I just wanted an excuse to hang out a bit. It's not like I have anything specific to say or anything, but well, you know, I just wanted to check in and see if you are OK. It has been a while since David, and I know you are OK. But, maybe Iris hit a chord tonight. It has been a while, since, well…"

"Well…?"

"Well, you are enjoying watching me squirm, way too much."

"Well…?"

"I just want to make sure that you are not lonely."

"Me lonely? That's funny. All I need to do is snap my fingers and I can have men swarming around me."

"Sounds delightful," says Dana. "You must teach me if I ever decide to switch camps." We laugh. "Listen, I am OK. I just need…" I pause.

"I know, I know, space, time and continuum. Whatever."

"Well yes, but actually, I guess what I was going to say is that I am lacking direction. I don't really know what I am doing. I mean, I already had a nice guy and I lost him. And you know me…"

"Yes, all angles and edges. Listen, you did have a nice guy, but he wasn't the right nice guy for you. Maybe you should take Iris up on her offer?"

"Iris was not offering to find me a nice guy. She was offering to find me a nice—"

"Well good night then," Dana cuts me off abruptly. I laugh. We hug, and part at the door of the supermarket.

Chapter 2

The next morning, I am woken up by the sound of my smartphone ringing. I try to ignore it by putting the duvet over my head. *Quiet, quiet, quiet, please be quiet,* I will the ringing noise to stop. But the ringing becomes more and more incessant. I pick up the phone. It is Iris. "What do you want?" I croak. "It is the crack of dawn. Leave me alone, you evil woman."

"Good morning sunshine."

"Not morning, and no sunshine. I need my beauty sleep."

"Nonsense, you are especially gorgeous when you haven't slept and are all grumpy. Now get out of bed, shower, and meet me for brunch at the port. There's this new place that I heard about that makes a brunch like every other place in the area."

"So if it is nothing special, why are we going there?"

"So that you can insult the people there my dear. I know how much you like to pick a fight."

"I do not."

"Do too."

"Oh forget it. Whatever. Wait, *why* are we going there?"

"The owner is a friend of a friend, and I want to introduce myself."

"At least now I have the truth."

"You can learn a thing or two from me. I'll send you the address. Now move it. See you there in an hour." She hangs up. "Wait—" I say, but the line is already dead.

I stumble out of bed and start getting myself ready. I have a quick shower. I pull on some comfortable leggings and a t-shirt and sandals. I stand at my window overlooking Rothschild Boulevard and take a few minutes to drink some tea with lemon, ginger and honey. The warm drink fills me up. I hold the mug with both hands, and watch the passersby.

All the regulars are already outside: the early birds who

have been up for hours cycling or running or swimming, or doing all three. They are sitting on benches drinking some freshly-squeezed fruit of the season: oranges, pomegranate or some ghastly mixture with kale or spinach. The Goth teenagers are in the kiddy corner, hanging over the sides of the jungle gym, comparing tattoos and piercings. The young kids play among them, darting in and out, not caring a bit if they have to climb over them to get to the top of the monkey bars. There are some elderly folk, in wheelchairs and walkers, with Filipino caregivers talking among themselves in Tagalog. I stare out the window, taking it all in. This has been my morning ritual ever since I moved to the city. I am not yet used to Tel Aviv. I can't say that I love the noise and the pace and the density. But, what I do love is that there is no judgement here. Everyone has a place. Everyone can belong.

I am at the Tel Aviv Port. Iris is already seated at a table. An attractive man is looking over her shoulder at the menu. He is smartly dressed with a button-down shirt and neatly pressed pants and good leather shoes. He is smiling at Iris. He has great teeth. "Hey babe," Iris says to me, as I seat myself. "This is Mike. He is new in town, all the way from the States."

"Hi Mike." I say, "Welcome to the country, I guess." I look away. I am not big on small talk. He says hi and thanks. "Mike is friendly with Dmitry; you know my ex-…" I can see her looking for a word. You can hardly describe Dmitry as an ex-anything. His phone number is still used frequently on Iris' speed dial. I nod discreetly. "Mike, Tamara here is into saving humanity from itself. Despite that, she is single and a lot of fun."

"Iris," I say gasping, "what are you doing? I am sorry; I think that Iris is a bit confused," I say to Mike. "I am *not* on the menu." My voice is stern and raised. Mike laughs. "It's OK." He directs the comment to me. "Dmitry warned me about her."

"What's going on?" says a familiar voice behind me.

It's Mattie. "Absolutely nothing, except Iris," I say.

"Iris, what have you done now?" asks Mattie with a smile. He pulls his wallet and keys out of his back pocket and puts them on the table and then sits himself down between Iris and me.

"Well, enjoy yourselves this morning," says Mike graciously. "And," he continues, turning to me, "incidentally, just in case you *are* ever on the menu, please do let me know." He walks off towards the kitchen. My face goes hot and red. For once I am speechless.

"What was that about?" asks Mattie, pulling a face in Mike's direction. "Wow, babe," says Iris to me, "look at that; even with your pathetic attitude, and dressed like a vagrant, he is still interested in you." I look down at what I am wearing, confused for a second.

"Iris, that was unacceptable. You will not do that to me again."

"Or what?" says Iris. "What will you do? I have decided to make it my mission to help you."

"No thanks," I tell her emphatically.

"Iris, leave her alone already," says Mattie with a mixture of amusement and annoyance.

"Both of you, my dears," Iris says looking directly at Mattie.

"What? Me too?" asks Mattie.

"Yes, my dears. Like I said last night, it's time for Auntie Iris to help you both get out of this rut that you have found yourselves in. You two are clearly too dense to get yourselves out by yourselves. So, consider this an intervention." Mattie and I look at each other.

"You hold her down and I will hit her," I say to him.

"That sounds good to me," he says. Naturally, we don't really mean it. Or maybe we do – just a bit. Iris laughs. "Come now. It will be fun. I will be your disciple, your guru. You will call me master."

"Listen, Iris," says Mattie, "as tempting as that sounds, I think I am out."

"Lesson number one:" Iris declares, "is never say no."

"Never say no," I say, "Iris, that's horrible, terrible, awful advice."

"I'm listening," says Mattie. "Let her finish."

"No you are not," I say to him. "Come on Mattie, we are storming out of here indignantly."

"Really? Indignantly. I don't think I know how to do that," he says.

"I'll show you how." I stand up, letting my chair scratch the floor and screech, as I push it back. I throw my napkin down on the table. Mattie dramatically does the same.

I walk around the table in the direction of the exit. Mattie follows me. "See you around, bitch," I say to Iris. I throw back my hair as if it were a long flowing mane, and I walk out. Mattie copies me, action for action, including a full-on falsetto and an imaginary hair fling, and follows me towards the door.

Iris just laughs and waves, "*Arrivederci* and *adieu* – see you my dears."

On our way to the car park, we grab some food to go. I get a muffin and freshly-squeezed orange juice, and Mattie gets an espresso and a brownie. The promenade is teeming with activities of all sorts. Rollerblades and skateboards speed past families, couples and dog walkers. A thousand photographs are being taken every second. We walk along the sea for as long as we can, until we need to turn off towards the car park where Mattie is parked.

"Never say no," Mattie chortles. "Classic Iris. That sort of advice can get us into a lot of trouble."

"It sure can," I say. He stops in his tracks and turns towards me.

"You know you shouldn't feel bullied by anyone to start going out. You always do things in your own good time. That's just your style."

"That's true, I say. "Thanks for your understanding. Maybe I am not ready yet."

"And you shouldn't be in a great rush. I almost rushed into

a marriage and that would have been a huge mistake."

"Yes, what a pair we make," I say. Mattie reaches into his pocket for his car keys. "Oh hell," he says, "I must have left my keys at the restaurant. Now I have to go back to the lion's den. Coming with me?"

"No way," I say. "Sorry, buddy, but you are on your own."

"Thanks a lot," grins Mattie, "I thought you vowed to protect me."

"Not this time," I say and head off towards home.

20

Chapter 3

It's Wednesday and I am at the Nest. I am there almost every day, including weekends and holidays. The Nest is a safe haven for teenagers from broken or economically downtrodden families. The program offered by the Nest guides these kids – or *Nesters*, as we call them – through their high school years: exactly at that critical turning point between getting lured into life on the street or sticking to the straight and narrow. The former option offers a spiraling web of vandalism, crime, drugs, alcohol and destitution. The latter guides them towards gaining support within their family unit – no matter what their personal and familial circumstances may be. The Nest focuses on enabling essentially good and smart kids to overcome their circumstances. It encourages and expects the Nesters to become productive members of the Israeli society and all that that entails: getting a high school diploma, getting called up for military service, continuing studies and/or finding gainful and legitimate employment.

The pressure on these kids is tremendous, and the Nest does its best to fill the gap, where parents and teachers cannot. To enter the program, these teenagers must have good grades, recommendations from their schools and approval from their parents. For some children, these standard conditions are insurmountable obstacles in themselves. Once the children are accepted, they have a place to come to after school. They eat a hot meal, even two if they stay late. They have volunteers to help them with their homework. They have a buddy whom they can talk to, bookshelves overflowing with books, a quiet corner for downtime and even a pair of slippers that they can slip into as soon as they step in the front door. I have been at the Nest for three years now. I basically run the place. It is my job to ensure the smooth flow of all operations: suppliers, permanent staff, volunteers, donors. I am also there for the kids, the Nesters.

The Nest and I are a good fit. I studied sociology and criminology in college, so the concept of easing kids into finding their way in the world just makes sense to me. Fitting into society – or not fitting in – are essentially two opposite sides of the same coin: one's sense of belonging and worth inherently influences the side of the coin that will face up. With my natural tendency to isolate myself, to keep my circle of friends small and my communication style direct, I feel like an interloper between the two sides. I know which side of the coin I need to root for, but I have pangs of sympathy for those kids who are teetering on the edge. Up till now, the Nest has felt more like an academic pursuit or a spiritual vocation than a job. To a great extent, it is about socialization – in the best possible way – not in a creepy "Big Brother" way. If society can be reverse-engineered and the Nesters can be socialized to stick to the right path, perhaps I might figure out how to fit *myself* in.

During the course of my studies, I was required to do some volunteer work. At first, I had a hard time settling down and I wandered from place to place. I started volunteering with the elderly, and moved rapidly from there to a center for the blind. Then I did a stint in a correctional facility. From there I worked in an animal shelter, and finally, finally, just as my supervisor was about to give up on me, she sent me to an organization that picks up runaways from the street. Some of these kids are doped out, others have emotional or mental issues and all of them are victims of society in one way or another: abused, misused, discarded and spat out, by family, friends or strangers. I stayed with the organization until college graduation and, frankly, would have continued, but the owner of the organization, Adam Stern, an investment banker and philanthropist, called me into his office and asked me to manage a new project of his – the Nest. It was my first proper job – my first paying job – and the transition was absolutely seamless and natural. Besides which, I absolutely love it, at least I used to. The hours aren't standard. The kids are complicated. Even the staff members and volunteers are not your run-of-the-mill folk; you need to be hard core to work here. There is no question that despite my normative family with its relative warmth and economic stability, I feel a certain empathy and kinship with these kids. And here, my distance and my sharp tongue are imperative. You cannot mollycoddle and mother this group. They earn my respect and I earn theirs. They know that I am tough, but fair.

I have a little office. It is tiny and has a bookshelf, a desk, a printer and a chair. When people meet me in my room for a serious conversation, I produce a collapsible three-legged stool from under my desk. When a kid just pops in to say hi or to ask a question, I have a few throw pillows that I lay on the old tiles and we sit cross-legged like Buddhas on the floor. I try to give each child some time alone with me, at least once every two weeks. For instance, just yesterday I sat here with Noa, a lovely kid with a lot of potential and even ambition, even though – like most of the other Nesters – nothing is simple for her. Noa is finishing school at the end of this year. She is a good kid with steady grades and a positive attitude. Like all the kids here, this was not always the case. Noa used to be the queen of truancy. She would wander and roam the streets of Tel Aviv, not wanting to be stuck with her younger siblings in their little apartment – both parents worked long and hard hours – and not wanting to be at school, which frankly bored her. She never acted out. She was never rude or obnoxious or abrasive. She just didn't do homework, and came to school only when she had to take a test. Incidentally, she had consistently good grades. The Nest gave her the framework that has allowed her to keep up with the school work required by the system, and it has even enabled her to tutor others, so that she has remained challenged.

When I think again about the conversation, I can almost feel Noa's frustration and confusion: "I don't know what to do," she says. "I am doing really well at school. No issues there. I will graduate and I will probably get really high marks." I nod and wait for her to continue.

"The problem is with the army. I have gone through all the required tests and interviews, and I have already been assigned to a unit. I have a call-up date and I feel like I am all ready." She sighs and continues, "The thing is, well, the thing is that my parents have other ideas. My father says that seeing as I am about to leave school, I should get a full-time job and do my bit to help the family. My mother is apologetic, but she says that they can't afford for me to be away from home and not contributing financially to the household in any way. I understand them. I really do. And I want to help out and take responsibility." She sighs an even bigger sigh and then pauses for a few seconds. "But on the other hand," she continues, "what about the army and the training that I will get there – surely that will enable me to get an even better job than anything I can get now? What about higher studies? If I find a job working in a shop or a restaurant now, I will not be able to aim for something bigger. What about the fact that you and the Nest also have expectations from me? I am expected to go to the army. So I either disappoint my parents, or I disappoint you. I know I am rambling on here, but there is one more thing I want to add. I know it is selfish to even think this way, but what about me? What about what I want?"

I nod my head thoughtfully, waiting to see if she is done talking. I think to myself what an amazing metamorphosis this child has gone through. When she began in the Nest two years ago, her grades were good, but she was all over the place. Apart from the truancy, she ran away from home a couple of times. She was frustrated, angry and lost. *Look at this amazing kid,* I think. *Look at her confidence, her ambition, her desire to learn and grow, and to do something significant with her life.* Noa has come a long way and her dilemma is real. I need to consider her situation from two main angles: should she place the needs of her family before her own personal desires? Should she choose basic employment now to supplement the income of the household, or study in order to achieve long-term employability?

When I am sure that she has finished talking, I clear my throat and begin to speak: "Noa, never mind that as a Nester, you are encouraged and expected to go to the army. Putting that aside for just a minute, you raised an important point: what is it that *you* want?"

Noa looks at me with her big, translucent eyes, slightly dazed by the impact of what I have said. Some of these kids never get over being asked that kind of question. It is emancipating and confounding at the same time. The old Noa would probably have sneered or mocked the sincerity of the question. But this new, mature young woman takes a few seconds and then says, "I need to think about it. I am not sure. All I know is that I feel stuck between a rock and a hard place. No matter how I look at it, I will just disappoint someone."

"You have a bit of time before you need to make any decisions," I respond. "I have a suggestion that sounds very simplistic and easy, but it's not. How about, before you jump to any conclusion, you try to figure out what you really want to do. At least then you will be able to put your whole self into figuring out how to get there . . . and I will be here to help you."

"I will do that," says Noa, with a sigh.

"All right, so let's catch up again next week and see what progress you have made," I say.

"Sounds good to me. Thanks," says Noa.

Just as we begin to wrap up our conversation, Perry, one of my more senior tutors comes rushing in. "Tamara, come quick. It's Eran. He's threatening Avi with a knife." Within seconds, I am up and out of the room.

I run to the back of the apartment where Eran and his math tutor Avi are supposed to be studying. Sure enough, Eran has backed Avi into a corner and is standing, pocket knife in hand, with a menacing look on his face. "Say you are sorry, you worthless piece of shit," threatens Eran, angling the pocket knife. Avi, who is himself just a high schooler, is trying to be brave but I can see that he is scared. His hands are up in a defensive position over his face. "Perry," I say calmly, "get everyone out the room quickly and quietly." Perry nods solemnly and starts to shepherd the remaining Nesters and tutors into the kitchen without a sound. The room empties within seconds. A strong sense of intense calm and concentration envelop me.

"Say you're sorry!" Eran snaps.

"I, I . . ." begins Avi, but the words refuse to come out.

"Eran," I call out. Eran turns to look at me when he hears his name. He glares defiantly at me.

"Everything will be OK," I say to both of the boys. I walk up to them slowly, my hands stretched out in front of me.

"He called me stupid. Avi said that I am stupid." Avi makes a noise somewhere between a groan and a cry. Eran turns back to him angrily.

"Eran," I say, "put down the knife."

"I am not stupid," he says, facing Avi.

"I know that," I say talking slowly and calmly, "I know you aren't. That's why you *must* put down the knife."

"Not until he says he's sorry." He waves the pocket knife again and Avi cowers further into the corner. He is now practically crouching on his knees.

"He *will* say that he's sorry, but not while a knife is pointed at him. Would you believe his apology is genuine if you force it out of him? Let him apologize to you because he wants to, and because he means it, not because you are threatening him."

Eran looks from me to Avi, his face locked with tension. Several long seconds pass. Avi stands up, shivering with fear, his eyes shut tight. "Look at him, Eran, look at what you are doing to Avi. Is this what you want?" I focus all my energy on willing Eran to come to his senses. "You are smart. You know that. Avi has been here for you for months now, helping you, helping others. Think about it." Eran starts to nervously shift in his place. "You are in the Nest because you are smart, because we see that you have potential. Do the right thing." I say.

"He called me stupid. I am not stupid!" Eran swipes the air with his knife.

"No," Avi cries out.

"Eran," I say, "listen to me. Think about what you are doing. I believe in you. Put the knife down." After several long seconds, it finally happens: Eran slowly begins to lower the pocket knife. His hand is tremoring. As he lowers the knife, I can feel the tension in my body begin to dissipate, like a hissing balloon. Avi also melts from his deep freeze and leans his head and shoulders against the wall. I maintain my composure and clear voice. "Put the pocket knife on the table next to you," I say. "I am going to take it."

Eran nonchalantly throws the open blade on the table. I walk over, pick it up, fold it shut and put it in my pocket. I stand between the two boys, like a bridge between two cliffs. I put one hand on Avi's shaking shoulder and one on Eran's.

"Now," I say, "Avi, you go first."

"I am sorry," he begins. "I didn't mean to say you were stupid; I just meant to say that you are not looking at the exercise correctly and that means you are not able to solve it properly. I really am sorry. I know you're not stupid. But—" he begins...and I stop him mid-sentence.

"No Avi, a genuine apology never has a condition in it. No buts."

"I am sorry," says Avi.

"Now," I say to Eran, "it is your turn to apologize."

"Me? He's the asshole."

"Eran, you pulled a knife on another person. Heaven knows if you would have actually used it. But that is unacceptable. It is unacceptable in the Nest and it is unacceptable in the world at large. So now you need to take responsibility and apologize." Eran huffs and puffs, but reluctantly spits out, "I am sorry, OK?" It doesn't feel absolutely genuine, but it takes all his energy to make the apology. Sometimes one has to accept what one can get.

With the situation now diffused, I say, "OK, you are both

finished with mathematics for the day. Avi, you can help Gali with economics instead, if you don't mind. She is in the kitchen with the others." Avi nods, relieved, and walks off to find Gali. "Eran, you are done here for the day. I would like you to take ten minutes to relax and breathe. Listen to music or read, and then head on home. Tomorrow, we will talk some more, the two of us, about what happened today and we will discuss the consequences." Eran nods his head and goes off to the quiet corner of the Nest. Situation neutralized. All the Nesters slowly get back to what they were doing before. This is by no means a regular occurrence in this tiny warm safe haven, but it is not the first time that we have had a crisis and it will not be the last.

I go back to my office. I would love to close the door and put my head on the desk and think, but I took the door off the hinges a long time ago. It was meant to be a statement that I am always available and accessible, but also that I am always connected to what is going on in the rest of the house.

Eran is a hard nut to crack. Instinctively, I feel that this is a good kid, a solid kid. I know that there was story of abuse at some point. Now there is an absent father, and a mother who is doing her best to support herself and Eran's siblings – all four of them. She is a good person, but there is no doubt that she has her hands full. Eran is the youngest, the only boy, with very few guidelines and instructions, and with almost no curfews and restrictions. He has the affectations of a spoiled child, the prince of the family, along with residual baggage from his period of abuse. Add to that general hunger, fatigue and lack of boundaries, and you have one angry kid. I am doing my best to rein him in, take care of him and set him on his way, but I would be lying if I said that I was absolutely certain that I can succeed. Absolutely nothing is certain. Of that I am sure.

I feel exhilarated by the incident – by the whole morning,

in fact – unable to sit down, unable to concentrate. It is hard to get back to the bureaucracy and spreadsheets after such an adrenalin rush. I have a graduation ceremony to plan. The year is more than halfway through. But I am incapable of processing details now and my thoughts are bombarded with feelings of self-congratulations and self-doubt. OK, so I talked Noa *up*, and I talked Eran *down*: I *neutralized* him. That's great. But, what is my role here? Am I like a meat grinder and it is my job to process the kids until they get to the right consistency? Who am I to do that? Who am I to decide what the right consistency is in the first place? Who am I to determine that any grinding should take place? Maybe society needs some hamburgers and some steaks? Maybe I am not meant to make Eran pliable and lean? Maybe it's OK that Noa isn't destined to be anything more or less than her parents are? They are honorable people. Maybe their roles in society are pre-determined, and that is the way it should be? All my successes and failures in the Nest are a mix of bitter and sweet, and it is getting more and more confusing.

That afternoon, Kobi, another Nest manager, comes charging into my office with a look of unmitigated contempt. I guess that he has just been updated about that morning's excitement. Kobi is good at his job; I will give him that, but he makes no bones about not caring for me. He asks me to come downstairs with him for a cup of a coffee. I know what that means. I reluctantly comply. We make something hot to drink and walk down three flights of stairs to the building entrance. There is a dilapidated old bench in front of the building. The bench is usually occupied, sometimes by a homeless man who wanders the neighborhood, sometimes by a Romanian caregiver and an elderly lady with Alzheimer's – out to get a bit of fresh air. Today it is empty.

We take a seat. I can see that Kobi has a lot to say. I can feel his tension. "Don't you think that we have taken enough crap from that kid?" he says, not mincing his words. "I say that we have tried hard enough with him and that now we should cut him loose. Did you call the police?"

"Kobi," I say, "I know that a red line was crossed, but I would like to give him another chance. And no, I did not call the police."

"You are making a huge mistake. Look at the bigger picture. What if next time he *does* stab someone and we knew about his tendency to pull knives and didn't do anything? What about the Nest? An incident like this could destroy the Nest. Don't you care?"

"Kobi, I understand what you are saying. But this is my decision."

"And it is a bad one. I don't understand you. You are so tough all the time. And now, you choose to be soft? Eran pulled a knife. He shouldn't be given a second chance. You are wasting your time, and mine. That kid will end up in jail anyway. You and I both know it. He cannot be controlled. What are you waiting for, for him to actually hurt someone?"

"That will not happen." I say emphatically.

"You don't know that."

"I can't be sure of anything. I am not naïve; I know that he needs more discipline, and like I said to him, there will be consequences for his actions. But as far as I am concerned, he is not a hopeless case." My heart beats faster. The phrase *wishful thinking* flashes through my mind. Maybe I am lying to myself? I push away the thoughts and continue to respond to Kobi. "Listen. Everyone has an obstacle that they need to get over. We all do. You and me both. I want to go out on a limb for this kid, because I believe in him."

"Well, that's very noble of you, and very stupid. For the record, I think you are making a terrible mistake, and I intend to tell Adam."

No big surprise there, I think to myself. Since when do Kobi and I agree on anything? "Well, then," I say to him, "I think that you *should* tell Adam. You should definitely do what you think is right. This is my decision and it is final. Frankly, your opinion has been heard and over-ruled."

"Like always. Right? Tamara does what Tamara wants."

"If it makes you feel better, then *yes*. Can you deal with that?"

"I have no choices, do I? When this blows up in your face, I will come and tell you I told you so."

Kobi stands to show me that he is done talking. We trudge up the stairs in a tense silence. Tiny dust clouds rise and settle with every step we take. I make a mental note to check with superintendent of the building to see if the person hired to clean the stairs has quit again. I go back to my office and finish my report about the event, including Eran's profile, background, a description of the event, how I handled it, and what I intend to do as a next step. With a reluctant sigh, I add Kobi's point of view. I send it off to Adam. Maybe Kobi is right? Maybe I am just kidding myself? Who is to say that I can do anything about anything?

I text Adam:

```
Hi, I sent you an incident report to your email.

Let's discuss in our next sync.

Not urgent on my end.

Let me know if you have questions
```

I don't receive a reply from Adam until much later, when I am already home.

```
Read the report.

Sound serious.

Sounds like you have it under control.

Give me a call if you need to talk.

We'll catch up at our regular 1:1
```

It's nice to get support from Adam. Now, if only I could obliterate Kobi's voice buzzing in my ear and believe wholeheartedly that I am doing the right thing.

Chapter 4

That evening, I catch a cab and make my way to suburban *Tsahala* – an affluent neighborhood in North Tel Aviv – to Aviva and Dana's lovely home. Aviva is at home for once. The kids, twin boys Roy and Amit – eight years old – and Yael, a gorgeous little red-head who is on the shy side of six years, join us for dinner and then retire to their rooms to do homework or play computer games. I have a soft spot for Yael. She reminds me so much of Dana when we were that age.

We adults head out to the Zen garden with a bottle of Sake that Aviva brought back from her latest trip to Japan and some macaroons from the local, rather snooty bakery, run by some graduate of *Le Cordon Bleu* in Paris. The Zen garden is one of my favorite places in the world. Dana has been practicing yoga for years and when they bought this place, Aviva designed it as a surprise for her. It is an enclosed and secluded area, but it has a little pond with Koi fish darting back and forth. On a grassy embankment next to the pond, there are rocks of various sizes that you can lean against or perch on. The garden is lit with subtle lighting and also has a well-used swing chair for two. Dana is a yoga instructor, but her students aren't brought to this area: it is her private space. She teaches in the basement when the summer days are too hot, or in the main garden when the weather is reasonable. This place is reserved for the family, and honorary family members like myself.

We are lying on the grass drinking wine and eating dessert and I am relaying the events of the day. I am exhausted, so I keep it short, not getting into too many details about how truly terrifying the experience had been. "Poor Avi," says Dana when I am all done. "He must have been scared out of his mind." She shivers. I have a mental flashback of Dana on the playground being pushed off the swings. Aviva puts her hand on Dana's leg; she must realize what Dana's thinking too. "My heart goes out to the other kid actually," Aviva says. "Think how troubled he must be to resort to a knife in order to make himself understood. Think about how many times he must have been told how stupid he is, before he decided to stand up for himself. Someone needs to reconfigure him. He needs to be reset to factory default and then to be reassembled."

I smile. Aviva is so geared to the world of technology and bio-med that even her metaphors are taken from there. "Well," I tell her, "we humans are funny that way. We can't really be reset – to wipe the slate clean – because we have hard drives and memory that never let us forget. But how awesome would that be," I say, thinking to myself of the many things I would like to will away. "My problem is that I don't know what to do with him. Obviously, my job is to support him and to help him to learn to move forward. But what about discipline? What about punishment? I am supposed to discuss this with him after the weekend. I haven't a clue where to begin."

Aviva and Dana are silent for a few minutes. The sound of Koi breaking through to the top of the pond travels in the air. "I don't know about discipline, but is there perhaps a way that you can show Eran the potential consequences of his actions? I mean, to discuss what might have happened had he gone through with it?" asks Aviva. I think about what she has said.

"Actually, you may have something there," I say in response. "I actually might have an idea that could work."

"What does Adam say?" asks Dana.

"Adam supports me whatever I do." I say. "He trusts me. Kobi, you know, my second-in-command, says that I am making a *huge* mistake and that I should kick this kid out on his ear: *do not pass GO, do not collect two hundred dollars . . .*"

"Is this the same Kobi that has been itching for your spot for over a year now?" snorts Aviva. "What a shit stirrer!"

"Well, maybe he is right," I say.

"And maybe he is an arrogant ass who is only interested in his own agenda," says Aviva.

"Besides which," says Dana, "Adam has your back."

"I suppose he has my back unless something terrible happens."

"Which it won't," says Dana deterministically. "Adam is lucky to have you."

"So is Eran," says Aviva. "He just doesn't know it yet."

"Thanks," I say, "Maybe you are both right. I'm not fishing for compliments or anything, but let's be honest. I am not the most well-adjusted person myself. You and the others are about the only society that I mix with. Maybe I am not the best judge of character? Maybe I am sorely mistaken about Eran's potential?"

"So you are a bit anti-social or shy, or *not well-adjusted . . .*" says Aviva. "So what? Do you need anything else? Are you lacking something? Do you feel the need to start folk dancing or join a tennis club? What is so maladjusted about your life, anyway? I have work and family and that's enough for me."

"It's the David thing, isn't it?" asks Dana.

"Well sure it is. I am not even talking about finding a soulmate or a partner, or procreating because my biological clock is ticking. I assume that I will eventually want those things, but for now, I just feel like a big, fat failure – like I torpedoed myself. All I want is to feel like I can fit in somehow. I am too comfortable being by myself. It is becoming easier and easier to shut everyone else out. I haven't made a new friend since before I got married. I feel stuck. It is easy and convenient to be stuck, but I know it is not the right thing for me."

"Firstly," says Dana, "I think that blaming yourself is ridiculous. We all liked David; he was a good guy, but he is equally accountable for your breakup and his role in it."

"But maybe if I were different it wouldn't have . . ."

"We wouldn't want you to be different," interrupts Dana assertively. "We want you just as you are." Aviva smiles and nods. Her wife's fierce devotion to her best friend is touching.

"Secondly, listen, you said you wanted to try to get out there a bit, so why don't you? Iris offered…"

"Iris…" I snort, "Iris would turn me into a geisha if she could. You should have seen her on Saturday."

"We heard," says Aviva.

"You did?"

"Yes," says Dana. "Mattie called Josh and Josh told Karina, and Karina was here for yoga yesterday."

"She was unbearable, practically tried to hook me up with some random guy that she had just met at the restaurant." Aviva and Dana laugh.

"She wouldn't do that, not really. She must have heard about him, or known of him through a friend. She would never set you up completely blindly," says Dana. "Besides which, whatever she did seems to have worked, because Mattie enjoyed his date on Monday."

I stare at her. "*Huh*? What's that?"

"Oh, I thought you knew. He met someone at the restaurant and they hit it off. Weren't you there?" I wrack my brain, but can't remember anything other than our dramatic storming out, the walk on the promenade, getting some food to go, and then parking at the car park. And then I remember. "Oh that's right, Mattie left his keys in the restaurant so he had to go back and I didn't go with him. That's when he must have met her." I have this weird feeling in the seat of my stomach. "Oh well," I say brightly, nonchalantly – "good for him."

"Absolutely," says Aviva. Dana gives me a thoughtful look. I lie back on the grass, and stare out into the Milky Way and wonder what it must be like to be a star looking down onto Earth. Does the earth look like a remote loner from the perspective of one of the billion stars in the path of the Milky Way?

Chapter 5

Eran is waiting in my office when I get to the Nest the next day. He is sitting on a stool and tapping his leg impatiently. This is a good sign. He knows this is a serious conversation.

"Good morning Eran," I say.

"Avi was wrong yesterday," he blurts out. "Avi was very wrong. And it made me mad." I say nothing, just take my seat behind my desk. "It makes me so mad when people say that to me. It really makes me want to break things. To smash things up into a million bits and then stomp on the bits and scatter them all over." His voice is getting higher and faster – his breathing, more rapid.

"Why does it make you so mad?" I ask him.

"Because, it isn't true. Duh."

"If it isn't true, why does it make you mad?"

"Because he thinks it is true."

"But you know that he is wrong."

"Yes, of course. I don't think he's wrong; I know he's wrong."

"So what do you care if he says it?"

"Because if he says it to me, maybe he will say it to someone who doesn't know me and then everyone around me will think that I am stupid and they won't know the truth."

"So what? If they don't know you, what do you care what they think? You are also entitled to think things about people you don't know. It doesn't make it true."

"You are just trying to confuse me," Eran says, "and that makes me feel stupid."

"Listen," I say, "we both know, that you are an intelligent person – you wouldn't be in this program if you weren't. As an intelligent person, you need to learn to practice restraint. You need to realize that for whatever reason, being called stupid is a trigger for you, and you need to be able to control your reaction to that trigger." Eran nods his head. He is listening intently. "I want to add something equally important – there will always be triggers and there will always be catalysts to our anger, fear and suspicion. Your reaction to these triggers cannot be to pull out a weapon, not just here, not just among people who know you and are here to work with you, like Avi – but also outside in the big bad world, among people who don't know you, who may have heard that you are not clever, or nice or trustworthy. That reaction will land you on the wrong side of the tracks in the best case scenario, and in prison in the worst."

"So maybe that is not such a bad thing! At least I would have some respect."

"Respect is overrated when your freedom is taken away from you. You are here because you are smart and people care for you. If you pull a knife like you did yesterday, you have no right being here. It shows a lack of respect for this place, for the people around you, for *me*." Eran hangs his head slightly. His fingers tighten around his thighs.

"You are a good kid," I say, "but this is a one-time mistake. There are no second chances."

"I suppose this is where you punish me," says Eran. "What's it to be?"

"No," I say, "no punishment. Unless you count making another calmer, more mature apology to Avi. The two of you need to talk. You scared him yesterday." I open my backpack, pull out my smartphone, and search for a number in my Contacts List. I scribble the number on a Post It note. "After you and Avi have sat down and talked, call this number and ask for a guy named Joseph. Tell him that I gave you the number and that I would like the two of you to meet him. Whatever help he asks for, you must comply. Before you go, I will leave a package for you to give him. Don't worry, it won't be heavy."

"Who is he?"

"You will meet him and he will explain."

"What's in the package?"

"If he wants to, he can show you."

"Why are you doing this? I don't need Avi. I don't need Joseph. I don't need this place. I can do everything on my own. I don't need anybody."

I sigh. "Have you heard of the expression *No man is an island*? Well it doesn't matter if you have or if you haven't. I really do empathize. Believe me. It is sometimes much easier to do things alone. I also tend to prefer my own company, because it is easier and it is quieter. But unfortunately, the saying is true: we cannot always do things because they are easy. If this were the case, we would be all pulling out knives or guns on people all the time. We need to find a way to make a niche for ourselves in society among people, even if it means that *we* have to make the effort."

"But why? Why do I need to do that?"

"Because the reward of being together, of being understood, accepted, supported, loved and remembered is so much greater than going from ashes to ashes without making an impact or without leaving a mark on anyone in your lifetime. You are not insignificant dust. You are more than that."

"Why do you care?" he asks.

"Two reasons. One, because I have to. It is my job. Two, because I happen to believe in you, and want to see you succeed." Eran gets up slowly, heavy with contemplation. He eases himself to a standing position. *This is no longer a kid; I think to myself; this is a young man.* He looks at me directly in the eyes, nods his head once, and walks out.

I want to believe that he will be OK. I want to believe that we all will be OK. *No man is an island,* indeed.

I reach for my phone and search for Iris' details. I text her:
```
OK, I need help.
```
```
When can we meet?
```

The message is sent off to that fantastical cyber postal cloud and I can see that Iris has read it on the other end. She types and the message pops up on my screen just seconds later:

```
Babe. Luv u

2 nite @ Terry's

dress like a girl
```

She adds an icon of applauding hands and two multi-colored hearts.

Chapter 6

Terry's is one of the oldest bars in the city of Tel Aviv. On the one hand, it has old-world charm – pictures of Tel Aviv, the White City – from a time where all you could see were dunes and sea, and low, stocky buildings like blocks of Lego. On the other hand, the clientele is a mixture of the most diverse cross-section that Tel Aviv has to offer: from diamond merchants, investment bankers and old timers who have lived in these parts forever, to hipsters, immigrants with Russian accents, refugees from the Sudan and the most colorful members of the LGBT community. Terry's is a leveler. Everyone is welcome. It is not a pick-up bar. It is a place to go with friends. The furniture is made of warm red leather and the tables are rustic looking butcher-block slabs on top of copper legs. Iris was wise to choose this place. I have come – not on the defensive, ready to ward off unwanted suitors – but with an open mind to listen to what Iris has to say. That is not to say that I completely trust her. That would be a mistake. I know her too well.

I get there before her, which is not surprising, because she is chronically late. Most people in this country are. Time is relative here. It is one of the things that I resent about society in general. I sit at the bar, and the bartender comes up to me. There isn't actually a Terry anymore, although there used to be. The bartender introduces himself as Alon. He is a clean-shaven and orderly young man, probably around nineteen years old. I briefly wonder whether he is one of Terry's blood relatives. He looks rather young to be running the bar.

"What are you having?" Alon asks.

"Please give me a red wine." I say.

"Would you like the house red, or something in particular?"

"Yes, that would be fine. The first one I mean." Clearly I

am not a connoisseur. He doesn't push me. I appreciate that.

While I wait for Iris, I sit at the bar and think of nothing in particular. There is a quiet and comfortable buzz. People are doing their own thing and there is no expectation of intermingling or working the crowd. It is a social bar for anti-social people like myself. When Iris does saunter in forty-five minutes later, it is like a gust of wind blasting in. That woman knows everyone. The business men fawn over her, the LGBT crowd give her adoring looks and cat whistles, and the hipsters, more nonchalant, call out:
"Hey!"
"How are you?"
"Call me."
Iris has an answer, a hug or a greeting for absolutely everyone. Like a true social butterfly, she flits in and then flies off. I can see that she has scanned the room to find me and is making her way in my direction. I give a nod of acknowledgment and turn back to the bar. I know her: she will come when she is ready. There is no use to even imagine that I could rush her. A few minutes later, we are all hugs. "Hi Iris. That is some entrance you made. Is there anyone who you don't know?"

"This city is a tiny pond, my dear. I am just a big fish," she says with a grin. And then she continues, "Tamara, my darling. This is not what I meant when I said dress like a girl." I am wearing blue jeans, sandals and a black t-shirt. Iris is wearing a sheer top under which you can make out a lacy bra. She is wearing skinny white jeans and high heeled sandals. She has her peroxided white hair up in a high pony tail. She has bright red lipstick and eyeshadow. She's my friend. I think that she's gorgeous, but I will never dress like her.

"Was that my first lesson?" I ask her. "Because you may as well flunk me now."

"No way babe," she says. "First alcohol, then school time."

"Alon, my darling. I cannot believe how handsome you are. Your dad must be so proud. Is he here tonight?" Alon blushes. I have never seen a bartender blush before, but that's the effect that Iris has on people. "Hey Iris. No, he isn't here tonight. We haven't seen you for a while. Do you want the usual?"

"Yes," she says. "That would be divine."

"I have been coming here for years," she tells me. "His dad," she says, beckoning to Alon, "used to be the one behind the bar. I came here with my first husband, that louse; my second husband, the deadbeat; and soon, I will come with my Roni. Just three more years till she is legal. This, my dear, is the place I bring people I love – or have loved."

It makes sense, I think to myself. "Awww thanks," I say to her. "I love you too."

"Yes babe," she says, "that means you."

Alon mixes her cocktail with cherries, arak and vodka. It is a powerful mix that even Iris needs to nurse carefully. "Thanks darling," she says. "When you see that this is empty, please send over some light beers for us."

"Of course, Iris," says Alon.

"Come, let's go," she says to me and I climb down off the barstool and we head to a little corner booth.

Once we are seated, Iris doesn't waste any time, whatsoever. She picks up from our last conversation, which I so abruptly stopped before it began. "Rule number one," she says dramatically, "is never to say no." I give a weak smile and remind myself that I contacted her for help this time, and not the other way around. "What I mean by that is that it is all in the attitude. If your state of mind is *no-no-no*, you will either find yourself with similar people of a negative persuasion, or else you will find yourself alone."

"But what if the person is an absolute jerk? Or what if I really, really don't think there's any potential? Why should I waste our time?"

"My dear, I am not trying to help you to find your soul mate – the one who wants you 'warts and all'. I have no doubt that you already know what you want. Right now, I am trying to get you back into the sandbox – to help you to find a playmate."

"A playmate?"

"Yes, and to find a playmate, you must be open to the game. You need to be able to imagine the possibility of making new friends. You, my friend, walk around with a *no-fly* zone around you. You shoot down people who enter the zone, whether they are friend or foe. All I am suggesting is that you buffer your guns. Before you shoot, consider the impact on yourself. Imagine the possibility that someone entering the zone might actually be welcome after all."

"I guess that makes sense," I say. "A bit militaristic, though. No-fly zones. Guns. Not quite my scene."

"I will leave the yoga metaphors to Dana. Besides which, I am kind of dating a pilot at the moment."

"Now I understand," I say with a smile. "I suppose I could try. Although there is the question of opportunity."

"Funny you should say that," says Iris. "I have to go to this party next Saturday night, and I have already told them that you are my plus one! They are thrilled because they need more women."

"Is it a singles thing?"

"Yes and no. It is my friend's birthday party. He is single, but he is also inviting all his friends and their respective partners." I pull a face. "Don't worry," Iris continues, "it isn't an intimate thing. It is his fortieth and he has hired a DJ, so it will not be a bunch of people sitting around and sipping wine in someone's lounge."

"I think I can handle that," I say. "I think I can."

"Excellent,' says Iris. "I will be there with you, every step of the way."

Chapter 7

The week passes uneventfully, despite the clouds of troubled thoughts that waft in and out of my consciousness. As the days go by at the Nest, Kobi continues to send furtive and critical looks in my direction. On Wednesday afternoon, he joins me for the last twenty minutes of my sync meeting with Adam, and his consternation comes pouring out like a torrential rainstorm.

"Eran's going to screw up, we all know it. We need to get him out the program now."

"No he isn't going to screw up Kobi," I say, "We have discussed this. We have to give him a chance. This incident is a turning point, a wake-up call. It's an opportunity for him."

"Adam, this is a mistake," implores Kobi. "They are so close to graduation and a foul-up of this magnitude is more than just a major indication of a problem, it is more than just another hurdle. It is grounds for not allowing him to graduate the program."

Adam remains silent, but I don't. "It is *because* we are so close to graduation that we need to give Eran the benefit of the doubt. No one believes in these kids, especially when it counts most. Eran needs us to believe in him."

"At what cost?" demands Kobi, "at the expense of our volunteers? Our sponsors? Our relations with the community?" After much deliberation, Adam supports me and the matter is closed, yet again. Kobi's eyes flash with irritation. More as a means to change the subject than to break the tension, I briefly raise the question about this year's graduation party. "We need a theme," I say, "an activity, something interactive that everyone can enjoy."

"What are you thinking of?" asks Adam.

"I am not sure," I answer, "I haven't really done any brainstorming yet."

"Any ideas, Kobi?" Adam asks.

"Maybe a few, nothing I want to share just yet," Kobi says gruffly.

"OK, then. Tamara, let's continue on for a few more minutes. Thanks, Kobi, for your time." Kobi grunts something and leaves my office in an indignant huff. Once he is gone, Adam says to me, "Are you sure that you are handling the Eran thing properly, Tamara? This is a big deal, and it *is* serious."

"I am sure," I say to Adam, "I am quite sure."

With those words, we say our goodbyes and the conversation ends. I know that I am not really sure. How could I be? There are no guarantees for anything. There are just a few more months before this group graduates from the Nest and goes into the army. At this point in the year, in previous years, I have been energized and motivated, but instead, right now, I felt like my batteries are running dangerously low.

Chapter 8

It is Friday morning. Typically, Friday is a quiet day at the Nest. It is usually the day that I catch up on administration. The kids are at school. There may be a volunteer or two who want to talk to me, or maybe, if someone finishes school early, they come by for some quiet time. There is no tutoring on Friday; the Nest becomes a quiet space to chill out. Volunteers are on call on Fridays and Saturdays. I am not on the volunteer roster; I am on call 24/7.

I am reviewing the volunteer roster at the Nest, making sure that we have no gaps. We have about forty volunteers. Some come every week, and others once a month, or even more infrequently. People do what they can. Some people find it easier to give money than to give time, and that's OK. But at my end, as the person who must manage it all, I do admit that it is a constant juggling act. Most of our volunteer tutors are students who are required to volunteer as part of their educational framework, and they have chosen to do that here instead of elsewhere. I wouldn't say we have an endless supply of help, but this is a relatively convenient place if you live in walking distance, and have a couple of hours to knock off every week. I can see that there is a gap for afternoon volunteers to cook lunch. I have a short list of grandmothers who will come at the drop of a hat. I give one of them a call.

"Hey Miriam, it is Tamara."

"How are you, dearie?" says Miriam, "do you need my help?"

"If you won't mind," I say, "I have bit of a situation on Sunday. One of my volunteers broke a leg and she is unable to make it."

"Do you think that they will ever install an elevator in that building?"

"I am afraid it is unlikely. We certainly cannot contribute to the payment, and most of the other tenants in the building are renters." The Nest is located in an old dilapidated building in central Tel Aviv, with a mixture of elderly people as well as, unfortunately, some unsavory types. We keep a low profile as much as possible, because not everyone is happy for us to be in the neighborhood.

"Anyway, would that be OK?" I confirm.

"Sure, says Miriam. "It has been a while since I came over. With pleasure."

"Thanks so much," I say, checking off that issue. One down. Now to call the plumber to fix the leaky faucet in the bathroom. Avi pokes his head around the door.

"Hey Tamara, I was hoping that you were here. Do you have a minute?"

"Sure," I say. "I am glad that you came by. Seeing as no one is here, let's go sit in the kitchen and have some coffee." I come out from behind my desk and lead the way. Avi is tall and kind of awkward around me. He follows me wordlessly. He is just in high school, but is already taking extra courses in mathematics and physics at the University of Tel Aviv. He is a good tutor for a subject that is not easy for most people to grasp. He is also a nice, gentle person. I make us two instant coffees. There are already some biscuits on the counter. I push them towards Avi but he shakes his head. "No thanks," he says. "Listen," he begins, "I came by to apologize to you."

"What for?" I ask.

"For the incident with Eran."

"Why are you apologizing?"

"Well, because it was my fault. I didn't have patience with him. I said something stupid. I was the stupid one." He looks out of the kitchen into the far corner of the apartment – towards the exact place where he was accosted by the knife-wielding Eran. "I was thinking," he continues in a voice a bit louder than a whisper, "that maybe this is not a good place for me to volunteer. Maybe I'm not tough enough. I am like a red flag to a bull with people like Eran. He can smell my fear. I have done my best up until now, you know, treading lightly, and I still managed to screw things up."

I wait a few seconds to make sure that Avi has finished. And then I begin. "Listen, I accept your apology if you want to apologize, but to put it bluntly, I am not letting you go. You may have hurt Eran's feelings, but his reaction was disproportionate: completely and to the extreme. Despite this place being called the Nest, it is not a warm, cushiony place. It is a place where we help to prepare these kids for the real world. In the real world, people lose their patience and say things that maybe they will regret. That's because they are real people. Just like you and me. Mathematics and physics are important for the Nesters, but learning how to behave, how to react … that is beyond critical; that is about survival."

"I hear you, and I accept that. But what if he pulls a knife again? What if next time you aren't able to stop him? At the risk of my pride, I'll admit that I am scared. I don't want to disappoint you, or leave you in the lurch, but every time I step into this place, since last week, I feel like I am suffocating with fear."

"Fear is not something that you should have to live with. At least not fear that can be eliminated by you not being here. I understand that. I can't force you to stay and I can't make any promises that if you stay, things will turn out as they should." I take a deep breath. "I also don't want you to stay if you are doing it for me," I say, a bit too forcefully. "You have no obligations to me and no need to do anything to make me happy."

Avi shakes his head distractedly. I respond, "What I do think is that you should consider what's in this experience for you. Can you spend the rest of your life avoiding people like Eran? Should that be an objective?" Avi tilts his head, deep in thought. "Eran is supposed to talk to you about an errand that I would like you to do together. All I ask is this: do the errand with him *for me,* and then make your own decision. A decision that works for you. OK?"

Avi nods. "OK. Fine." He gets up and leaves the kitchen, with the still untouched coffee steaming on the table. *I don't think that I handled that very well,* I think to myself. Maybe I am mistaken. Maybe it is wrong to push Avi to stay. He is scared, and rightfully so. Maybe it is a mistake to think that Eran can adapt and soften. Who am I anyway to think that I can change either of them? It is presumptuous, egotistical and selfish.

I go back to my office. My smartphone is flashing on the desk. There are three messages. The first one is from Dana:
```
Want to come over tonight?

It's just us and the kids
```

I text her back:
```
No, thanks

Rough week

Need time alone
```

She replies straight away:
```
OK, you can always change your mind
```

The next is from Mattie:
```
Call me

Speak later
```

I briefly wonder what is up with him and his new girlfriend. I will call him later.

The last one is from Iris. She sends me the address and the time of the party. And then a final sentence:
```
Darling, I beg of you, dress for a party,

not for trekking in the desert
```

Chapter 9

The next morning, I wake up early and go for a brisk walk to the sea. I charge into the water and swim out as far as I can, tread a bit of water for a while and then take a slow swim back to shore, languishing over every stroke. I stand ankle deep in the water, looking back out to sea. This is one thing that I love about living here in Tel Aviv: the welcoming stretch of the blue sea, the ease with which I can just go and swim, the soothing nature of the cool water. But I have a party to go to and an outfit to choose. I sigh and turn abruptly away from the panoramic view, bumping into a group of joggers who are making their way swiftly across the beach. One manages to avoid me and shouts rudely: "Watch where you are going." I collide with two others and the three of us fall onto the sand. "Dammit," says one and heaves himself up. He gives his friend a hand. "This totally ruins our time. Thanks a lot," he says to me. I ease myself into a sitting position. "Thank you?" I say. "All I did was turn around. You guys ran into me." But the jogger is already gone. The third one extends a hand to help me up. "Are you hurt?" he asks.

"I am not hurt, I am fine," I answer "But you should be more careful."

"I would argue that we all should be more careful," says the man, in accented Hebrew that sounds familiar. I look at him carefully this time. It is that guy from the restaurant. Iris's friend. Some English name, with an M . . . Marvin? Mark? "It's Mike," he says, as if he is reading my mind. "The name is Mike. We met the other day."

"Yes," I say. "Oh, I didn't recognize you at first. You know, dressed like this."

"You mean undressed like this. Yeah, the clothes are a work thing. For whatever reason, customers would not appreciate me coming shirtless to the restaurant."

"I can understand that," I say.

"So did you bump into me on purpose? Are you finally on the menu?"

"Don't be ridiculous. Of course it wasn't on purpose." Shaking my head at him, I wave my hand and start to walk off.

"Wait," he calls after me, "remind me your name."

"Tamara," I say and walk off towards home.

I get home, have a shower and wash the sand, shell fragments and sea smells off of me. I spend the next few hours trying to decide what to wear. I have jeans and more jeans and a bunch of sloppy, casual t-shirts. I would like nothing more than to call Iris and say that I am not coming. But I can't bear to tell her that it is about clothes. She will make me go shopping. So I call Karina.

"Hi," I say.

"Hey, Tammy," she says, "We haven't seen you for ages. What's up?"

"Well, listen," I say. "This is totally embarrassing, but I am going to a party tonight with Iris and she has threatened me that I need to dress up, and I just can't find anything suitable. Can I borrow something from you?"

"Are you kidding? Of course it's OK. I would love to dress you up."

"You are not getting a blank check, you know."

"Sure, whatever. Just come over. If you come in the evening, I will make you up as well."

"No way. Not going to be a painted lady."

"Everything is relative; a little color never hurt anyone."

"There's always a first," I say. "See you later."

"See you!" says Karina with laugh, and then she adds: "This is going to be such fun!"

"For you maybe, but for me, it will be excruciating."

"Thanks a ton! You asked me for help."

"I know, I know. I am just being difficult."

"Wouldn't have you any other way." said Karina, "except maybe with a touch of make-up."

"Ciao," I say with a sigh. Karina sounds way too enthusiastic. But at least I have one friend who understands this sort of thing.

At eight thirty in the evening, I walk over to Josh and Karina's. It is a lovely clear evening. In fact, it is a perfect evening. I try to recall why I am ruining it with a night out. I ring the intercom in the lobby. "It's me," I say into the grey intercom. "Come on up," says Josh and beeps the door open. I take the elevator to the third floor, where the door is wide open. It is quiet in the house. The kids must be sleeping. I go into the lounge and sit myself down. Karina peers around the corner. "Nadav just wants a good night kiss from you."

"OK. I'm coming." I get back up and walk into Nadav's room. It is a spotless pastel blue space. I wouldn't mind resting here for a while. "Hey monster," I say bending down to him, "need a kiss from your favorite aunt?"

"Yes," he says and buries his head in my neck. I give him a massive monster kiss with fake growling and a big bear hug. "Have wonderful dreams about me," I say. "If not, I will have to come back and give you a monster hug." He giggles and lies back down. Karina comes over and says in a stern motherly voice, "And now to bed. See you in the morning. All monsters out." Josh is in the doorway. The three of us sneak out and close the door most of the way. We go to sit around the breakfast table in the kitchen. Josh gives me a kiss on the cheek. "Hey, Tamara," he says. "Joshua," I say using his formal name with a smile. No one ever calls him that. "What's up?"

"Nothing with me," he says, "unless you're asking me about mortgage rates."

"Not tonight," I say. He picks up a dish towel and starts to dry the dishes on the drying rack and put them away piece by piece. "Anyway, it sounds like you have more exciting things to talk about than us old folk."

"What is this party tonight?" asks Karina. "Are you meeting a date there?"

"No, not unless you count Iris as my date. It is her friends. She wants me to practice meeting people."

"Is that what you want?" asks Josh, looking up from the sink.

"I am not sure," I say. "It's not like I have to have someone in my life at the moment, but I do realize that there is a fine line between not wanting and avoidance."

"Do you think you are maybe avoiding meeting people?" asked Karina.

"To be honest, I am not sure whether I am not interested, unmotivated, or just scared. I know people divorce every day, and so far as divorces go, mine was uncomplicated: no kids, no property; we both got back what we brought in. But I do feel burned by the experience. You know, if two people like David and I – who got along, liked each other and loved each other – could split, then perhaps expectations of future relationships are completely unrealistic? I mean, how can I possible hope to find something better than what I already had?"

Karina and Josh look at each other. And then look at me. They have both known me for a very long time. That is a lot of sharing that I have just done. Quite unlike me. "Sorry," I say, "not what you were expecting from me? I am not feeling like myself lately."

"I think Iris is right," says Karina. "Your aim for now shouldn't be to find your next serious relationship. It should be to put yourself out there and to, you know, well, practice."

"Could be fun," says Josh with a grin.

"Sure," I say. "I guess it could be. But I would rather be at home than going out."

"That's the avoidance rearing its ugly head," says Karina.

"Sometimes it's nice to get out. Who knows? With Iris there, it is sure to be fun."

"Yes," I grimace, "anything could happen."

"Let's go look at my stuff," says Karina.

"I guess I will finish up here," says Josh.

"Yes, don't dare show your face in the room," I say.

Karina and I go into the master bedroom. It is a stylish and impeccable room with a neatly made bed with silk covers and at least five throw pillows. Karina goes over to the side of the room and opens her closet. My mouth drops open with surprise. In stark contrast to the elegance and orderliness of her room, her wardrobe is bursting and bulging with stuff. As soon as she slides open the doors, at least four garments come tumbling out. This is not one of those wardrobes that you see in home styling magazines. To say it is a mess is a polite understatement. It is a huge shock to me. Karina is one of the most organized and well put together people I have ever met. This closet is space that belongs to a hoarder of the worst kind. Karina is completely undisturbed by the mess. She doesn't even notice my wide-eyed shock. In fact, she seems to know where everything is. She scans the closet and pulls out five or six clothes hangers. "Let's begin…" she says. "But before I give these to you, my assumption is that you are going to hate everything I give you. Even if I say that it looks nice."

I nod my head. "You are almost definitely correct."

"So given my assumption, this is not going to be a democratic decision. You will try on everything and I will make the decision. OK?"

I smile. Karina knows exactly how to deal with me. "OK," I say, "I will say thank you, but I won't pretend to like it."

Karina makes me try on five different dresses. They are almost all the same length – just above the knee – but each has a different style. The floral one she rejects immediately. I am glad because, despite our agreement, I would have had to put my foot down. Flowers and me are just not compatible. The navy one with the halter neck she puts aside as a possibility, even though the neck makes me uncomfortable. The red dress is figure-hugging and it shows way too much skin. I feel very uncomfortable and fidgety. I keep pulling it down. The black dress is plain and kind of nondescript. It is OK. She calls it classic. I call it mostly comfortable. The last dress is a plain maroon color, with a maroon diamond shape cut into the back. "I think this is it. This is the one," Karina says. "I can see you are not as fidgety with this dress as you were with the blue one."

"Don't you think I should just go with the black one? It is more comfortable and simple."

"*Naah,*" she says, "you can wear *comfortable* another time. This maroon one looks good." She helps me pull my hair back, gathers it up off my face. I am wearing these strappy black sandals, which she says are *good enough,* gives me just a slither of eye liner and eye shadow, and pronounces me *ready for action…*

By the time I step out the bedroom and into the lounge, it is time to call a taxi. Josh sits in the lounge listening to music in the background and reading a newspaper off his tablet.

When he sees me, he stands up and whistles. "Stop it, Josh!" I say, feeling downright silly. "Tamara, I just can't remember when you dressed like this, since, well, ever."

"Just tell her that she looks nice, you idiot," says Karina to Josh.

"You look nice, you idiot," Josh says to me and flashes a grin. "Just kidding. About the idiot part. You do look nice, seriously. The others are going to flip. Wait till Iris sees you." He fishes out his smartphone from his pocket. "No way," I say. "No pictures."

"Spoilsport," says Josh.

"Bye," I say, and walk out of the apartment in order to wait downstairs for the taxi. Just before I close the door, I turn around. "Thanks Karina," I say. She smiles. Josh continues to stare at me as I walk out of the apartment. It makes me smile. I can still remember him coming to school wearing his shoes on the wrong feet.

Chapter 10

The taxi pulls up outside Karina and Josh's building and I get in. "Take me to number six Sea Drive, Herzliya," I tell him. It is nine o'clock on the dot. The driver nods and gets back to the national obsession: listening to the news. Every hour on the hour. We drive silently, listening to the five-minute bulletin: every word in the news is sacrosanct. The windows are rolled up and the air conditioning is on. It is hot outside. When the bulletin is over, the driver sighs and eyeballs me from the front seat, trying to gauge my reaction to the news. He is probably wondering whether or not he can engage me in a lively discourse around the highlights – or the lowlights – of the news. Yet another terrorist attack – a stabbing at a Jerusalem bus stop, political bulldozing from all sides of the spectrum, whether or not additional budget will be found for health… education… national security interests… But I am not one who engages easily. The driver can see that my gaze remains steadily on the billboards, on the highway and on the car lights as they flash by. He is not bothered by my impoliteness. To each his own. There will be someone else to argue with after I leave the taxi. Instead, the driver lowers the volume of the radio, and allows the oriental music to fill in the empty space in which conversation has been denied. He sings softly, *sotto voce*, an Arabic melody that ululates in and out of the blasting air conditioning. A few minutes later we arrive. I pay him and say *thanks* and begin to step out of the car with a big sigh. For the thousandth time that evening, I have a moment of stabbing doubt that I am doing the right thing… even if at the very least, I have the proper attire. I *would* rather be at home. "Don't worry'" says the driver to me, "everything will be alright in the end…it has to be." I give him a little smile. This is the answer to the conversation we never had about the situation in Israel, the sentiment about the state of the world in general, and maybe, just maybe, this is the answer to my feelings of dread. Everything will be OK. It has to be.

The villa is located in a prime location just by the Herzliya beachfront. There is a buzzer on the door, but there is also someone standing at the entrance, ushering everyone in with a cocktail and a big smile. The place is busy but not packed. It is still too early. I rebuke myself for not coordinating with Iris so that we arrive at the same time. With my heart sinking in my throat, I realize that I am pretty much going to be on my own, knowing how Iris favors lateness and grand entrances. *This cocktail isn't going to be enough to calm my nerves*, I think, and I head over to the bar, which is currently the rocking center of the party. I have my empty cocktail glass in my hand, and I look forward to getting rid of it, and getting a tall glass of red wine to take its place. The dance floor is already choc-a-bloc with party die-hards and acrobatic showoffs who can't stop themselves. The bar has a Hawaii theme: floral garlands, waiters in beach shirts, fake palm trees and coconut decorations. Totally tacky. If they greet me with "aloha," I am pretty sure that I will walk out of here.

I make my way through an easily shifting crowd. No one takes the personal space thing too seriously. By the bar, the crowds are packed more tightly. However, no one seems to mind or even notice being gently pushed or moved aside. I redirect the crowds so I can make it to the bar. On my way, I catch snippets of idle chatter and people swapping details and anecdotes. I can also see old friends hugging and new friends exchanging numbers. In front of the bar, there are a few people who I need to move in order to make myself seen. "Excuse me," I say and gently squeeze in between two men. The one in jeans and a white t-shirt moves aside easily, moving someone else in the process. The other one, in black pants and a buttoned-down shirt, turns to me with a big smile and says "Well, hello!"

"Mattie," I say. I am so thrilled to see him – finally, a familiar face – that I throw my arms around him. "Tammy, I thought it was you from your voice, but when I turned around, well, you confused me for a second."

"Yes, well, Karina. This is her doing. It's stupid I know, but Iris said…"

"No, no, it's not stupid. You look… you look really beautiful," he says slowly.

"Thanks, man," I say, "you do too. I meant to call you back by the way. I totally forgot. I had a heavy week. Sorry."

"No problem," he says, pushing his hair out of his eyes.

"We can talk now," I say. "Thank goodness you are here. I thought that I would be all by myself. You know how Iris is. Always late."

"Yes," says Mattie with a laugh. "I do know, but actually, I am not here by myself. I am with Orit."

The girlfriend. "Oh, that's right." *I totally forgot!* I think to myself. "Right, of course, yes, Dana mentioned something."

"Actually, that's why I called. I wanted to make arrangements so that the two of you could meet."

Already? I think to myself.

"Now I guess is as good a time as any." Mattie continues.

"Sure, yes, absolutely, sure. Lead the way," I say with shrill enthusiasm. We leave the bar – without a drink. I deposit the empty cocktail glass on a random surface and make a mental note to find another cocktail soon, or else to make a second attempt to reach the bar. Mattie leads me to a side room where there is a group of people chatting in a circle. He breaks into the circle easily and effortlessly. The people make room for him, as if they are waiting for him. He guides me by the elbow, until I am more-or-less in the center of the circle. A place that I cannot tolerate being in. He knows me so well. He stands with me, his arm around me, so I am not alone. "Hey everyone, this is my best friend from school, Tamara." He goes through the group mentioning each person's name and a sentence about them. The hosts are among them. I am overwhelmed by the situation, and it is all a blur to me, except when Mattie stops at Orit. "This is Orit," he says. She is tall. Much taller than me, with curly black hair and dark eye liner and bright red lipstick. She is wearing a short skirt and heels and a black shiny shirt. She is pretty. I feel small and child-like next to her. She looks really mature and elegant. "Hi," I say to her.

"Hey," she says, "I have heard a lot about you."

I am unable to respond. I cannot lie, and I cannot do small talk. So I just nod. "It's nice to meet you," I say to her and can think of nothing else to add. Mattie nods from me to her and puts his arms around us both.

"Now," he says, "I will try again to go and get those drinks." He turns to me, "What were you going to order," he asks me, "a red wine?"

"No," I say, "a beer." Not sure why I said that.

"OK." He says, "Wasn't expecting that. Orit, Sangria?"

"As long as it doesn't have grapes inside. Yes, please." Orit answers.

"Coming up . . ." says Mattie and he walks off. I shift out of the center of the circle and fall in between Orit and another man. Orit says to me, "Mattie says that we must find some time to get to know each other."

"Yes," I say and I nod. "Perhaps we can go outside for a bit and talk," I suggest.

"Not now," Orit says, shaking her head. "Definitely some other time." I shrug and agree with her by nodding my head vigorously. *Where is Iris?* I think to myself. It would be wonderful if she would just magically appear. The man on my other side taps me on the shoulder. "Hey, I am Elon. We were already introduced." I nod helplessly. "Shall we go dance?" I weigh up my options: stand here awkwardly and not get to know Orit, or go off with Elon whom I just met and get away from this circle. It's a no brainer. "Sure," I say. "I am not much of a dancer, though."

"Neither am I," he says, "who cares?" I walk off with him. Thankfully, Elon isn't interested in speaking. We head in silence to the dance floor. We dance near each other, but not with each other. He moves and sways to the music, his feet planted solidly in one spot. I do my own thing. Hardly Fred and Ginger, but at least I am not standing awkwardly with a group of people who I don't know, and my best friend's girlfriend. Elon and I stay on the dance floor for another fast song. From the corner of my eye, I can see a flash of movement and I sense a change in the loudness of the room. *Iris must have arrived*; I think with relief. I am about to make my get-away from Elon so that I can join her when the music turns slow. I step forward to Elon to excuse myself and he steps in and puts his arms around me, pulling me closer. "One last dance," he says, "and then you can go." I say nothing. *Why not?* I can allow myself to enjoy this moment of intimacy with a complete stranger.

The song croons slowly on, and I can feel emotion building up inside of me, thinking that the last time I danced like this was with David on our wedding anniversary. I realize in horror that if I don't leave, I am going to burst into tears here, in Elon's arms, on the dance floor. My throat feels groggy and my eye lids heavy with tears. I refuse to break down here in front of everyone. "Elon," I say to him mid-song, stopping both of us in our tracks, "I am sorry, but I don't feel well . . . I have to go." He lets go of me immediately and we head off the dance floor, him slowly and cautiously; me, two steps at a time. I go as quickly as I can without making a scene or a disturbance.

"Tamara, babe, come here," I hear Iris calling me. I wave to her and motion that I will call her. "Tammy," I hear Mattie calling out my name, and I look in his direction. He is standing where I left him, one arm around Orit, the other holding the beer that he took for me. I can feel the tears ready to burst like an angry cloud. I wave to them and run out of the villa, past the couples only just arriving. Once I am outside, I finally burst into tears. *God. What a baby I am. I don't even want David, or miss him. What the hell is wrong with me?*

The sky is black and scribbled with stars. The noise of the air conditioning, music, people and clinking glasses is gone. The fresh air and the new-found silence wash over me and my tears begin to dry.

As I slowly recover, I realize that my phone is vibrating incessantly in my little purse. It is Iris. I cancel the noise and send her a text.

```
Sorry, didn't feel well.

Had to leave. Speak tomorrow
```

As I press Send, another message comes through from Mattie:

```
Are you OK? Where are you? I will come to you
```

I reply to him:

```
Thanks. I'll live. Just felt a bit sick.

Enjoy the party
```

He sends me a thumbs up icon. I can see that he continues to type away. But in the end, the typing stops and no further messages are sent. I walk from the villa all the way down the beach road towards the hotels on the beach front. From there, I hail a taxi and I head back home.

Chapter 11

The next day at the Nest, I am doing paperwork in my office. Miriam is cooking up a storm in our tiny kitchenette. Smells of couscous and soup waft through the apartment. She brings me some steaming tea with mint leaves, lemon and honey. "You look like you need this, sweetheart," she says. "Come and talk to me when you are done."

"I sure will," I say. "I just have to sift through some things before *rush hour*. Rush hour is when the kids come to the Nest after the school day is done. My phone rings. I don't recognize the caller.

"Hi," I say, "Tamara speaking."

"Hi Tamara," an accented voice speaks to me. "It turns out that I am more impatient than I thought."

"Who is this?" I ask.

"It is Mike. You rammed into me on the sand the other day on the beach." The guy from the restaurant.

"I didn't ram into you: we bumped into each other," I respond.

"Whatever. I am sure Freud wouldn't agree. There are no coincidences."

"I refuse to argue over this."

"Then don't, let's just discuss it like two adults. Over some ice cream."

"Ice cream?"

"You don't eat ice cream? That is going to be a problem for me."

"Of course I eat ice cream. Everyone eats ice cream."

"Good, so it's settled."

"What's settled?"

"We meet tonight at ten o' clock."

"Tonight at ten o' clock, I will be sleeping."

"You can sleep another time; tonight we eat ice cream."

"Don't you have a restaurant to run?"

"I don't have to be there all the time, but thanks for your concern."

"Have I given you any reason to think that I am interested in you?"

"None whatsoever."

"So why are you doing this?"

"I like a challenge. I like to break down resistance. So will you be there?"

"I don't know where 'there' is. I don't know."

"I will send you the address. See you later." Mike hangs up.

Iris. I think. Dammit. OK fine, so I didn't make it through the party. She is still schooling me from afar. My phone beeps, once, twice, then a third time. It must be Mike sending the address. What do I need to do to shake him off? I don't even bother picking up my phone to read the message. I just take a sip of my steaming tea, cupping the mug with my hands. As I am drinking the steaming liquid, Noa appears suddenly in the doorway.

"Hi," she says, "can I come in?"

"Sure," I say, "pull up a chair." Noa pulls out the collapsible stools out from under my desk and settles into it. "I have given this program a lot of thought" she says, "and why I am in it. What my parents want, what *I* want," she stresses, "and I have decided that what I would like is to go into the army. I think that the long-term gain for my family will be more beneficial than if I end my studies after high school and find a job for which I don't need any special skills."

I take a deep breath. This is great news. I am so pleased that she has made this decision. I allow myself to give her a fleeting smile. "I understand," I say.

"The thing is," she continues, "I am happy with my decision and confident that it is the right one, but I don't know how I should tell my parents and I was wondering if you could be there with me."

"Noa," I say, "of course. If that is what you want, then that is what I am here for. I will be happy to help. Let me call your parents and we will set up a date." Noa looks at me with intense relief. She exhales loudly. "Wow, that would be great," she says. "I am so nervous. I know that they are going to object."

"Let's see what we can do. Noa, I am so proud of you," I tell her.

"Thanks," she says with a big, shiny smile, elated at my compliment. "The decision seems so obvious now, but I have really been tossing and turning over this. It would be so easy to just give in and do nothing and not have to live with resistance from my parents."

Resistance. There it is again. I nod. *It is so much easier to do nothing* – I think to myself – *these kids are educating me.* "You are terrific," I tell her. "I will call your parents and we will figure this out."

"Thanks," Noa says, standing up and stretching. "That's great. Thanks so much." She leaves the room, a skip in her step. Moments like these give me a great sense of worth and purpose. I pick up my phone. Here goes. Ice cream with Mike. How bad can it be? There are two other messages, both from unknown numbers, and one from Mattie. The first one is Mike. There is an address, time and some text:

```
the path of least resistance is to just be there
```

Persistent fellow. I send him a thumbs up. It disappears into cyberspace with a heavy finality. I open the message from Mattie. It says:

```
Can we talk?

Please call
```

I don't have the time for this now. Probably wants a critique on his new girlfriend. I will call him later. I open the third message.

```
Hi. It's Elon

We danced on Sat night
```

Just wanted to check that you are OK

Do you want to meet up?

Iris. Damn her again. I get hot and flushed when I think back to last night. I dial her number, not even waiting to cool off. She picks up after the third ring. I don't wait for her to greet me; I just launch into an angry speech. "Iris. I can't believe that you are handing out my number to random people. You need to ask me first. We have discussed this. I agreed to your help, but not like this."

"Darling, you are on speaker. I am at the hair salon." I can hear the sound of air from the hair dryers and I can just imagine the ladies all listening in as they get their hair done.

"Iris, what have you done, you naughty girl? Do tell," says a voice from the background.

"You just focus on my hair," she says in response.

"I don't care where you are, or who is listening… you were meant to help me, not pimp me out." A chorus of gasps and *oohs* echo over the line.

"Darling, pimp you out," said Iris, "very harsh, but an interesting choice of words. Also, very dramatic, but I guess it is a phase you are going through. Disappearing like Cinderella like that – all doe-eyed and teary. What a grand exit! I couldn't have done it better myself."

"Did she also leave a glass slipper…?" asks a voice in the background.

"Nope, no glass slipper, and not at midnight," says Iris, and then adds dramatically: "leaving me, her fairy godmother, to face the music, all alone."

"Oh please Iris, give me a break." I say.

"Iris, poor child, perhaps she wasn't feeling well." chimes in another voice. "Maybe she had a bout of the flu?"

"Who are you kidding, babe?" Iris says with a laugh, "I don't know what was up, but it certainly wasn't the flu."

"Whatever," I snap, "that's not the point. What am I supposed to do? Both Mike and Elon are now sending me texts. It's too much."

"Two men! Wow!" sounds the peanut gallery.

"Who's Elon?" asks Iris. "Bravo, my cherub. Sounds like you don't need me after all."

"What do you mean *Who's Elon*? Don't play all innocent."

"My darling. Mike called me. He told me you met at the beach again. He told me you knocked him right off his feet and…"

"I did not knock him off his feet," I interrupt.

"Sure babe, whatever. Anyway, he wanted to call. So I gave him your number. If you have found someone else, I am thrilled, but I have nothing to do with that."

"Then who was it?" I ask her. And then I realize. *Mattie*.

"OK, whatever, never mind," I say, "I have got to go." And I abruptly hang up.

I storm out of my office and into the tiny kitchenette. Miriam looks at me and sizes up my mood within seconds. "My child," she says, "I find that there is nothing more comforting and therapeutic than chopping up vegetables. Here, take a knife." She opens a drawer and retrieves a simple, sharp knife. She makes room next to her at the countertop. I retrieve cucumbers and tomatoes from the massive bowl in which they are soaking in salted water and begin to chop away. We work in silent synchronization, and all my thoughts dissipate into nothingness.

The rest of the day passes uneventfully. I leave the Nest and when I am at home, after a quick and refreshing shower, I send a long, overdue, but polite text to Elon:

```
Thanks. I am better

Sorry I left like that. We can meet.

On call 24/7, so can't commit.
```

I hope he gets the message loud and clear. I am holding

him at arm's length. He types back straight away.
>   So am I.

>   Emergency medicine doc. You?

Dammit. I should have been more direct. He continues:
>   BTW...   we don't have to call it a date

>   if it makes you feel better

He did get it. I send him a smiley with a sheepish grin. And then continue to text:
>   I manage an after-school center for youth

>   After school means at all times

He responds:
>   OK... Are mornings OK?

I say:
>   Sure...

>   Perfect. Next Monday?

>   Unless I have a better option

What? I think to myself. I send him a string of question marks:
>   ???????

>   Sorry –

He adds an icon with googly eyes –
>   I meant, unless an evening becomes available

I sigh and send my second thumbs up icon of the day. It disappears like a flash.

I make myself some tea. I have a tiny herb garden on my porch. It has lemongrass, mint, oregano and myrrh, and several other goodies. Tea is really the only food stuff I invest in. Everything else needs to be quick and painless. Otherwise, I can't be bothered at all. David used to do all the cooking. He loved it. I am in a t-shirt and short shorts sipping tea when there is a knock at the door. "Who is it?" I call out. "It's Mattie." Shit. I never called him back. I open the door and let him in. He bends down to kiss me on the cheek. "You smell nice," he says.

"It's probably the tea," I say.

"Nope," he says, "it's you, your hair."

"Yes, I just washed it." He comes in with some grocery bags.

"What are you doing here?" I ask. "I should be angry with you."

"Actually, I should be angry with you for not calling me back. So I decided to come by."

"What if I weren't home?"

"I took a calculated risk that you would be."

"Actually, I am going out tonight."

"Like that?"

"No, I was planning on changing."

"With Elon?"

"Not with Elon, you jerk. You should have checked with me."

"I tried to tell you, but you didn't answer me. I take it you have time to eat with me?" Mattie asks. I nod. I have over two hours before I need to head out. Mattie makes himself at home, taking out my one and only frying pan, heating it up and preparing omelet batter. Grating a bit of cheese to put in the batter. Spicing it up with salt and pepper. While he does that, I cut up some more herbs: myrrh and parsley for me, oregano and parsley for him. He lays the omelets side by side in the pan, and toasts bread in the toaster. For the second time that day, I chop up vegetables and clear my mind.

We sit at the table and eat. "This is your best omelet yet." I say.

"Thanks," says Mattie. "You are an easy customer. Orit is fussier. She doesn't like eggs to be *eggy*."

I smile. "That could be a problem when one is preparing an omelet," I say. "Orit seems nice," I tell him. "Elegant. I need to spend more time with her."

"She is elegant. Makes me wonder what she sees in me. I can barely dress myself in the morning." He laughs and shifts his hair out of his face. "Anyway, we must make some time to get together. I think you will like her. She is… intense. You know, deep."

"Good. That's nice. That will be nice. I am sorry I didn't call you back. I have been a bit overwhelmed. Last night's party especially. It's so stupid. I did feel sick. But you know, emotional sick. Residual divorce stuff. I guess the slow dance broke me. Who would have thought it would be so hard for me to move on? I feel like such a weakling."

"Don't be silly. You are doing just fine," insists Mattie. He continues, "Anyway, I have a good feeling about the Elon guy. He is a doctor, you know."

"Yes, I know, but I am not going out with him, I am going out with someone else. Mike something. I don't know his last name. And it isn't a date. It is just ice cream."

"Since when isn't ice cream a date? All he needs to do is order you one scoop of plain vanilla and one scoop of pistachio and you will be his for all eternity."

"Wow! Am I that predictable?"

"Not predictable: decisive and sure of yourself."

"You make me sound like a woman who I would like to date," I tell him. Mattie laughs and gets up. "Now that you have been fed and we have properly caught up, I am making my exit. See you later." He scoops me up in a big hug, lifting me slightly off my feet. He leaves the apartment as he entered it, quietly and quickly and without a fuss.

Chapter 12

E-cicles is the trendiest ice-cream spot on the Tel-Aviv beachfront. That's why I hate it and why I would never have chosen it myself. Not that I am childish and keeping score, but if I did, Mike would be in deficit.

The concept of the place is very simple and like most things nowadays, it goes the distance to eliminate human interaction. As you enter the ice cream parlor, there is an array of touch screens on the wall, which you use to place your order. You choose cup, cone or bowl, size, flavor or texture. You drag-and-drop scoops and flavors and toppings. You can add any number of dishes to your cart, from milkshakes to coffees to soft drinks. You can also calculate calories and get a full dietary and nutritional breakdown. Once you have confirmed your order, if you are a member, you get a member's discount and can pay independently. If you are not a member, your next step is to go to the register, where the teller reluctantly and disdainfully takes payment.

The human element hasn't completely been eliminated after all. The display window of the many creams, sorbets and toppings isn't gone. It is still there, and it is tempting. Several workers – straight out of Willy Wonka's factory – efficiently and smoothly make up the order and ensure that it is delivered to the pick-up counter.

Want a taste before you order? No problem whatsoever. There is a counter just for that. It is not encouraged, mind you. It is at the far corner of the shop, where the line will not be held up and efficiency will not be compromised by fussy kids and nervous adults.

Mike and I meet outside at the back of the long line of people waiting to make their choices. I don't know him very well, but I can tell that he is raring to go. He has a nervous energy that is just radiating impatience.

"Tamara," he says, "just on time." He kisses me on the cheek, as if he has known me forever. "Have you been to this place before? This is my first time."

I shake my head. "Looks awesome, doesn't it," he continues. "For a restaurant, you kind of want a slow and lingering experience, but for ice cream, this is the way to do it." We edge forward in the line. "How was your day? Mine was to be expected. Chewed out the shift manager for not cleaning up properly last night. Waited for the meat supplier who never came. Bastard. Second time. I am shopping around for someone new. Any ideas?"

"No," I say. "I don't work with meat suppliers."

"Lucky you." We have just about reached the touch screens.

"This place looks clean, well run, efficient," he says as he takes in his surroundings with a critical eye. "I wonder whether their ice creams are organic. What a racket. Do you eat organic?"

"I don't object to eating organic."

"Quacks and charlatans. Let me tell you about the organic food industry…" I sigh and prepare myself for a rant. "Wait, wait, hold that thought; let's order." Mike is like a gamer trying something out for the first time. I stand at a safe distance as he zips through the options. "Would you allow me the honor of ordering for you?" he says with surprising chivalrous formality. It surprises me, given the fact that up until now we haven't exactly been having a balanced mutual conversation.

"Sure," I say. "Thanks. My favorite flavors are…"

"No, no, let me guess. You will tell me later if I am correct."

"OK, are you sure?"

"Absolutely! Do you want something to go with that? Coffee? Mineral water?"

"Maybe a mineral water. Thanks."

Mike plays around on the touch screen. He pulls out his credit card. I guess that he is setting up a membership. Club music is blaring. The intensity and brightness of the colors is blinding and the swarm of people is incessant. "This may take a few minutes, he says." Pity not to get the membership discount..."

"Sure," I say. "Hey, do you mind if I go catch us a table outside?"

"Sure," he says. "No problem. Good idea," and then as an afterthought he adds, "Choose well."

Choose well – what does that mean? Whatever. It's not like this is going so well anyway.

"OK," I say, my voice a bit uneven. "I will try." I am tempted to just leave, but I will resist the temptation.

I exit the bustling shop. There is a bar with high chairs running the length of the shop. There are low tables around the perimeter. The tables and chairs are built in. You can probably squeeze ten people around a table. The only intimate spaces are also the only portable ones: several high tables, around which two to three people can stand and talk. Like at a wedding or a cocktail party. In the near distance, closer to the beach, I can see a solitary bench. Quiet, intimate, away from the noise of the crowds. It will give us an opportunity to talk. I might as well try to make an effort, to conquer my own resistance. Maybe his nervous energy and incessant chatter will have dissipated now that he has had his E-cicles experience? I walk briskly to the bench before someone else takes it and perch myself down at an angle so that I can signal to him when he exits the shop.

It is not a long wait. He comes out balancing a carrier bag with bottles and three bowls of ice cream. I wave him towards the bench. He looks over to the bar winding around the side of the shop, but doesn't hesitate to walk over. I consider maybe that I didn't choose so well, because perhaps it was a little bit inconsiderate to sit so far from the entrance. But I am reluctant to get up and help him, just in case we lose this prime spot. When he is safely near and I am confident that no one can hijack our bench, I rush over and help him. He gives me two of the three bowls.

"Sorry," I say, "I just thought it would be easier to talk here."

"No problem. Keeping me on my feet. I like it." He gives an easy smile. "And you are probably right. It is a bit noisy by the shop. I like being immersed in the action, but I am guessing you prefer something a bit more intimate." I give him a sheepish smile and say, "Now that you mention it, I am not mad about crowds and people and noise."

"So on a scale of 1-10, how excruciating was the E-cicles experience for you?" he asks.

"Better you don't know," I say. "Let's just say, I wouldn't do it again."

"Fair enough… let's just hope that I didn't screw up on the ice-cream flavors as well." He takes out those fluorescent plastic spoons from the carrier bag.

"So what did you get me?" I ask him.

"Well, I got chocolate fudge and forest fruits in this bowl, and vanilla and rum-and-raisin in this bowl. I figured chocolate or vanilla. The probability of success is 50/50."

"Wise thinking," I say. "I am in the vanilla school." I hand him the bowl with the chocolate. "On the other hand, I don't like rum-and-raisin, so either you eat that too, or it gets thrown away," I add.

"OK, I am sure that we can figure something out. I would hate to see a good scoop neglected. This third bowl is the mystery bowl. I couldn't resist it. There were so many interesting flavors, I figured we should try at least one. This time I picked, next time you can…"

I don't respond to the inference, and instead I say: "So what is the flavor?"

"*Uuuh*, that is for me to know and you to find out."

"Mike, I really hate games. Taste tests included."

"Don't be such a killjoy. Try once, and if you don't get it, I will tell you."

"Fine," I say. "Just once." I take a spoon of the ice cream

and look at it, and it is greenish in hue. I smell it. It has a familiar smell. A good smell. "There is definitely ginger in here." I say.

"Yes!" says Mike. I taste it. The flavor is slightly tart, and not overwhelmingly sweet.

"Ginger… and cinnamon…" I say taking another taste.

"Yes, well done. What a palate! One more flavor… you can do it," he says. "What's the main flavor? What can it be?"

"Is it… is it perhaps green tea?"

"Wow," he says, "that was amazing." I am also a bit amazed and in awe of myself that I guessed correctly. "I like it," I tell him. "It's really good… refined, interesting. Good choice!"

"It's also organic," he says, and after a slightly long pause, he adds, "What a shame; I don't think that it is going to work between us." I look up to the thronging crowds on the promenade and the gently crashing waves that I can only hear, but not see in the evening darkness. A virtual ping goes off in my head, a threshold has been breached. "Well, I guess that's it then." I get up and stretch.

"Just kidding… just kidding" says Mike. "It's a joke."

"Yeah well," I say, "I'm not. Thanks for the ice-cream. Can I pay you back?"

Mike shakes his head incredulously. "Ciao," I say and walk off.

Chapter 13

Joseph Segal is four or maybe five years younger than me. We met when I was a sociology student and was wandering from volunteering framework to framework. He was then – and remains today – one of the most inspiring individuals I have ever met. He is also one of the shortest men I have ever met. At 148 centimeters, most people tower above him. Today, he sees his height as a blessing, but when we met he was still coming to terms with it. We met at a juvenile facility in the south of the country when he was about seventeen years old. He was one of its many inmates. By the age of about ten, when Joseph stopped growing, all of his troubles began. Children can be cruel. So can adults. On a regular basis, Joseph was assaulted, insulted and humiliated because of his miniscule size. Classmates and teachers alike were the perpetrators. Random people on the street snickered to see him walking with his peers. At home, his parents did what they could to love him and protect him, but unfortunately, one of his greatest tormentors came in the form of his own flesh and blood: his younger brother, Eitan.

Eitan took pleasure in small cruelties, placing random objects out of reach on a regular basis: Joseph's favorite cereal, his toothbrush, one of the shoes that he was planning to wear that day, or his glasses. No matter how much his parents tried to discipline Eitan, and to teach him compassion for his older brother, Eitan got more abusive and more creative in his bullying. And indeed, at first Joseph was an easygoing boy: he met his abusers with good humor, even when the spirit of the bullying was not intended to be funny. But eventually, even easygoing people get worn down. After a particularly difficult week of abuse, beginning with a teacher who decided to punish him for chatting by making him stand in the corner of the classroom while standing on a chair, continuing with his classmates taking a snapshot and circulating it among the entire grade, and culminating in his school bag being thrown on top of a bus stop by Eitan as they were walking home from school, Joseph began to plan his revenge. He was a short boy with an ambitious plan of tall revenge.

The plan was simple. It rested on three basic principles: timing, patience and shortness of height. Like most boys his age and height, Eitan enjoyed playing basketball. The basketball court was a home away from home for many of the teenage boys trying to avoid nagging parents or excessive homework. It was a sorry excuse for a court with one old, sagging hoop and a faded and peeling backboard. Anyone playing on the court needed to double up and shoot at the same hoop. Eitan and his friends had a regular Thursday afternoon meetup. He was a domineering boy, and luckily for Joseph, he was a creature of habit. Eitan would often do the first round of layups and being full of bravado, his first layup would always be an attempt to slam dunk into the net. Joseph's plan was to loosen the screws of the net only enough that at the right moment, Eitan would hang on and go tumbling, net in hand. Joseph would laugh at the tumbling sight, and no one would know that it was him. He would then say to everyone: *"You see, that could never happen to me."*

Loosening the screws would be a slow and arduous job. It would be carried out over a period of about a week, in which Joseph would painstakingly sneak out in the early morning and wheel a ladder on a dolly – both taken from the caretaker's unlocked office – to the basketball court. He would climb the ladder and slowly loosen five of the screws of the net, just enough so that the sixth would hold as his bullying brother would feel himself slipping in midair. The last bolt would be the failsafe that ensured that Eitan would not hurt himself so badly, so as not to detract from the sweetness of this revenge. The act was foolproof. No one could possibly suspect that he of all people would be able to pull this off. Eitan would be humiliated and maybe even the school would be forced to invest in some more modern equipment, instead of those old, decrepit structures from the Jurassic era. He might even be declared a hero.

The night before the day of reckoning, Joseph had loosened all five screws to the extent that one had fallen out completely. It took him twenty minutes to find the one that had fallen and to screw it back in place just enough so that nothing looked amiss. He went home as soon as he was done so that he could be woken up by his mother as usual. The whole day was a day of excitement and buzz. He could barely concentrate and for once, the looks, insults and jokes were like water off a duck's back. It was a good day. His anticipation was huge and his spirits were high. Instead of getting on the bus after school, like he usually did, he followed his younger brother and friends as they swarmed to the decrepit basketball court. He sat in the first row of the court, as close as he could get to the hoop. He wanted to have the best seat in the house.

"Come to see how the big boys play?" asked Eitan with scorn.

"I sure have," Joseph answered him. "Why don't you show me, brother?" Eitan looked at him quizzically, unable to decipher his brother's uncharacteristic audacity. He shrugged and walked away. As predicted, Eitan and his friends very adeptly kicked out any contenders for the court.

Stage two was the layups. As usual, Eitan pushed his way to the front. "Me first, me first," he shouted as he pushed past the others and made a grab for the ball. But for once, his friends good-naturedly fought back. They kept the ball swiftly flying in the air out of Eitan's reach. Normally, Joseph would have enjoyed the spectacle of the boys keeping the ball from his brother, but this time, it was important to him that Eitan be the first. However, sometimes the stars do not align as we intend, and Eitan charged down the court after two boys who were passing the ball between them. In the last seconds, the three of them were in the circle together and they all charged at the same time towards the hoop: two to shoot and one to defend. Joseph stood up abruptly. "*No!*" he shouted as the three charged the hoop. "*Stop!*" he shouted as the three boys and the ball collided with hoop. "*No!*" he shouted again, as the hoop, the backboard, the boys and the ball, came tumbling down in a massive heap.

There were a few seconds of deathly silence, followed by a furor of activity. Eitan, at the bottom of the heap, was out cold. His friends were moaning with pain, the hoop partially on top of them. Joseph ran out of the court to get help. "Call an ambulance, call an ambulance," he shouted. "There's been an accident on the basketball court." Two adults walking by the school saw that this miniscule boy was serious and scared, and they whipped out their phones and ran into the gym. "Oh no, oh no," cried Joseph and he continued running, all the way home.

As Joseph sat on the floor in his room, swaying back and forth with the door shut and the lights closed, he missed the ensuing events in the gym. Eitan's friends got away with a dislocated shoulder and a broken arm respectively. Eitan himself was less lucky, given the fact that his friends fell on top of him as he tried to get the ball back. He suffered from broken ribs, a punctured lung, a concussion and what would turn out to be chronic back pain, a constant reminder of the day's events.

After the incident, Joseph came forward to confess his clandestine activities. After deconstructing the years of bullying and humiliation leading up to the events, Joseph, Eitan, their parents and the staff at the school were subject to observations and sessions aimed at figuring out what went wrong and how it could be corrected. It was decided that the Segal boys would undergo counselling and that, as a direct consequence of his actions, Joseph would be sent to a juvenile facility for several months.

From the very first time that I met him, Joseph made a huge and irreversible impression on me. It was not only that he was profusely and profoundly apologetic and understanding of the consequences of his activities, it was also that a spark had been ignited within him. He became an inspiration to and an influence on others to embrace and take responsibility for their actions and to become the best person that they can possible be.

Joseph was tireless in fighting for the good in each person, indefatigable in helping people to see that they are worthy and valuable. It made no difference to him that people continued to laugh at and humiliate him about his size; he didn't hear or see or even comprehend. He was a young man on a mission, and even the biggest miscreant and delinquent understood that he could not be worn down by words and taunts. If anything, Joseph's stature in the facility was larger than life, and he became a confidante and a mentor to the other boys.

I remember him stepping in between two boys who were about to lose control and have an all-out fight. Such a small person could have been knocked out within seconds, pushed into oblivion. I started to lunge forward to separate the boys, but one of the staffers stopped me... "Just watch," he said. So I stopped in my tracks and watched as Joseph talked the boys down from their clenched fists and their tense shoulders. It was an unbelievable sight. It was not long before Joseph told me his story and it has stayed with me ever since. We have kept in touch all of these past years.

Nowadays, Joseph is a counselor and a guide. He runs a community center, as well as a program that focuses on eradicating bullying. He works with both victims and bullies to try and mediate and defuse tensions. He works with schools and youth movements: running workshops to build and reinforce the societal infrastructure that was missing when he was younger man and to some extent is still missing today. Occasionally, I send people to him, like Eran and Avi. I give them a parcel to bring to him: a big carton. It is large, but it is light. Although I am never there at the time that they deliver the parcel, I know exactly how the scene plays out.

Joseph always opens the box in front of the visitors that I send. He makes a dramatic show of pretending to wonder what is inside, asking the visitors if they have any idea. Then slowly, he removes the lid from the box, to reveal the contents. For the visitors, it is a puzzling moment of bewilderment. For Joseph it is a signal that I need his help. Not that he needed the box to understand that. He takes the contents out gently and holds it between his two small hands. It is bigger than his head. He holds it with reverence and care. "I have a great idea," he says, looking at the gift with a half-smile. "Let's go play some basketball."

Eran and Avi come tumbling into my office. They are excited and talking a hundred words a minute. Eran's eyes are shiny and intense. Avi – usually the more guarded of the two – is charged with energy. I smile. Joseph has worked his magic.

"We met him," says Eran. We met Joseph." Avi nods vigorously. Eran continues, "He is... he is —"

"Spectacular!" finishes Avi. Eran nods his head in agreement.

"But he really sucks at basketball," says Eran and both boys laugh.

"He asked us to give this to you," says Avi and pulls out an envelope. I take the envelope and without opening it, put it on my desk. "So tell me," I ask, "why is Joseph spectacular? What did you discover?"

"It's hard to say," says Avi. "There is just something about him. Obviously he has a real presence for such a little guy."

"Yeah, but, it's not that," continues Eran. "It's his story that makes me think. If I had known him, if I had been at his school, I would have... I would have bullied him. I would have teased him."

"Maybe you would have and maybe you wouldn't have. You don't know that," says Avi placatingly."

"No, I do." says Eran. "I would have been the guy who pushes him into the locker, or throws his pencil case on to the highest shelf. I know I would have. Look at… look at what I did to you…" Avi places his hand on Eran's shoulder.

"But you didn't. You stopped yourself."

"Tamara stopped me."

"Tamara couldn't *make* you stop. *You* made you stop."

I listen to the boys with pride welling up from within. "Anyway," Avi continues, "maybe you would have been his bully or maybe you wouldn't have. Regardless, it's hard not to stare at him. I also would have stared. When we first came into the office, it felt like my eyes were burning."

"Yeah, me too. I thought to myself, 'Why did Tamara send us here to see this freak show?' " Eran hangs his head. "*That* was what I was thinking. I am such a jerk." I am about to interject, but Eran continues without pause: "I guess that I am scared that I will always be the biggest jerk with the shortest fuse – like a firecracker about to go off – unaware or uncaring of who gets hurt and to what extent. What if I do major damage to someone?"

What a huge declaration from this amazing young man. My heart swells at his words. Avi, with his acute sensitivity, also understands the momentousness of what he has said, and he looks at Eran with wide eyes, saying nothing.

"Eran," I say after a few seconds, "I am so proud of you. What you said now was not easy. It takes maturity and self-awareness and courage. With those three things, you are fully equipped to move forward and to be the best possible person that you can be."

"But what if I screw up?"

"We all screw up," Avi says.

"Yes we do," I say. "The question is what we do after the fact. Look at Joseph. He made a terrible mistake that had some very high costs." I pause. "On the other hand, look at what he has made of himself since then. We all deserve second chances. Hopefully none of us will ever get to the point where we need a second chance due to something extreme or dangerous. But, if we do, there is always an opportunity to grow from the mistake."

"Have you ever needed a second chance? Have you ever screwed up?" Eran asks. Avi shifts uncomfortably at the personal nature of the question. But he listens intently.

Me, second chances, I think to myself. I think of my divorce, so amicable and genteel that I have been left feeling incapable, not undeserving, of a new relationship. *Does that count?* I think irrationally. Perhaps it would have been easier to move on if I had cheated, or if he had been a complete jerk, or if one of us had had an intolerably bad habit. *Second chances in love and marriage. Does that count?* I think to myself. But, aloud, I say to the boys, "Well, everyone screws up. As a teenager, I went through a bad patch with my parents. I guess most of us do. It is part of growing up." I pause and then begin again. "In a way, being divorced also feels to me somehow like I screwed up, even if I know exactly how and why it happened, and even if I know that statistically, it happens to about one in three couples here in Tel Aviv." Eran nods thoughtfully, but doesn't say a thing.

"Thanks… for everything… I mean, you know… for sharing," says Avi. "I guess we should go study," he says, turning to Eran.

"Yes," says Eran, "I just want to add… *ummm.* What I want to say is…" he says, searching for an appropriate response. "Well, for now, I just want to say *thanks.*"

"Thank you," I say, "thank you both. And also for running that errand for me. I assume that you both will be seeing Joseph again." The boys nod in unison and with unabashed enthusiasm. When they are gone, I pick up the envelope and I open it. There is a single post-it note with an almost illegible scribble – a quote that I recognize from the Talmud: "Whoever saves a life, it is considered as if he saved an entire world."

I smile. Kindred spirits we are, Tamara and Joseph.

Chapter 14

It is Friday night and we are all at Dana and Aviva's house. Kids and adults are intermingling. There is a buzz of motion and an undercurrent of loud and soft chatter. As usual, there is too much food. Aviva is back from India, so the smells of curry, turmeric and mango fill the house. I like Indian food, but I can see that Karina has quietly gone to the kitchen and made a couple of nondescript sandwiches. Bread with some colorless spread or other – cheese? Hummus? Peanut butter? She places them strategically between the Naan bread and the chicken tikka.

As usual, an exuberant Iris is the center of attention. "So you all remember my nephew Oren, right?"

"The one with braces and peroxide blonde hair?" asks Josh.

"Yes, but that was years ago. He is now a strapping and gorgeous man. He just got out of the army."

"OK, sure."

"Well, my sister told me that he got into a bit of trouble recently."

"What happened?" asks Mattie.

"Oh no," says Dana with concern, "is he OK?"

"He will be OK," Iris grins, "and it is quite a funny story actually. He still lives with his parents. You know, saving money and all that. Life is so expensive. Especially in Tel Aviv if you are just starting out." We all nod in commiseration. This is a story that is way too familiar to all of us. "So anyway, he brought this girl home one night and they decided to get into a bit of role play." We all listen with big eyes and bated breath. Iris continues. "She lay naked on the bed. He tied her hands to the headboard. He stripped down and put on a superman cloak. He climbed onto the desk in his room, and was about to jump down, cape and all to 'save the damsel in distress' when the desk toppled over. He fell and broke his leg and couldn't get up. She was tied to the bed naked like the day she was born, so she couldn't get up to help him. In the end they had to call my sister and brother-in-law into the room. Can you imagine what they saw? A naked girl strapped to the bed, and Oren in a superman cloak in a crumpled mess on the floor."

Josh laughs. "What a great story!"

"Poor girl," shivers Dana. "The sheer embarrassment. I would rather die."

"It is kind of funny," says Aviva. "What a failed superhero intervention."

"It just proves that Batman is superior – yet again!" says Mattie.

"Actually, it proves that Oren and Iris are blood relatives,"

I said. "I can totally see that happening to you," I say to Iris and laugh.

Iris laughs too. "I wish I were as creative as that...I still prefer a good old nurse-patient routine."

"Please, spare us the details," says Karina.

"Yes, besides which," says Dana, "there are kids running around."

"Rather they learn from us..." says Iris. "Besides which, what about you, Tamara? Don't think I have forgotten for one minute the mischief that you are up to. Hypocrite! How many of us are stringing along two guys? Dry spell is over; I guess? What happened with them anyway?"

"Which two guys? Tamara, you never said anything," says Karina.

"Wow," says Josh. Mattie tilts his head, listening intently.

"It's not a big deal. Really." I glare at Iris. "I am not stringing anyone along. I went out with the one the other day. You know, the restaurant guy. A total disaster."

"Oooh, pity. He was delicious," says Iris.

"No he wasn't; he was an arrogant bore. And I am going to go out with the other one this week. He just needs to give me a time when he is not on call."

"On call? What does he do?" asks Karina.

"He's a doctor."

"*Oooh*, what your mother always dreamed of," says Iris.

"Nope, my mother doesn't really care. Never did. At this point, she would settle for a sperm donor."

"Not true," says Dana.

"No she wouldn't," says Mattie.

"Your mom? No way," says Josh.

"Oh, leave me alone, all of you…" I huff. "Anyway, we'll see what happens with this other guy."

"Mister Doctor. Have fun. And you, peanut?" says Iris, putting her hand on Mattie's shoulder.

"Me, I guess everything is OK."

"Still with your gal, Orit?"

Mattie pauses, "I guess. I mean yes. All's good."

"You sound fabulously enthusiastic."

Mattie grins. "Just don't feel like sharing is all."

"Spoilsport," says Josh.

"He's a gentleman," says Karina. "I respect that."

"Me too," says Dana.

"Not me," says Iris. "Gentleman. How boring. Anyway, that doesn't exempt either of you from your obligation to me."

"What obligation?" Mattie and I ask at the same time.

"For lessons in the opposite sex. Saturday night, at Bloom's Pub."

"Give me a break," I tell Iris. "Bloom's is a total meat market. No self-respecting person goes there."

"I will have you know that I am a regular." says Iris.

"I rest my case." I say with a laugh.

"My darling cherub, self-respect is over-rated."

"Could be fun," says Mattie turning to me. "I double dare you."

"Not a double dare!" I say in mock horror. "How can I say no to a double dare?"

"Don't you want to see the beast in her natural habitat?" he asks, looking at Iris. I think about it for a few seconds and then answer. "You got me," I say. "Yes, that would definitely make it worth my while."

"Can we come too? We also want to see a live hunt," says

Josh. *"Pleeease?"*

"No way!" says Iris. "Anyone who has been with the same person for over three years is *persona non grata*. When you settle down, you lose your survival instinct. Going to Bloom's could harm you irreparably. It is for your own sake that you are definitely not invited."

"Lost our survival instinct, have we?" says Aviva.

"Absolutely," says Iris. "Easy prey. The bunch of you."

Chapter 15

Saturday morning floats in slowly and lazily. In the early morning, I go to the beach for a swim. I come home and shower, and spend an hour getting ready for my meeting with Noa's parents, which will be taking place this week. I prepare all kinds of facts and statistics relating to how military service is beneficial professionally, personally and financially – although, of course, there is a short-term versus long-term factor that needs to be taken into consideration. My challenge in this meeting will be to help them see the bigger picture: to focus on the long-term benefits. After I complete my preparation, I go over the presentation that I have prepared for our next manager's sync session. Kobi will be there as usual, probably goading me and pointing out everything that he could do better. He's always angling to replace me. Adam will be forced to referee between us. I hate that. Kobi is a good guy, despite the politicking. He could do well leading a place like the Nest, I am sure – if it weren't for his combatant attitude. Just as I am about to put my work aside and decide what I want to do next, my phone buzzes and a message pops up:

```
Hi. Wed + Thurs night are free

What do you prefer?

Ethiopian sound good?
```

I smile. It's oddly satisfying to be courted. I hit the reply.

```
Definitely Thurs night

Never did Ethiopian

Sounds like fun
```

I send the message and am surprised by the fact that I actually mean it. Something is different. Elon answers within seconds.

```
Cool. Will send time + details

Call you tomorrow

Back to work
```

That was easy, I think to myself. Now I can get back to my weekend, and chill for a bit before heading out to Bloom's. I shut down my laptop and clear away the papers I have been scribbling on. Suddenly the phone rings. I pick it up and check out the screen. The call is from the Nest. This can only mean that something's happened. "Hi," I say.

"Hi," says Lily, one of our weekend volunteers. "So sorry to disturb you on the weekend."

"Lily, what's going on?" I ask.

"Avi called a few minutes ago."

"Avi the volunteer?"

"Yes, he and Eran were in a fight. Eran is in the hospital. Emergency ward."

"Oh no! Which hospital?"

"Ichilov."

"Do you know what happened?"

"No. But Avi did say that the police were involved."

My heart sinks. "Do you know how Eran is?"

"No. Avi asked me to call his mom. I am about to do that now."

"OK. If she can't make it, tell her that I am on my way there right now." I grab my things and head out.

Ichilov Hospital is twenty-five minutes away by foot. I grab my bike and peddle. There is no point in calling a cab. By the time one comes, I will already be there. My mind is flooded with questions and concerns – mostly for Eran and his welfare – but pesky little thoughts sneak in as well. *What if I was wrong about Eran all this time, and Kobi was right?* Perhaps he is a bad seed. Perhaps we have been wasting our time. *If the police are involved, this could be trouble for the Nest.* We vouch for these kids. We care for them. I make a mental note to myself to call Adam as soon as I get to the hospital. I try to focus on Eran and his health, but I keep hearing Eran's own voice in my head saying "I am such a jerk," and "What if I do major damage to someone?"

Come on Eran. I think to myself. *Be OK. Be OK. Be OK.* With that mantra in my head, I peddle as quickly as I can to the hospital.

By the time I have locked my bike in the nearest bike stall and reached the emergency ward, I am sweating a river. The halls are illuminated with neon lights. The walls are supposed to be soothing, but their pastel-colored drabness makes this place feel like the institution that it is. Eran is still technically a kid, so this is the emergency area for children. Most of the patients are post triage. Parents sit around with kids dulled by fevers and others try to calm those who are crying due to cuts, bruises, burns and breaks. Eran is nowhere to be seen, but all of a sudden I see Avi. He is pale and has clearly been crying. "Avi, what's going on? Are you OK?"

"I called the Nest, but you weren't there. I spoke to Lily."

"Lily called me. What happened?"

"I called his mother, but she couldn't come. She has to look after the other kids."

"Are you OK, Avi?"

"They took him. I came with them in the ambulance. But they took him right away and told me to wait here."

"Who took him?"

"The paramedics tried to revive him in the ambulance, and when we got to the hospital, the doctor took him." Tears are streaming down his cheeks. He is shaking.

"Come here, come with me . . ." I say and I walk him to the nearest vending machine. There is an empty bench in front of it. "Sit here," I tell him. But he doesn't move. I put my hands on his quivering shoulders, and gently ease him down onto the bench. He settles down. His shoulders relax slightly, but he is still shaking. I buy him a coke from the vending machine and open the can for him. "Drink, drink. Get some energy."

He drinks and some of the coke spills. He breathes in, slightly calmer. "I told him not to do it," he says. "I told him to leave it alone," he continues. "But he just wouldn't." The color is coming back to his face slowly.

"Drink, drink," I say to him in a calm, soothing voice. "Take a few minutes to just sit and drink. I just need to make a quick call. I will be right here near you."

I step about three meters away from Avi, and find Adam on my smartphone. I hit the Enter button and it starts to ring. Adam picks up after two rings. "Hey, what's wrong? Is everything OK?"

"I am OK. But I am at the hospital with one of the boys."

"What's going on? Who is it?"

"Eran."

"*Eran*, the same Eran that you disciplined a few weeks ago?"

"Yes. The same."

"Is everything OK?"

"I don't know. He seems to have gotten into some trouble. One of the volunteers is here as well, the boy he threatened with a knife, Avi."

"That's not good."

"I don't know. He seems to be in shock a bit, and he isn't talking much sense. They weren't at the Nest. I don't know where they were and what they were doing. This is such a mess!"

"Do you need me to come down? Where are you?"

"Ichilov. No, no, don't come. I will let you know."

"OK. I am here if you need me."

"Thanks, Adam. I hope I didn't screw up."

"Whatever happened now, you are not responsible."

"I know, but perhaps it was a mistake keeping him on."

"If that is the case, then we'll know soon enough."

"I guess."

"Take it easy, OK?"

"OK, I will try."

"OK, speak to you later. Bye."

"Bye."

"Hey, hey." I see Avi get up abruptly as a white coat flashes past him.

"Avi, what's going on?" Avi turns to me, distracted for a minute, and then he turns back to the fast-moving figure.

"Wait, excuse me, wait a minute," he calls. He turns back to me. "That's him. That's the doctor. That's the doctor who took care of Eran when the ambulance arrived. Hey wait a minute," Avi calls.

"Hey. Doctor, stop please!" I call. The doctor stops abruptly and turns in his tracks. He looks busy and harried, but manages to crack a half smile on his face. "I thought we agreed to meet on Thursday?" It is Elon. I turn red and then shake my head. "Sorry, you threw me there. I wasn't... expecting... thinking. It's just that you took in one of my kids," I say.

"Your kids?"

"Yes, from my work. Came in unconscious? With this boy." I gesture at Avi.

"Ahh, yes."

"What's going on? Is he OK?"

"You know that unless you are a relation, or have some sort of legal status or guardianship, I can't really say much."

"I understand; I don't have any of that. His mom can't be here right now."

"I know you are both worried. What I *can* that say he is going to be OK."

"Oh, thank goodness for that. Can I call the mom and tell her that?"

"You can, and if she finds a way to come by later, I will fill her in."

"Can we see him?" asks Avi.

"No, unfortunately, not yet. He'll definitely be here overnight. My suggestion is that you come by tomorrow morning during visiting hours. He is going to be happy to see you. Listen, I'm sorry but I need to run."

"Yes, sure, thanks for the help."

"No problem. Don't worry," Elon says, turning to Avi. "Your friend is going to be OK. He is a lucky kid."

"Oh thank goodness," says Avi and sits down abruptly in the nearest chair and covers his face with both of his hands. I walk over to him, and stand in front of him, deliberating whether or not to sit down next to him, or to give him some time alone. As I am considering what to do, I feel a gentle tap on my shoulders. I turn around. It is Elon. "Tamara, see you later this week…Thursday . . .?"

I nod. Who can think that far? My brain is frozen at the moment. Elon turns briskly and walks off.

After a few minutes, I say to Avi, "Let's get out of here. He nods wearily and stands up. We head to the exit. It opens out onto a large grassy area. Nervous parents and tired doctors occupy the space, some smoking, some trying to regain lost energy. "Let's lie on the grass here for a few minutes." Avi nods and follows me off the path and onto the grass. I lie on my back and look up at the blue sky and breathe in deeply. The air fills my lungs. Avi does the same. His color is now restored and he is back to his regular self. Without looking at me, he says, "I am sorry. This whole thing was my fault."

"Avi," I say, "just relax and tell me all about it from the beginning." Avi takes a few seconds to gather his thoughts and then he begins to speak. "Eran and I decided to meet to play some basketball. He was meant to, you know, teach me, to help *me* – for a change. We were playing on the court. There was another group there, a rowdy group of kids. We ignored each other. They were a group of kids that I wouldn't normally play with. But, they kept to themselves and so did we. Only, I am really bad at basketball," Avi gives a bitter laugh and then continues, "I was so bad, that at one point I threw the ball really hard and it ricocheted off the backboard and knocked this big scary-looking guy right on the nose, which began to bleed immediately. I quickly apologized. He came towards me angrily and menacingly. He began to threaten that he would really hurt me. He was about to throw a punch, when Eran stepped in the middle." Avi pauses, remembering the moment. "Eran was so awesome. He stood there and said, 'Let's work this out. Let us get some ice for your nose.' The big guy swore at him and said, 'Ice? Do you think that will help, you piece of shit?' His friends just laughed. 'What I want is an eye for an eye, or a nosebleed for a nosebleed.' The guy was so angry." Avi shivers as he relays the events, and then begins to speak again.

"Eran said to him. 'We aren't going to fight you. We came here to play ball.' The big guy kind of looked at us with this weird expression and then said to Eran, 'OK, then, I guess I can be more sporting, more friendly. I guess I can forget this ever happened.' And he turned to walk away. At that moment, I felt as light as a cloud. It was a moment of pure relief and joy, and Eran felt it too. I could tell. He was so proud; he was so happy. And then the big guy turned back and threw a punch. I can still see it in slow motion. Eran never saw it coming. He got hit in the nose and the impact was so great that he fell right over. Next thing I know, he is out cold on the floor and there is blood everywhere. I thought he was dead. And it was all my fault. The punch was meant for me," Avi says in a small voice.

"I can barely remember what happened next. One of the passersby must have called the police. I guess someone else called an ambulance. I was useless, crying and calling out for Eran. The other guys just ran. They didn't stick around to help or anything. The ambulance came first and as they were loading Eran into the back, the police arrived. I didn't know who to call, so I called the Nest to see if you were around. I asked them to call Eran's mom, and to say that we were on our way to Ichilov. I guess you know the rest."

This has been a long speech for Avi, but it is a speech made with the relief of knowing that his friend is going to be OK. For me too – without even knowing the potential consequence of Eran's medical situation – the relief that I feel is palpable and absolute. With Elon's assurance that Eran will be OK, and now, having understood the circumstances around the incident, I feel vindicated: majorly proud of Eran and his restraint in the face of a situation that might have turned out completely differently.

"You both are wonderful," I tell Avi. "What a situation to be in. Think of where you were a few weeks back and now this. And how Eran looked out for you. It wasn't your fault. It was a split-second decision that might have turned out even worse. It also might have turned out better – at least for Eran. We will know more tomorrow. But I am really grateful that you are both OK," I tell him. We both sit up slowly.

"I must get home," says Avi. "I can't believe that I am here. In this situation. It is quite surreal."

"Do you want me to walk home with you?" I ask, getting up. "I just need to get my bike."

"No, I am good. I think I need to just get out of here. I need to just lie on my bed, you know, and be a bit aimless."

"I hear you," I say. "Let's talk again tomorrow morning."

Avi walks off, his awkward skinny gait still slightly off-balance from the events of the day. On the way to my bike, I make two quick calls. The first is to Eran's mother. "Rita," I say, "don't worry; Eran is going to be just fine. I don't have any details, but I have the doctor's assurance that he will be OK." I think of Elon in his white coat. "Eran is in good hands," I tell her, "and the doctor says to come by any time and he will fill you in."

"Thank goodness," she says and bursts into tears. "I will be there soon," she says. "I have made arrangements. Bless you for being there. I am so grateful."

"Of course," I say. "You have a great kid and I mean it." I then make a quick call to Adam. He answers immediately. "Hey," I say.

"Tell me what's happening," he says.

"The bottom line is that Eran will be OK. He was hurt and I don't know the extent of the damage, but he will be OK. The doctor says that he will be OK."

"Do you know what happened? Do you know whose… I mean who did what?" asks Adam as delicately as he can.

"He got blindsided by a bully when he refused to fight with him, Adam. He did great. He did great!" My eyes well up with tears. "That's good news, Tamara. You did great too. Well done." We end the call. The adrenalin of the afternoon is wearing off quickly and I feel like I am about to cry. I am too tired to cycle and too weary to be alone. So I walk beside my bike, holding the handlebars. I call Mattie, but he doesn't answer. I call Dana, and she answers right away. "What's up, Tammy?" she asks. I burst into tears and am simply unable to stop.

A few hours later, I have mostly recovered, after Dana has talked me through my shock as I walk home from the hospital. Then I shower and even manage to rest. I am sitting in a pair of shorts and a t-shirt, drinking my tea and listening to some music when the phone rings. It is Mattie. "Hi," he says, "I saw you called. Sorry I couldn't take it."

"Don't worry, it's OK now."

"Did you need something?"

"No, I had a bit of a rough morning. A kid from the Nest is in the hospital."

"God, that's awful. Is he OK?"

"He will be. I was so worried. I called you because I just needed to talk, I guess. As I was leaving the hospital, I just needed… some company." I think back to my own sobbing and shaking. "Company is a bit of an understatement. Comfort I guess is more relevant. Anyway, I am OK now. And looking forward to absolutely nothing. No noise, no mess, no fuss."

"What are you talking about? We are meeting in a couple of hours. Iris will kill you if you don't come."

"Oh shit. That's right. I can't, I am so finished. It's the last thing that I need."

"Don't be silly. After the awful day that you have had, this is exactly what you need. Besides which, it means that we get to hang out. How often does that happen these days?"

"True, but still, I don't know…"

"Come on, Tammy. Please be there."

"When you ask like that . . . it makes me not want to come on principle."

"Always the sentimental one… I love it," Mattie goads.

"You blow me over with your compassion." I laugh. The day's tension begins to slowly dissipate. "I'll see. I'll think about it. I am not saying no…even though I am leaning towards it."

"Don't lean towards *no*, lean towards a fun night out." says Mattie.

"I'm leaning towards *maybe*…"

"Good enough for me, says Mattie. "See you later."

"See you . . . maybe . . ."

"Oh just be there, and stop playing hard to get," says Mattie and he hangs up.

Chapter 16

I sit at the bar and wait for Mattie to arrive. I cannot believe that I am actually here. This day has been so intense. As usual, I am on time and he is late. I have to learn to make more dramatic entrances, or at least not to be the very first to come in. The bartender, a young man in a white string undershirt, looking like he came out of a *Right Said Fred* music video from the 80's, slides up to me and asks, "What can I give you?" I am too embarrassed to ask for something non-alcoholic, so I answer, "Just give me something light, a cocktail that's not too strong. I need my wits about me tonight." He gives me a quizzical look. *Why did I say that?* I think to myself with a red face. "You got it," he says and shuffles off to mix up the concoction in his alcohol lab. I must have been sitting there for a good few minutes before I can sense someone coming up behind me. I can tell that it isn't Mattie. Something about the smell and the size of the presence doesn't quite match up. I start to swivel the bar chair, getting ready to punch if I have to.

"Hey, baby," says the man, coming into full view. "I see that you are all by yourself. Are you lonely? Want some company?" He is a tall man with a large build and greased back hair. He is wearing a shiny black jacket and a purple metallic shirt underneath. If Mattie could see this, he would laugh at me. I kind of want to laugh as well, but I don't want to hurt his feelings.

"No thanks," I say, "I am waiting for a friend," and I swivel back to the bar. The greasy-haired man turns my bar stool around again. "When is your 'friend' coming? I have plenty of love for more than one," he says. I shudder.

"I don't mean to be mean," I say, "but I am not interested, what's your name?"

"Jeff," says the man.

"Jeff," I say, "I want to be crystal clear: I am not interested."

"Sure you are baby; you just don't know it yet."

"Oh, I think I do, Jeff. You are not my type."

"I," says Jeff, puffing out his chest, "am everyone's type. I am versatile, baby." The barman slides over with my drink. I take it gratefully. Although I have just told Jeff that I didn't mean to be mean, that compassionate sentiment has now completely vanished. I am no longer in the mood for being polite. "Listen, Jeff, let me be blunt. You are very forward, and your endgame is very obvious – you want sex, right?" Jeff goes silent. Perhaps he is not used to people being direct with him. "Well," I say, "isn't that what you are after, to leave here by the end of the night assured of a sexual escapade with some random woman that you have just met?"

"Well, yes," he says hesitantly.

"Well, let me tell you why it won't work with me." Jeff comes closer to hear. The barman leans forward to listen. "You see Jeff, your appetite and voraciousness point to aggressiveness. Your unwillingness to listen to me or to take what I am saying seriously points to selfishness and egoism." Jeff breathes in deeply, and takes a step back. "Your inability to read the writing on the wall signifies obtuseness and a lack of emotional intelligence. Now you tell me, Jeff, why would I want someone selfish, egotistical, aggressive and obtuse in bed with me? What I want in the bedroom is the opposite of what you are offering, Jeff, do you understand me?" Jeff exhales loudly and takes another step back. "I want a partner who gets me, understands me and gives me what I need. Do you get what I am saying, *Jeff*?" I say.

"Bitch," he mutters and scurries off.

"Wow," says the bartender, "I learned something today."

"Yeah, well," I say, "he caught me on a rough day. And I have a big mouth. I'm Tamara," I tell him and extend a hand.

"Sasha," says the barman and shakes my hand back. "Come here anytime, sweetheart. After that diva display, I would love to see how you make nice…"

"I am afraid you may need to wait some time to see that." Mattie interrupts us. "Hey, Tamara. Good you made it. I was convinced that you wouldn't come."

"I almost didn't," I say.

"What are you having?" Sasha asks Mattie.

"Beer, anything cold and dry." Mattie gives me a big hug. Crushes me in his arms. "So what's this place like?" he asks once he has let me go.

"Interesting," I say, watching Jeff at the back of the room, trying his luck with another woman. "I am not sure that I can get used to coming here regularly."

"Who says that you have to?"

"*Yoo hoo,*" we hear, "my babies…". Mattie and I turn around to see Iris floating in. As she comes in, I swear I can feel the noise level rise in the room.

"Can you hear it?" I ask putting my hand to my ear.

"Yes," Mattie says, smiling. "Iris is in the house."

"For you a kiss," she says to Mattie and she steps up to him and gives him a kiss on the cheek. Iris is not a small lady, and she somehow makes everything seem loud. The smacking sound of kiss resonates like a loud messy slurp. "And for you," she says to me, "a hug." She wraps her arms around me, not a bear-crushing hug like Mattie, but a deliberate hug in which, in one fell swoop, she releases my hair from its hair band, gets me out of the shawl that is covering my shoulders, and lowers my shirt line by a couple of centimeters.

"That's better," she says.

"Wow," says Mattie to Iris, "you have a talent that is totally wasted on you."

"Who says the talent is wasted?" asks Iris with a wink. "I always like to keep all my options open."

"Am I the only one who feels violated here?" I ask.

"You shouldn't," says Mattie. "You look great," he says and I feel an ache in the pit of my stomach.

Sasha appears at the bar in front of Iris. "Well, my darling," she says to him, "you look like a creative type. What do you feel like cooking up for me?"

"Anything you would like," he answers magnanimously. "Your wish is my command!"

"No, handsome," Iris says, "anything you would like is what I want." Sasha smiles and goes back into his quarters. Iris has given him a challenge in which he intends to excel.

Iris sits between us, and she puts a hand on each of us. "Now dears, we are about to get serious, because tonight, neither of you is leaving here unless you have a date with someone lined up. Tonight we begin with you Tamara, because if we don't, I know you will back out."

"But I have already been propositioned, just before you came," I tell her, "and besides which, I already have a date on Thursday night."

"You do?" asks Iris. Mattie turns to listen.

"Yes, I do. The doctor guy from the party."

"Fine, so this will just be a practice round. OK?"

"OK, fine."

"You get to choose who you want to practice on."

"Thanks very much." I say. Iris begins to count off the potential contenders: "Option one: nerdy looking hi-tech dude at the back of the room. Option two: metrosexual with sunglasses, two booths away. Option three: any one of the guys drinking beer in that group over there." She beckons to a table nearby.

"And what if I don't?"

"*Don't* is not one of your options," she says.

"And what if I still don't?"

"Not an option, babe!"

"And will you judge me based on who I chose?"

"What do you think," says Iris. "Don't you know me by now? Of course I will!"

Mattie laughs infectiously at Iris's impossible mission and my misery in facing it.

"Laugh it up," I say to Mattie. "You are next. Iris, so all I need to do is get a phone number?"

"*So all I need to do* . . . Listen to Miss Confidence. Go for it," says Iris.

"Fine," I say. I take a long sip of my drink and think. The nerdy-looking guy is the least scary. Metrosexual is out. I can't go out with someone who cares more about the way he looks than I do. Finally, there is the group of guys. Well, it's a crapshoot – an embarrassing and humiliating crapshoot. I will be like a gazelle parading in front of a hungry pride of lions. If those lions don't feel like a bite; I will be mortified in a very public way. I hop off my bar stool and start walking towards the nerdy guy. "I knew it!" said Iris, just loud enough for me to hear. So at the last minute I make a beeline towards the table of laughing guys. There are four of them sitting in a booth, laughing and drinking beer. *I can do this!* I think to myself.

I get to the table and slide into the booth, as if they were all sitting there just waiting for me. "Skootch over," I say, and push myself in, practically sitting on top of one of the guys. "Make some room." They are startled into silence by my arrival and stare at me incredulously. But the guy shifts aside wordlessly. *How funny,* I think to myself. *They are the gazelles and I am the lion.* This is easier than I thought. I plow forward. "Oh excuse me, I think I made a mistake," I say with fake embarrassment. "I saw you guys from the bar where I am sitting with some friends, and you looked like some friends of mine. How silly of me," I say, but I stay seated. One of the men finds his voice. "Sorry, where are our manners?" He does a quick round of names. I don't even listen. I am too busy thinking – *now that I am here, what next?*

"Are you with that blonde up there?" one of the guys asks, pointing at Iris. "Yes, she is a good friend of mine. She is amazing."

"Excuse the question if it is inappropriate, but do you happen to know if she is available?"

"Are you interested?" I ask.

"Sure," he says, "I am."

"Well, she is my friend, so how do I know if your intentions are good?"

"I can't promise my intentions are good, until I know what she wants my intentions to be."

"Actually, you have a point," I say, my mind moving fast.

"If you would like," I say nonchalantly, "I can give her your phone number."

"If I give you my phone number, will she call?"

"I can't promise she will call, but I can promise to encourage her."

"Fine," he says. He gives me his name and his number and I plug them into my smartphone. *That was easy-peasy*, I think to myself. *I got a phone number.* "Alright then," I say, getting up. "Sorry to have disturbed. Please get back to your beers."

"Wait," says the man sitting next to him. "What about you?"

"What about me?"

"Now that you have come all this way, can I have your number?" I look at him and then look at Iris and Mattie who are still watching me intently. *Is this the way it works? Is it possible that this is how this works?* I try to get a good look at the speaker without making him feel like a bug under a microscope. He looks normal enough. Even good-looking in a boyish way.

"I don't bite," he says with a grin. "Promise —"

"At least not on the first date," laughs one of his friends. He fake-punches his friend on the shoulder good-naturedly.

"Don't listen to him. I am normal. I don't live with my parents and I don't raise cats."

I laugh. Sounds like a match to me. "And your name?"

"Yonatan."

"Well, Yonatan, OK," I say, "I guess that would be OK, but I will call you."

"Fine," he shrugs, "I can handle that," he says. "But you will need to give me your name, so that I know who is calling."

"Tamara," I say. "My name is Tamara."

"OK," he says, and he reaches for my phone, plugs in his number and hits dial. When it rings, he quickly hangs up.

"There now," he says, "now that you have called me once, calling a second time, won't be so awkward."

"*Aaaaw*, sweet," say his friends.

"That's my cue to exit," I say. And I head back to Mattie and Iris – triumphant.

"Tamara, you savage beast, that was magnificent," says Iris. "You have surpassed my expectations. Did I see that you got two numbers?"

"Yes," I say sheepishly, "but honestly, the first one is for you."

"Really," she says. "I would love to say that I am surprised, but that would be lying."

Mattie and I laugh. "Which one?" she asks. "White t-shirt and jeans." I point to him and he waves his hand. "OK," she says.

"He will do." She blows him a kiss. I forward her the contact information. It reaches her with a satisfied ping.

"Which one is yours?" Mattie asks.

"He is not mine. Blue shirt and jeans," I say.

"Niiiice," says Iris, "tall, dark and handsome. So tomorrow you will call him," she states matter-of-factly. I shrug nonchalantly. The adrenalin has worn off, and I'm not sure whether I have it in me to call. Sasha comes up with a new round of drinks.

"Did you see our girl, Sasha? She did it!" says Iris, already on a first name basis. Sasha laughs. "I have seen her in action; I am sure that she can do anything," he laughs.

"Now it's Mattie turn," I say indelicately, changing the subject. "Mattie, Mattie, Mattie!" I cheer.

"I am ready!" he says, "ready and inspired by Tamara to succeed." He gets off his bar stool and pretends to flex.

"Alright," says Iris, "let's break it down. Girls generally travel in packs, so you don't have too many options to approach individuals. So there are those rowdy girls near the kitchen, the depressive girls near the entrance and one girl all by her lonesome at the other end of the bar. She is either easy prey or someone you shouldn't approach under any circumstance."

"Alright," says Mattie, pretending to crack his knuckles.

"Bring it on." As he turns to make his decision, a voice calls him from the entrance to the bar. "Mattie, over here. Mattie!" I recognize her; it is Orit.

Mattie looks startled. She walks up to him. "Karina told me you would be here," she says to him, ignoring me and Iris. "I would really like to talk with you. Would that be OK?"

Mattie seems to think about it and then says, "Fine, OK, let's go sit over there." He gestures towards a vacant booth, turns to us and shrugs, and walks off.

"You lose on a technicality," yells Iris. I exhale loudly. My eyes follow the two of them as they walk over to a darker corner of the room. I turn back to the bar. I can feel Iris eyes on me. It is only the three of us left at the bar: Iris, Sasha and me. I look at my watch. It is already half past eleven. It has been such a long day and I am suddenly exhausted. "Iris," I say, "It has been an education, but I need to get out of here. I have an early start tomorrow."

"It *has* been an education," she says to me. "You did well."

"I did, didn't I?" I say. "And I had fun. But now I must go." I get off my bar stool and give her a hug. She doesn't try to dissuade me or encourage me to stay. She just says, "Bye, darling." I can feel her eyes on me as I exit the bar. As soon as the bar door swings shut behind me, I take out my phone and open the Missed Calls list. I select Yonatan's number, and hit Delete.

Chapter 17

Next morning, I wake up early and go for a run on the beach. I get home and showered and then make my way to the hospital in time for visiting hours. I am not the first one there. Joseph and Avi are already by Eran's bedside. He has a bad concussion and a broken nose. He looks like hell, but he cracks a smile when I come into the room.

"I am sorry," he says, "again!"

"It wasn't your fault," says Avi.

"Even if it wasn't my fault, I am still responsible for my actions."

Joseph smiles at me and grabs my hand and squeezes. I am sure that he can feel the pride bursting from my heart.

"Eran," I say, "I am so happy and relieved that you are OK. I was worried. Now you just need to focus on getting better, quickly. Graduation is soon and we expect great things from you."

"From me?" he asks incredulously.

"Yes, you. When are they releasing you?" I ask.

"I need to be under observation for another day or two, and then I am out."

"That's good news," I say, "and the boys who did this to you?"

"We don't know," says Avi.

"Don't worry about them," says Joseph. "For now, think about yourselves. And when you are fully recovered, I could use some help in the center, if *you* don't mind," he says, turning to me.

"As long as Eran would like to get involved and it doesn't disrupt his studying, I think that is an excellent idea." I couldn't ask for anything more . . . Eran under Joseph's wing. It's funny how things just work themselves out.

My phone vibrates in the side pocket of my bag. I fish it

out. It is Mattie. "Excuse me just a second," I say, and step out the room into the hospital corridor.

"Hey," I say.

"Hi," Mattie says. "I didn't get a chance to say goodbye yesterday."

"Don't worry about it. It was pretty late and I had to get up early. And I knew you would find a way to chicken out."

"Very funny. Anyway, I don't want to disturb you now. I know you are busy, but just in case you are flexible, I wanted to check whether you can meet for lunch on Tuesday. I need to be in Tel Aviv, near the Nest, and I thought we could grab something together."

"I guess a girl needs to eat," I answer, "and I can definitely get out for a few hours," I say scrolling through my calendar.

"That is super, just terrific," Mattie says. "Can't wait. I will book the place."

"No need to be so formal," I say. "There are plenty of restaurants in the area."

"Yeah, but Orit is pretty fussy about food, so she wants some place specific."

"Orit, oh," I say. I am taken aback for a second. "Oh, OK…"

"Is that OK?"

"Yes, fine, just fine; I just wasn't expecting it."

"OK, great, see you later."

As I finish my call, Joseph steps outside. I give a big momentous sigh. "Things can't be that bad," he says. "Eran seems well enough. Not only that, but look at this amazing turnabout. He exercised the ultimate restraint, and he is not even remotely angling for revenge."

"Yeah, sorry, I'm not actually sighing for that. Just, you know – life. It's a bit complicated and tangled at the moment."

"When isn't it?"

I smile weakly, "True."

"Want to talk about it?" asks Joseph.

"No, I just need to grow up already." I say.

"Tell me about it," he says with a laugh. I laugh too.

"Alright," says Joseph, "I got to run. But you are not getting off that easily…"

We say bye. He heads out and I head back into Eran's room.

Noa's parents live in a scruffy apartment building in one of the southern suburbs of Tel Aviv. It is an area that has become trendy over the years, but that trendiness hasn't brought with it much visible change to the dilapidated neighborhood. Even in these early evening hours, the hole-in-the wall kiosks are still open and young teenagers slink around like street cats: after having skipped school, they are now dragging the hours out together on rusty old park benches, avoiding going back home. On the sidewalks, men in white undershirts, old pants and open shoes are sitting in *ad hoc* circles, heatedly debating the political situation in a mixture of Hebrew and Arabic, over the sound of dice being thrown into well-used sets of backgammon. The smell of smoke and coffee mixes with dust and a distant sea breeze. It is evening time and Noa's parents are expecting me. They know what this is about and their defenses are up. We sit around the family table in the kitchen.

This is not a family with a lot of means, but they are proud and they are loving of one another. They offer me tea, which I readily accept, not because I am thirsty, but because they have offered. I sip it slowly.

"Nava, this is delicious," I say to Noa's mother. She nods her head. "Eli," I say turning to the father, "and Nava," I say turning back to the mother, "thanks for allowing me to come here tonight." Noa sits anxiously and quietly with us at the table. "We are so proud of Noa at the Nest. She has done so well. Her grades are remarkable, and everyone loves working with her." Nava beams, but doesn't say a word.

"We are proud of her too," says her father. "She will graduate – unlike us. It is a wonderful achievement. We thank you for your part in this."

"Well, thank you, but it is a group effort and Noa herself is responsible for the lion's share of the work," I say.

"Yes, we know. Noa is wonderful." There is silence. Neither of us is willing to break the spell by bringing up the elephant in the room. Noa is shaking with tension. I begin gingerly and delicately. "I understand that you have some reservations concerning Noa's conscription." There is an awkward silence. "It's not so much about her going into the army," says Nava.

"Although we are not sure how she will benefit from it frankly," interjects Eli.

"It is just a long time, and we want her, we need her to…" continues Nava. "We think it is time that Noa took more responsibility around here." Noa bursts into tears.

"I know, I know," she cries, "I want to, but I also want to go to the army."

"You are young and you think you know what you want," says Eli, "but helping your family is more important."

I think of all the information that I have gathered about the advantages of the army and I begin to say, "Eli, Nava, the long-term gains of Noa being in the army will be way more beneficial to the family than if she doesn't go. She can learn a trade, find a career, she can make contacts and she can grow."

"Long-term gain doesn't interest us at the moment. It doesn't help us to support Noa's brothers and sisters, and it certainly doesn't put food on the table right now!" says Eli emphatically. "We knew what we signed up for when we allowed Noa to join the Nest," he continues, "but we also hoped that our circumstances would change. And if anything, if anything, they are a bit worse . . ."

"If things were different," adds Nava, "we would perhaps reconsider, but we cannot at the moment."

"Noa's had her opportunity and now she needs to help us to help the others" says Eli.

I can see that there will be no further discussion on the subject with them tonight. Noa is teary-eyed and resigned. Eli is authoritative and clear. Nava is looking down at her hands with sad, tired eyes. "It is late," I say, "and I don't mean to disturb. I truly do understand the issue. I know that your minds are made up, but let me see what I can do. Maybe, let me think. Would it be OK if I called on you again some time?"

"You are always welcome in our home," says Eli.

"Thanks," I say and get up. "Noa, we'll see you soon at the Nest." Noa nods. She is pale and trying hard to fight back more tears. Nava gets up slowly and walks me to the front door. "I am so sorry," she whispers as she closes the door behind me. I walk about eight meters before I feel the buzz of my smartphone. I check the message; it is from Noa.

```
I am sorry

I knew this would be a waste of time
```

I write back immediately:
```
It is my job to help you,

Let me see what I can do

Don't give up
```

And then, in a feeble attempt to lighten the mood:
```
Now GO and study!
```

And I add a winky face icon.

I contemplate the situation as I walk to my bus stop. Of course, it would have been so much easier to have resolved this issue without further delay, but the outcome was to be expected. It is gratifying to know that Eli and Nava have no objection to conscription, but that other obstacles need to be overcome. The bus comes quickly and as the doors open, a cool rush of air conditioning hits me and makes me shiver. I take a seat facing forward and watch the world rush by like a blur. *Life is like a fast, blurry smudge*, I think. *Nothing is ever clear, and nothing can really be broken down into a neat sum of its parts.* I think of Eran at the hospital: it would be easier for him to succumb to his surroundings – but here he is, fighting. I think of Noa: it would be easier for her to succumb to her parents – but here she is, fighting. And here I am, I think: jumping in to fight alongside them. *Let me see what I can do* – a tacit promise that I hope I can fulfil. Here I am, rolling with the punches, and then going back home to my quiet flat and my herbal tea, and the deafening sound of my thoughts.

The next day passes quietly at the Nest. I am on the phone with Adam, talking about the meeting with Noa's parents, when Kobi steps in to join us for our regular managers' meeting. He is a few minutes early, but I signal him to stay; he needs to get an update about Noa anyway. He pulls up the stool and settles down to listen. Adam gives me some ideas for stipends and financial assistance, as well as the names of a few people whom I can ask for support and ideas. I write them all down, and I agree to get in touch with him in a few days' time to give him some updates.

We then discuss the monthly roster of volunteers, our donors and sponsors and each of the kids and their progress, including Eran's hospitalization. Registration for next year's program is already underway, and Kobi talks about the selection process and his communication with the respective schools. Finally, the discussion turns toward the graduation ceremony. This time, Kobi and I have come with a few ideas.

"How about rock climbing?" asks Kobi. "There is an indoor center that we can go to, take part in an activity and then have a celebratory toast. I have already checked and they are prepared to donate their facilities and a guide."

"A nice idea, can everyone do it? I mean, in terms of physical fitness." asks Adam.

"That shouldn't be an issue. We have no real physical limitations among the Nesters. The activity requires pairing off, which is always a good lesson in teamwork," Kobi says. He goes over his notes, and then he continues: "Apart from the climbing activity, I also thought about a tour in Haifa. There is so much to see there: historical and modern. It is also fascinating place in terms of co-existence. There is so much to talk about in terms of good citizenship and values. We have one or two tour guides who are prepared to lead us in the excursion. We just need to figure out what we would like to do."

"Both are great ideas," I say. "I kind of prefer the second one, because it is more inclusive, and it offers more possibilities. Having said that, my idea was actually more like your first one. I was thinking about basketball. We have some connections to some pro-players and I was thinking that we could do a workshop on the court and then watch a game together."

"That sounds really cool," says Kobi. "We should do that."

"Interesting," says Adam. "Is it a sure thing?"

"Well, honestly, my connection is tentative, and I need to do more homework, but I am somewhat confident," I respond.

Adam summarizes the discussion: "It sounds like we have some solid ideas. Kobi, you look into the Haifa excursion and Tamara, you look into the basketball. When we have something more concrete, we can make a decision."

"OK," Kobi and I say in unison. When I hang up the phone, Kobi says, "I can't believe that after all the progress Noa has made, she may not finish the program as intended."

"Yeah well, the parents are quite adamant, and I guess the situation is not easy. We know our community here. Their troubles are very real and even if we get them additional financial support, who's to say that it will be enough? I have no way of knowing how much is enough."

"What did the parents actually say?" asks Kobi.

"Their words were that Noa's *had her opportunity*, and now she needs to help to give the other kids theirs." Kobi looks at me thoughtfully.

"Of course they are right," I say, more miserably than I intended, "but I am not giving up just yet."

Kobi says, "Sounds like mission impossible; can I lend a hand? Run with a few ideas?"

"Sure," I say with a sigh, "the more the merrier."

"By the way," he says, "about Eran..." I catch my breath –

we have had a nice conversation up till now and I don't
have the energy for any more tension. Kobi sees me stiffening
up and he smiles and says, "Don't worry, I just want to say
that I am sorry that he was hurt and that I heard he was
fantastic." Then, softly, he continues, "and I am so happy,
really and truly, that I was so horribly wrong about him – and
about your decision."

"Thanks, Kobi," I say. "That is really nice to hear. You
have made my day," I say, and I mean it.

On Tuesday, after a quiet morning of routine at the Nest, I
slip out for a few hours to meet Mattie and Orit for lunch.
Mattie has made reservations for "Rabbit Food," one of the
many vegan places that have popped up in Tel Aviv over the
past few years. I don't really care one way or the other what
kind of food is served. On the one hand, I am particular about
food, but, on the other hand, I am not big on eating anyway.

Mattie and Orit are already seated when I get there. Orit is
squinting at the menu. It is written in chalk on a blackboard
above the counter. Mattie gets up when he sees me, a huge
smile on his face, and reaches over to give me a hug. Orit stays
put. She gives a small "hey," and settles back to her staring
competition with the menu. As I get settled, I say to Orit, "Hi,
how are you?" She looks at me, nods, and says "OK." I wait
for reciprocity, and when it doesn't come, I shrug and look up
at the menu myself. What is so fascinating up there? I get the
feeling that Orit is angry. Not sure whether with me or Mattie.
I steal a look at him and gesture discretely to Orit as if to ask
delicately – *what's going on?* He shrugs it off.

"So, what's to eat?" I ask cheerfully.

"Well," says Mattie, "if all else fails, you can always have
tea to your heart's content."

I smile. There is a special section just for teas on the board.
It is decorated with hand-drawn leaves: mint, myrrh, sage and
lemongrass, to mention a few. "My kind of place," I say.

"Tea isn't food. I need something more than that," says

Orit. "I thought you said that there would be some options for me," she says to Mattie, putting her hand gently on his.

"I think there are quite a few options," says Mattie. "See, look there, there's Quinoa salad."

"It has mint."

"Lentil hamburgers."

"They are made with coriander."

"Rice with chick peas."

"It has cumin."

"I am sure that you can get some of those without the condiments and spices," I say.

"Perhaps," she says. "Well, I will have to try something," Orit says with a sigh.

"I told you she was a fussy eater," says Mattie with a smile.

"Why did you tell her that?" asks Orit with a frown.

"Not a big deal. I was just explaining why I was booking some place specific instead of just popping into a random restaurant," Mattie answers.

"It's not a big deal. I am a bit difficult myself," I tell Orit, trying to be reassuring. She shrugs and clams up.

"What's up, Tammy?" asks Mattie.

"All's OK. Having a few issues at work, but trying to sort things through."

"Isn't it graduation soon?"

"Yup, it's that time of the year."

"I told Orit what amazing work you do." Orit nods, but doesn't say anything.

"What do you do?" I ask her.

"Copywriting," she says.

"Interesting," I say, trying to sound like I mean it.

"Not really," says Orit, "I just kind of do it."

"Are you looking to make a change?" I ask her.

"What do you mean?" she asks.

"Well, if you're unhappy, are you thinking of what to do next?"

"I didn't say I am unhappy. It is just a job." I can't think of anything to say to that, but luckily I don't have to because the waiter steps up to get our order.

"What are you folks eating today?" he asks cheerily.

"That depends on how flexible you can be," says Orit.

"I will certainly do my best."

"Can the Quinoa salad be prepared without mint?"

"Of course."

"Are the pine nuts roasted?"

"No, they are fried."

"Not good!"

"Can I have sunflower seeds instead?"

"Roasted?"

"No, plain."

"You sure can."

"Would it be possible to have lime juice instead of lemon?"

"I will check and get back to you."

"Fine."

"And to drink?" asks the waiter.

"I will try the beetroot and celery juice," says Orit.

"Good choice. Next," he says, turning to me.

"I would like the Portobello steak without the spinach risotto."

"No risotto. Got it. Would you like something else instead? How about roasted vegetables with rosemary and almonds? I recommend it," says the waiter.

"Sounds delicious, OK."

"How come you can roast the vegetables but not the pine nuts?" asks Orit with consternation.

"Good question. Would you like me to ask?"

"No, don't bother."

"He can ask, if you would like," says Mattie.

"No," sighs Orit, "I will be fine. I always manage."

"And to drink?"

"Fresh apple, mint and ginger," I say, "sounds delicious."

"That does sound great," says Mattie. "Make that two of the drink. And I will have the lentil burgers with fried onions and sauerkraut. No special instructions."

"OK," says the waiter, "just reading it back: Quinoa salad. No mint, sunflower seeds instead of pine nuts and lime instead of lemon. Portobello steak with roasted vegetables and almonds. No risotto. Lentil burgers with the works. One beet and celery juice, two apple-mint-ginger juices. Good choices. Enjoy your meal." And the waiter goes off to the kitchen to start the orders.

"So, how did you get into copywriting?" I ask Orit.

"It was something to do. I studied linguistics."

"That's interesting."

"Is it?"

"I think so. Words are powerful. Especially the written word." Orit shrugs.

"I guess you are right," she says, "But I think that after all the studying, I just wanted to do something practical."

"Don't we all," says Mattie.

"Copywriting made sense to me. What about you? What made you do what you do?" she asks me.

"I guess a bit like you: I fell into it. It was a practical next step after my studies."

"I couldn't be responsible for kids like that, especially not troubled ones." Orit shudders. "Taking care of myself is hard enough. You must be a real people person. I personally need my space."

Mattie smiles and looks at me. I smile back at him. "Well, not really; I need my space too, and I am not really a people person. You can ask Mattie. I suppose that in my job, being detached maybe helps a bit. Especially when you deal with issues related to people and their welfare, it is probably easier to not be too sensitive."

"Amazing that you can deal with real issues and not care," says Orit.

"I didn't say that I don't care," I say somewhat defensively.

"I think being detached means not caring," says Orit with a shrug.

"I agree with Tamara – not only because detached and caring are not synonymous – but also because I happen to know how much Tamara cares," says Mattie. "But, anyway, Tamara is good at what she does and she enjoys it, right?" he says, looking at me. I am pondering whether or not he is correct. Being good at it and enjoying it are two different things. I am not so sure of either point at the moment. Before I can respond, Mattie continues, "What are you planning for this year's graduation party anyway?" adeptly steering the discussion to safer ground.

"I was thinking of something with basketball."

"Basketball," says Mattie, "cool, what do you mean?" The waiter comes back to us with a nervous look on his face.

"Excuse me, miss," he says to Orit, "but we don't have any lime, only lemon."

"Well that just stinks," says Orit. "Typical. Fine," she says, "I will just have lemon then." The waiter goes back to the kitchen with a relieved spring in his step.

Our orders come quite soon after that. The rest of lunch is eaten in relative silence with the occasional banal comment about the zestiness of the spicing and the inevitable "this-tastes-just-like-meat" comment about the vegan steaks and burgers. After we pay the bill, we get up and begin to walk out into the Tel Aviv afternoon. Orit and Mattie are hand-in-hand. "You guys, thanks so much for the invitation for lunch." I say.

"Yes," says Orit, "thanks for joining us," she says with a smile. "Mattie has told me so much about you and he was right." I look at her. I have no idea what she is referring to, if anything, so I just smile. I shut my eyes tight, because I fear that if I keep them open, I will roll my eyes in Mattie's direction.

"Tammy, are you OK?" Mattie asks.

"Yes, fine, just tired. I heard that almonds can make you slow and sluggish," I reply.

"Really?" says Orit. "Interesting."

I nod, say "Bye guys, see you later," and walk off. I start walking away as quickly as I can without seeming like I am running. "Tammy." I hear my name being called in my tail wind. "Tamara, stop a second." Good lord. I can't stick around anymore. I turn around; it is just Mattie. What a relief.

"Hey," he says, "are you OK?"

"Fine, fine," I say. "Lunch was interesting."

"Don't patronize. She is really nice once you get to know her."

"I know Mattie; I guess I just need time."

"Listen, let's talk, just the two of us. I will be in touch."

"OK," I say. "But now I got to go," I say and I scuttle off.

After a brisk walk, I get back to work within ten minutes. Just before I start making my way up the stairs to the Nest, I try to shake off the heaviness and fatigue that I am feeling. On a whim, I pick up the phone and call Iris. She answers straight away.

"Tammy, sweetheart, love you, miss you, want you." Her words are an immediate pick-me-up.

"I am in a sucky mood. Cheer me up. Tell me something funny."

"I am not wearing any underwear," she says. It's not really funny, but I can't help giggling.

"But wait, there's more. I am not wearing any underwear and there's a rip in my skirt." My giggling turns into a burst of laughter.

"Front or back?" I ask.

"Back of course."

"What will you do?"

"What any normal person would do: take off my skirt and staple it together. And then go home and change."

"But how will you do that? Won't everybody see you?"

"I need to find a way to get to the bathroom with my back to the wall."

"Oh man, you are so funny. I needed that."

"Thanks for laughing at my expense."

"Anyway, what's up, darling? Why are you down?"

"Just had lunch with Mattie and Orit. It was a bit rough.

She kind of rubs me the wrong way."

"Perhaps you just need to get to know her."

"Yes, I suppose so. That's what I said to Mattie."

"Hon, I got to go, I see my chance to make a dash for the ladies."

"See you Friday at Napoleon's. Bye."

"Wait, what about Napoleon's?" I say, not sure what she is talking about. But Iris has already hung up. I will ask her later.

The rest of the afternoon stretches out uneventfully. I make a few phone calls on Noa's behalf with some moderate success. It seems that there may be some support that her family can get from the municipality – if they are not getting it already. I also find the name of another contact that could potentially help me from within the framework of the IDF draft office. I send the details to Kobi and ask him to look into it. Satisfied that I have done what I can for today, thoughts of Orit and Mattie begin to seep back into my mind. Not wanting to deal with them, I pick up my phone and call Eran.

"Tamara, hi!" he says.

"How are you?" I ask. "We miss you!"

"Thanks," he says. "I will be back next week, thank goodness. I have never been so still in my life. My mother can't believe that I am actually at home. Usually, she barely sees me during the week."

"So, is it a good thing?"

"Yes, she is thrilled, and my brothers are thrilled. And, I have been so bored during the day that I have had no choice other than to study."

"So you are completely ready for finals."

"I am ready. Avi has been helping me as well."

"Over the phone?"

"No actually, he has come around a few times."

What an unexpected friendship! I think to myself, and how far they have both come.

"That's terrific." I say. "You two make quite a formidable pair."

"Yes, it makes me feel bad about how I threatened him."

"It's a good thing that you feel bad. That incident was a growing experience. Look where you are now."

"True, but still."

"At some point, you need to take that experience and decide what you want to do with it. You need to decide if and how it has changed you, and then, you need to let it go."

"Like Joseph."

"Exactly like Joseph," I say.

"He has also been around to visit me," says Eran. "He has been so great, so supportive."

"I'm glad," I say.

"He also talks a lot about doing something that is meaningful. Like what he does, or what you do."

"And what do you think?"

"I think that I am not like either of you. I don't have the same skills – or, you know, the same way with people that you have."

My brain halts for a second at the sentence. It's the second time today that my people skills have been commented on, unjustifiably. I know for sure that my people skills are not my strong suit. But, no time for introspection or analysis. "Everyone has different skills, and as for the way one deals with people, that it is a work in progress for all of us. There is no set recipe for who should do these kinds of jobs. It all begins and ends with motivation. Do you want to do it?"

"How do I know if I want something?"

Good question – I think to myself. "I am not absolutely sure I know the answer to that. Some people do things because of opportunity, some people do things because of inertia, some people do things out of fear and some people do things because they feel that it is the right thing to do. I can tell you that all of those reasons are true for me at some point or other."

"What would you do now, if you could?" asks Eran.

"I am not sure," I say honestly. "I like working at the Nest. I get great pleasure from it and from the people I work with. I am not sure what I would do if I were somewhere else. I do think about it though. That's normal. Most people move between many frameworks throughout their lifetime."

"Food for thought, I guess." says Eran.

"Absolutely," I say. "And you have a few years before you have to really make a decision. Because you are about to move into your next framework!"

"Yes," says Eran. "My call-up is for right after graduation."

"I can hardly believe that. I am so proud of you."

"Actually, I am proud of me too!" says Eran.

"Well you should be."

We say our goodbyes and hang up.

Shifting frameworks – it should be so easy. It should be organic, natural, and seamless, but it isn't. For Nesters like Eran and Noa, the shift from high school to army call-up requires a tireless community of volunteers and professionals. And what about the rest of us: those who can supposedly undergo the shifts on their own. What about me? Failed marriage, tentative personal life, doubts about the professional front – my frameworks are like quicksand. Don't they say that in quicksand, it's best to simply stay still?

After a few minutes of silent contemplation, I shrug my thoughts aside, pick up my phone and call Joseph. It rings for a few minutes and then a voice says, "Hello."

"Hey, Joseph," I say.

"Hi, Tamara. What a nice surprise."

"I just wanted to thank you for your interest in Eran. You really seem to be having a huge impact on him."

"He is a terrific kid. You have done a great job."

"I had a few moments of doubt."

"Don't we all."

"You can say that again," I say. "Listen, on another subject, before I forget. I know that you guys integrate basketball a lot into your youth center activities. Do you have any connections with any of the professional teams? I would like to do a graduation focused on an interactive workshop and then maybe the group could catch a game."

"Great idea, and yes, definitely. One of our major sponsors is connected. Do you want me to hook you up?"

"Absolutely, please. That would be terrific."

"On one condition . . ."

"Name it," I say.

"OK, "says Joseph, "you speak to me."

"I speak to you all the time."

"Not like that. What I mean is that I want to hear what's up with you. At the hospital, you were a bit off."

"You do remember why we were there, right? I was worried."

"I know, but I know that Eran's situation was only part of the issue. I want to hear all about it. What's going on?"

"Are you ever off duty?"

"Absolutely never. A man's work is never done . . ."

"I am pretty sure that that is not how the expression goes."

"Maybe not, but it still happens to be true . . ."

"And you won't take no for an answer?"

"Is *that* a real question? Not a chance."

"Alright then, let's meet. I will set something up for us. My calendar is open. Is Monday afternoon good for you?"

"What time?"

"Around two-ish? At you?"

"Yes to both. Sounds good. I will try to get you what you need by then."

"That would be awesome."

"*Awesome* is my middle name."

I laugh. "Good to know."

We hang up and I start to pack up my things and leave for the day. My phone lets out an impatient little buzz: a new text message. I pick it up to read. It is from Mattie. I can't help but sigh again when I think about lunch with him and Orit. Excruciating.

Can we meet sometime?

The text says.

    Sure. When?

I answer.

    Friday night at Blooms? 9:30?

    This Friday is no good

I try again.
    Next Friday?

    Sure.

He sends me the thumbs up icon.

Chapter 18

Before I know it, Thursday is upon me. On Thursday afternoon, I make my way to Karina and Josh's place. Only Karina is in. The kids are at their grandparents and Josh is still at work.

"What's up, Tammy?" asks Karina as she expertly pulls out clothing options from her bulging wardrobe. Several items come rolling out of the closet. "Apart from your hot date . . ." she says with a smile as she kicks all the tumbling garments into a messy little pile at the foot of the closet.

"Hot date? Let's not jump the gun," I answer, as Karina continues to pull more and more clothes out from seemingly random places. "Whoa, don't go wild there," I say, feeling increasingly uncomfortable with the growing pile of textiles.

"Don't deny me my fun!" says Karina. "Same rules apply. My decision is final and you will suck it up."

"OK," I say with resignation.

"I heard you went out with Mattie and Orit."

"Yes, did you hear from Mattie?"

"Yes."

"What did he say?"

"He said it was a bit rough"

"Funny, I said the same thing to Iris. Those words exactly!"

Karina smiles. "Here, try this on," she says, throwing me some black slacks and a white flowy top.

"Won't I look like a waiter?"

"Not if you accessorize," she answers, and hands me a red leather belt. I go to the walk-in bathroom to try it on. "In what way was it rough?"

"I don't know," I answer. "Orit, she seems OK, but she is a bit . . . a bit difficult to get to know." I come out of the bathroom wearing the improvised outfit.

"Nope, I don't think so," says Karina. "A bit too formal. Let's remember it for another occasion. Try this instead." She hands me some brown corduroy jeans and an orange button-down shirt. "Wow, this is really intense," I say, pretending to squint at the orange, as if it were blinding me with its radioactive glow.

"Don't exaggerate," says Karina, laughing at me. "It is burnt orange, not volcanic lava." I walk back into the bathroom.

"Orit seems, you know, like a mixture of introversion and stubbornness. It was a bit exhausting," I say as I come out of the bathroom again.

"Oh no, that's awful. Try on this blue top with those black slacks." She hands me a powder blue short-sleeve silk top.

"This shirt has everything. It is simple and elegant, and casual and smart all at the same time," Karina muses. I go back into the bathroom.

"You know, I did try to get to know her, but it was a bit difficult – like drawing water from a stone," I say. "Gosh, this shirt has buttons at the back. I am going to need your help." I come out to Karina and stand with my back to her so that she can do up the buttons.

"Introverted and stubborn. Difficult to get to know . . ." she repeats as she buttons me up. "Sounds exhausting." I can hear the smile in her voice. I look up, facing a full- length mirror.

"This looks great," Karina says. "Just take this scarf in case you are cold and drape it around yourself like so." She hands me a silvery grey scarf and shows me how to put it on.

"Wait." I say, "What are you suggesting?"

"Nothing, just advising you about the best way to wear the scarf."

"Not about that! About Orit. What were you trying to say to me?"

Karina laughs. "Listen honey, I am not suggesting anything, except that it sounds like Orit needs more time. Sometimes people who are more introverted and stubborn just need a bit more time. Don't you think?" she asks, looking directly at me.

"You are implying that she is like me. Or that I am like her."

"Well, isn't she? Aren't you?"

"She seems stuck, kind of regimented, maybe even a bit lost in her routine."

"Well Tammy, I kind of thought you were feeling a bit stuck yourself."

"I mean yes, but mostly, you know in the personal arena. And I am working on that . . . apropos this ridiculous makeover session. And, professionally, I am . . . I guess I am, plowing forth."

"Plowing forth?"

"Yes, you know, rolling with the punches?"

"Rolling with the punches? Plowing forth? Sounds a bit reactive to me."

I consider that for a moment. "You know what, maybe you are right."

"About what?"

"This does look good on me…"

Karina laughs and gives me a hug. "Have a great time," she says. "Don't forget that we are meeting on Friday morning for Iris' birthday breakfast."

"Dammit, Iris mentioned something, and I forgot to ask her about it. Good that you are reminding me. Where are we meeting anyway?"

"According to the email that Iris sent, anywhere where there is alcohol."

I laugh. "So it isn't really a breakfast then."

"We can tell ourselves that it is," says Karina, fixing my scarf.

"OK," I say, heading to the door, "but how will I find that oasis of good cheer?"

"Napoleon's in Jaffa, ten in the morning."

"Ah, OK. I will be there."

"Enjoy Tammy, have fun!"

"Thanks, I will. Bye."

Elon and I are meeting at an Ethiopian restaurant in the center of Tel Aviv. The restaurant is near the central bus station, and the neighborhood is a hodgepodge of color, noise and motion. Middle-sized buildings, maybe five to seven stories, none of which are in great condition. On street level there are multiple stores – the old juxtaposed with the new. There is designer shop for bathroom tiles next door to a television and VCR repair shop – who still goes there? Adjacent to them are a 3D printing studio in between a cobbler shop and a butcher. The neighborhood is populated by a tapestry of folk. There is only a smattering of Hebrew: instead, Tagalog and Mandarin mix and mingle with Arabic, Amharic, Tigrinya and Russian. This is the bustling center and home for refugees, manual laborers and immigrants – a field day for anthropologists and sociologists.

The restaurant is practically a hole in the wall. There is enough room for about eight tables inside the place and three tables outside, precariously balanced on the tiny wooden deck that was built about two meters above the busy street. The diners are a mixed group: Tel Aviv locals, like myself, who eat out almost every meal instead of cooking, vegans who have found a home in this establishment, and trend makers who have heard that this is a cool place to try out. I don't see a single Ethiopian in the restaurant. But I can see that the general manager-slash-concierge-slash-waiter is an Ethiopian in his late twenties. In the kitchen, there is another Ethiopian lady about the same age, standing behind a few massive aluminum pots, stirring vigorously, occasionally stopping to add additional spices to the cooking brew. They briefly confer on an order and I can see that they are more than just manager and employee.

Elon has already arrived. He is sitting at a table on the little deck. He gets up when he sees me and gives me a peck on the cheek. I am close enough to smell his cologne, and he smells nice. "You look nice," he says.

"So do you," I say with a smile. "Somewhat different from

the hospital scrubs that you were wearing the last time I saw you."

"Yes." He says. "But hospital scrubs are uncomplicated. I don't need to think about what I should wear."

"Amen to that," I say with a laugh, thinking of Karina and her endless efforts to style me.

"Maybe we should start a trend of uniforms for people who just can't be bothered to make clothing-related decisions?"

"I agree." I say, "or specify what clothes should be worn for every day of the week. On Mondays, we wear brown, on Tuesdays, we wear blue . . ."

"Sounds perfect. Uncomplicated . . ."

"Yes," I say, "that is what I am going for: uncomplicated."

"Talking about uncomplicated, whatever shall we order?"

"Have you been here before?"

"No."

"Do you know anything about Ethiopian food?"

"No."

"Are you a foodie in general?"

"No."

"Excellent," I say with a laugh. "Tel Aviv is already overflowing with them. I can't bear the obsession people have with where to eat, what to eat and how the food is prepared."

"I agree completely," says Elon. "Is now a bad time to show you my Facebook page with a blow-by-blow account of me preparing macaroons?"

I laugh – Elon is clearly joking. "So how will we order?" I ask.

"By calling the waiter," Elon quickly responds, and I laugh again. Elon gives the universal hand signal for summoning servers and within seconds, the waiter comes over.

"Hi," says Elon. "We are new here."

"And ignorant," I add.

"Absolutely, totally ignorant," says Elon. "Can you recommend something for us?"

"Sure," says the waiter, eyeballing the both of us one at a

time. "Absolutely!" he says with conviction, and abruptly turns around and walks off. We stare after him as he heads inside the restaurant. "Did we order?" I ask.

"I think we just did," said Elon.

A few minutes later, the waiter comes out with two massive platters. "This is *injera*," he says. "You break off a piece of the bread and then you dip it in the different sauces and into the *wat*. *Wat* is our vegan stew. Some of it is spicy."

"I like spicy," said Elon.

"Me too," I say. "This looks delicious."

"This platter," says the waiter, "is *ful medames*, a dish made of beans, garlic, lemon, cumin… also very tasty."

"Yummy," I say.

"In Ethiopia, we eat with our right hand," says the waiter. "So I challenge you to do the same."

"Not a problem," I say. "Dipping into humus has been my only staple meal for two years now."

Elon laughs. "No wonder you hate foodies," he says to me. To the waiter he says, "Thanks. This looks great." The waiter nods his head regally and walks off.

"I am curious," I say. "Does eating with your hands affect your sanitary sensibilities? You know, as a doctor."

"Not as long as I am not going into surgery. Also, as a rule, doctors aren't actually sanitary and ascetic individuals."

"They aren't?"

"Nope, most of the doctors I know smoke like chimneys, eat unhealthy loads of oil, sugar and caffeine and like to muck around with the best of them."

The waiter comes back with two large beer mugs. "Ethiopian beer," he announces proudly. "Enjoy."

"Thanks," says Elon. I also give a nod of thanks to the waiter.

"You, as well?" I say, coming back to our conversation.

"Yes!"

"What do you muck around in?"

"It just so happens I sculpt."

"You sculpt?"

"Yes, I am afraid so."

"In what medium?"

"Clay."

"Wow! Sounds amazing . . . really!" I say. Silence ensues for a few seconds as my thoughts wander.

"I know what you are thinking," he says suddenly, breaking the pause in conversation.

"What am I thinking?" I ask.

"About that scene in Ghost."

"That movie from a thousand years ago?"

"The one and the same. Whenever I tell people that I sculpt with clay, that far-away look is always the same reaction."

I laugh. "I can't help it," I say.

"Well," he says, "I hate to disappoint you off the bat, but I don't have a sculptor's wheel."

"Very disappointing," I say with a laugh.

"So we will just have to improvise," he says flirtatiously.

"Cheers to that," I say, and we raise our beer mugs and clink them together.

About an hour later, I can barely breathe, I am so full. "I cannot believe that we managed to finish all of that," I say with a groan, looking at the empty platters. "I feel like I am about to explode."

"Why don't we just walk it off?" suggests Elon. "It is an amazing evening." He is absolutely right. The sun has already set. The street lights are on. The traffic has slowed down and all the locals have come out to play. From now until five in the morning, the city will not rest. Bars, restaurants, theaters and beach-side cafes will be open for the endless streams of people who come to the city to feel alive. From the resplendent Tel Aviv opera house, to the makeshift comedy clubs in the more southern parts of the city, all the way up to the souk in Jaffa with its Middle Eastern and Western infusion – there is something here for everyone.

There is an endless stream of people, flowing in multitudes

of directions. What is clear is that there is no way to compartmentalize, to generalize or to assume where the passersby are going. The senior citizen in a string undershirt and sandals may be heading to folk dancing or to an opera. The twenty-somethings with the multiple piercing and tattoos may be headed out to a club or to an art exhibition. The thirty-something metrosexuals may be headed out to the latest sushi, or Thai, or Cambodian, or whatever restaurant with friends, or maybe they are off to visit their parents, who will welcome them with hugs, food and drink, as if they had spent hours in preparation. Tel Aviv is a city where you just can't tell what is up and what is going down.

It takes us half an hour to walk to the sea and another half an hour before I realize that I have walked him back to my apartment. "I can't believe it. We are at me." I say.

"And here I thought that we were just walking randomly through the city," he says. "Little did I know that you were luring me back to your home."

"We *were* walking randomly. I guess I came here like a homing pigeon."

"Freud would disagree."

"Freud can kiss my ass."

"I am sure that he would do a lot more if you would let him."

"What would he say about you sculpting? What do you sculpt anyway?"

"Sorry, I can't tell you."

"Can't or won't."

"OK, won't."

"Why?"

"Because you will read too much into it."

"I won't, I promise." I put my hand on my heart solemnly.

"Will you leave Freud out of it?"

"Absolutely."

"Fine. I sculpt famous architectural structures," he says. I scrunch my lips so that a smile won't escape. "Particularly skyscrapers," he continues. Too late, the smile escapes. "You promised . . ." says Elon indignantly.

I bite my top lip. "You sculpt skyscrapers? That is . . . that is so . . ." I say scrunching up my mouth, trying desperately not to laugh.

"That is *not* phallic," Elon insists.

". . .very *artistic* of you. Is what *I* wanted to say!"

"A woman of your word . . ." says Elon.

"I try to be." I say.

We are at the front door of my building. I punch in the code and the door buzzes open. I step inside and turn back towards him. "Well, doctor," I say, "are you coming inside with me or not?"

"Sure," he says. "Wait, are *you* sure?"

"Absolutely," I answer, "I want to hear more about your sculpting."

"Very funny," he says. He follows me up the stairs. Our footsteps echo in the stairwell. I pull out my key at the front door, and turn it in the lock. We step inside. I close the door behind me and lock it from the inside. When I turn around, Elon is standing right behind me. "Tamara," he says, and takes a step forward. *What the hell*, I think to myself, *why not*? I step right up into his personal space. I put my arms around his waist and pull him towards me. He puts his arms around me and lifts me clean off the floor. We are now face to face. I kiss him. Over an hour has passed since we ate, but he still has a faint taste of Ethiopian beer. We continue to kiss as he leads me to the bedroom and puts me down on the bed. I can feel his weight on me. *God, I have missed this*, I think to myself.

As we kiss, I run my hands down his back. Where his shirt meets his pants, I release the fabric so that I can feel his skin. I press my hands down on the small of his back going as far as my arms will reach. Elon climbs off of me for a second to pull off his shirt. I try to do the same with my shirt, but then remember that the buttons are at the back. "You are going to have to help me with this," I say. Elon laughs. "Come here," he says. We both stand at the edge of the bed. "Sorry about that silly shirt. So complicated," I begin to say, but he unbuttons me before I finish the word. Surgeon hands, I guess. The powder blue shirt flies through the air to the foot of the bed, followed by my bra. I laugh and begin to turn around to face him. Before I make it all the way around, I feel his hands on my breasts. He kisses me down my neck and my skin prickles. I inch closer to him so that we can be skin to skin. His hands wander down from my breasts to the button of my pants. I feel my pants and my underwear open and slide down to the floor right on top of his. Before I can give it anymore thought, I feel him angle his pelvis. Instinctively, I arch my back towards him and lean over the bed. He pulls me nearer, placing both hands around me. All of sudden, I feel him inside me, and it takes my breath away. My insides quiver at his movement. He holds my breast with one hand, and the inside of my thigh with another. With every movement, my head feels light and my body feels electrified. I realize suddenly that I am groaning with pleasure. I don't remember myself like this. We move together. Elon is agile and strong. His body is warm and muscular. His hands are strong and determined. They know what they want. My body responds to his. Each thrust of passion is like a crashing wave that builds slowly, lifts me up, carries me off and throws me down with increasing urgency – pushing me nearer and nearer to a magical destination. The waves become more deliberate and stronger until I can feel that the journey is about to end. I am totally consumed by Elon. My body is almost impossibly helpless and weak, but he holds me up, supports me. I feel like clay in his hands. He molds me with his every movement. I can feel the biggest wave about to come and pick me up. Soon, I will have to let go.

The final wave crashes inside of me, and I am released suddenly. Like a helium balloon, my mind floats off into a white hazy mist of unreality. We lay there, Elon and I, spent, naked and satisfied. His arm rests casually on my thigh. He kisses my shoulder. I take his hand and put it on my breast. He reaches up to my face and I kiss his fingers. He puts his hand back down. I snuggle even nearer to him until I can feel the pulse of his heart beating on my back. We fall asleep.

The next morning, I wake up because the sun is streaming into the room. I know immediately that I have overslept. I think to myself, what did I do last night? The bedcovers are strewn messily across the bed, and I am not wearing any pajamas. Elon! I suddenly remember. "Elon," I call out, but the apartment is clearly empty; it resonates with silence. I walk naked to the lounge area, grabbing an oversized t-shirt along the way. On the kitchen counter, I find a note scribbled on a napkin.

Tamara, thanks for last night

It was delicious and the food was good too

Sorry got to go. My parents are expecting me for

breakfast.

Call you later

Breakfast. A little bell goes off in my head. What's the time? I pick up my mobile phone. The clock says ten forty-five a.m. I have seven missed phone calls, five text messages, as well as one audio message. Of the missed phone calls, three are from Dana, one is from Mattie, one is from Karina, one is from Iris and the last one is from Elon. Elon's call was just five minutes ago. *Dammit.* My phone was on silent. *Oh no,* I think to myself – Iris's birthday breakfast in Jaffa. Even if I throw on some clothes quickly, by the time a taxi picks me up and I get there, the breakfast will nearly be over. And besides which, I don't feel like the questions. *No,* I say to myself. *It is done for now.* I have missed the breakfast. I will make it up to Iris. I consider calling Elon, but then decide to read the text messages instead.

From Elon:

8:15 – You were sleeping so deeply

I didn't have the heart to wake you up

Hope you saw my note

Call you later…

From Dana:
9:50 - Feel so stupid should have picked you up.

Aviva and I are first to arrive, as usual.

When are you coming? Calling…

10:10 - Mattie + Orit have arrived.

No Iris - typical. No you.

Should I order you something?

Calling again…

10:15 - Karina + Josh just got here

Where are you?

Is your phone broken?

Karina says maybe your date was that good ;-)

10:20 - Iris is here.

She says that she hopes the sex was worth it.

Sorry. I have no control over her.

Pick up your phone! ☹

Dialing again…

A voice message from Iris. I hit the button so that I can listen.

10:25 – My darling. I am not angry at all provided that the good doctor satisfied you.

In the background of the recording I can hear Dana, objecting: "Perhaps she is just sleeping or late, or not feeling well?" I can hear the others scoffing in the background. Iris continues loudly and rambunctiously: "I hope he has you stretched out, and is doing a full body examination. You can never be too careful. Your birthday present to me is that I get to hear all the dirty details. Say bye to him from us."

"Bye," call the voices in the background.

"Sorry," says Dana. "*I* tried . . ." but she is cut off by Iris, as Iris ends the recording.

From Karina:
```
10:20 - I knew the outfit was killer!!!

Can't wait to hear it all

Orit says he's nice & yummy looking

Will you see him again???
```

Karina's clothes! Forgot about them completely. I walk around the apartment and gather the items one by one. The grey scarf is in the lounge; I don't even remember taking it off. The shirt is at the foot of the bed, and the pants are on the side. Those I remember. I am going to have to dry-clean everything. What a mess. I am never going to live this down. I drop the clothes in a bag by the front door so that I will remember to take it in tomorrow. I walk to the bathroom. I start the shower, pull off my shirt and step inside. The water is steamy and hot. I soak my hair and lather it with shampoo.

What *about* Elon? I think to myself. It *was* a great date. He is fun company. We talk easily and comfortably. He is funny and intelligent. The sex was great. I think and shudder with pleasure as I remember being naked in his arms. *Sure*, I think. *I could go out with him again. He's good company. He's definitely, nice.* I wonder why I can't muster more enthusiasm than just 'good' and 'nice', but I block the thought out and I pick up my phone and shoot off a text to Elon:
```
I think Ethiopian food brings out the best in me
```

But, need to go again to prove the theory

Up for round 2?

Within seconds, Elon texts back:
Sure, but it isn't the food

that brings out the best in you,

It is the company

Call you later

Of the missed phone calls, only Mattie has left a voice mail. I hit Play. The message consists of a two-way conversation with Mattie talking to me and Orit talking to him:

Hey Tammy. Missed you today . . . In the background, I can hear Orit shout: "Come Mattie, let's go into the water."

We all missed you, Mattie continues. "Coming in just a minute," he shouts to Orit.

I know that everything is almost definitely OK, but just checking in anyway, says Mattie.

"Can you lather this on my back?" Orit chimes in.

"Right away," says Mattie. "Like this?" he asks.

"Make more circular motions. Yeah, like that," says Orit.

Anyway, I need my hands. Gotta go, says Mattie.

"Please put the phone away," Orit says.

Orit says hi and bye. Speak to you later. Bye, says Mattie.

"Like this…?" I hear him ask Orit.

"That's fantastic honey," I hear Orit say. The voice message gets cut off. I put down the phone, and put on my running shoes. I think I just need to run this morning off.

Chapter 19

On Saturday, I pack a bag and cycle over to HaYarkon Park. As usual, the park is teeming with people. Picnics are a serious business here. Families come *en masse* from very early in the morning. They cordon off sections with ropes and streamers in order to have a semblance of private space. By the time I get here, the park is segmented into messy chunks demarcated by different radio channels blaring out music and talk shows in Arabic, Hebrew, Russian and English, smells of grilling meat, portable furniture, and various games. I walk from the Frisbee section, through multiple soccer games and a makeshift volleyball court, as well as a rather violent dodgeball game, until I get to *Zapari*, a local, private apiary in the center of park. This is my meeting point with Dana and Aviva and the kids. Not that we plan to join the masses; none of this is quite their style – or mine. They are more of an organized educational-adventure type of family. We are meeting at the park, after they have spent the morning in the Tel Aviv planetarium. Once we meet up, we will head away from the smells and noise and find an area where grilling is forbidden and there we will sit and have our picnic.

We arrive at more or less the same time. Dana and I hug. She whispers in my ear, "Don't give me details . . . just tell me that you had fun yesterday." I smile and say. "I am fine, Mom. Everything is fine."

"Hey, Tammy," says Aviva. "Nice of you to join us today. We were worried that you might still be indisposed," she teases.

"Aviva – leave her alone," says Dana.

I laugh. "I can handle it," I say.

The kids come over to say hi and then go off to find the best spot for our picnic. When they are out of earshot, I ask, "So was Iris really mad at me? I didn't have the courage to call her."

"*Naaah*," says Aviva, "she was more amused. We all were."

"It's not really – you know – like you," said Dana.

"No it isn't, and it wasn't exactly planned."

"But you had fun, right?" asks Dana, and then adds, "Is he nice?"

I consider my answer for a few seconds and then say, "He's nice and funny, and we had a good time."

"Sounds to me like there's a *but*," says Aviva.

"Well, there were two butts actually," I laugh.

"Tamara," says Dana, aghast.

"Just kidding. I don't know whether there is a *but*. We had a nice time. He is a good guy. On paper, he is perfect: a doctor, kind, intelligent, we have great chemistry, we spoke non-stop and you know, he seems to get me."

"A good guy," says Aviva – "not exactly a superlative."

"Well it's still early," I say. "Why should there be expectations for anything more? I know that we have kind of jumped to intimacy, but we are both consenting adults, and we had a good time."

"So what's the problem?" asks Dana.

"I'm not sure that there is one," I say.

"So, what now?"

"Well, I guess we go out again."

"That's great," says Dana.

"Cool," says Aviva.

"I guess," I say.

"As long as you are having fun . . . that is the main thing," says Aviva.

"Is it?" I ask.

"For now," Dana says.

We sit down at our designated picnic spot – one of the only shady spots near an open area peppered with rocks of different shapes, sizes and textures. Dana and Aviva never cater in excess, but what there is, is never your typical spread.

We lay out a blanket and bring out the food. There is a mango and spinach salad with pecan nuts, barley, feta cheese and olive salad. Three types of sandwiches on whole wheat bread: tuna, lemon and avocado, or goat cheese and antipasti, or aged Gouda with mustard seed and sun-dried tomatoes. I am always responsible for desserts. Today I have brought grapes and apricots, a dozen different cupcakes and tahini cookies with white chocolate chips. We will not starve.

After we have all eaten, the kids pull out TAKI, a card game. Real hold-in-your-hands stuff, which you can play with and pass around – nothing digital. The cards are divvied out and we play a group round. No one can be born and raised here without succumbing to the pleasure of the game. It is fast-paced, competitive and fun – an excellent way to channel aggressive tendencies and pent-up frustrations. Aviva takes the first few rounds with ease. She is naturally competitive and a really strategic thinker. In the next round, the kids realize that if they work together, they can impede her progress.

"Put down the hand card if you have it," says Roy to Amit, "and then Mom will have to miss her turn."

"I don't have it," says Amit, "but I can change color."

"Too dangerous," says Roy. "She has quite a few cards. Chances are she has all the colors. Maybe we should change directions?"

"OK."

"You are being so unfair, says Yael. It's not nice to gang up like that, right Mom?" she says to Dana.

"You are right, you precious thing," says Dana.

"Little Miss Perfect," says Amit.

"Precious angel," says Roy.

"Don't worry about me, honey," says Aviva to Yael. "Who said I am going to lose? These guys only think that they have me, but it ain't over yet." But soon, Aviva finds herself picking up more and more cards, losing the advantage that she had in previous rounds.

"What's going on here?" she says. "I am actually falling behind, you little scoundrels. Yael was right! This does feel like you are ganging up against me."

"We are not ganging up against you; we are just learning how to stick together, like you always tell us," says Amit.

"Exactly," agrees Roy. Dana smiles. Aviva isn't often out-maneuvered and out-witted.

"Smartasses!" says Aviva with a smile and picks up another card.

"Anyway," I say, "what does it matter? As long as you are having fun, that is the main thing. Right?!"

"Touché," says Aviva.

Chapter 20

Sunday morning, on my way to the Nest, I drop off Karina's clothes at the laundromat two streets away from my work. It is my first time there. I never go to laundromats if I can help it. The air always feels stale and humid. The clothes look like flattened bodies hanging tightly one against the other on a massive conveyer belt. Those places give me the creeps. As I open the door, a bell jangles and the customers turn around to see who has entered. I give a big smile when I see that Mattie is among them, the last in line.

"Hey," I say, and go up to him and give him a hug. "What are you doing here?"

"Orit's flat is two blocks down."

"Of course, right," I say. "I mean, I didn't know that she lived here, but sure."

Mattie smiles. "I spilled some red wine on my shirt at Iris's birthday breakfast." He looks at me with amusement. I hold up my hand before he can begin. "Don't even start on the subject," I say.

"You know," says Mattie, ignoring me, "the breakfast that you missed because your date went overtime."

"I am aware that I missed it," I grimace. "I am also aware why I missed it."

"So are you going to tell me about this hot date of yours?"

"Why would I do that?" I ask him.

"Because I'm your friend."

"Since when do we talk about this kind of thing? Nah, I don't think so."

"But I am interested to know."

"Still no."

"*Quid pro quo*, I will tell you all about me and Orit."

"Hell no," I say, a bit too emphatically.

"Why not?" he asks, a bit defensively. "Maybe *I* need to talk."

"Sure, you want to tell me the best way to lather sunscreen

on your half-naked girlfriend. Like I really need to hear that," I laugh.

Mattie gives a shy smile. "There may be other things that I have to say as well," he says.

"Sounds mysterious. Isn't that what we are meant to be doing on Friday night?"

"Yes, good, I was just about to remind you."

"So start making a list of what you want to talk about."

"Starting with your date."

"We'll see about that . . ."

Mattie is next in line. The old man behind the counter takes an old ticket and the wine-stained shirt from Mattie. He walks off slowly. A few minutes later he comes back and says to Mattie: "Here's the receipt for your shirt, and here's your wife's dress from last week." He places the ticket on the counter.

"Wife?" I say to Mattie. "That was quick!" I hand over my clothes to be dry-cleaned and the old man writes it all up. "All this happened at Iris's birthday party?" I ask. "I will never sleep late again. It sounds like I missed out on all the fun." Mattie laughs. "You would have heard about it from me," he says with a grin, "if you ever decided to call me back . . ."

". . . Oh you sensitive soul. Sorry about not calling back." The old man looks up from his work. "I am done for now," he says. "Your clothes will be ready on Thursday."

"Thanks," I tell him. Mattie and I take our tickets from the counter and walk out of the shop together. The bell rings as we exit the store. "Don't worry about not calling me back. You will make it up to me by keeping me thoroughly entertained on Friday night," says Mattie.

"OK," I laugh. "See you on Friday."

"Bloom's at nine thirty," says Mattie, "we'll talk then."

"See you . . ." I say, and we both walk off.

That afternoon, Kobi and I work together intensively on trying to resolve the Noa issue. It takes time to get into a rhythm. Kobi is prickly with me, and I am edgy in return. But circumstances require that we put all that aside. We are carving out a package that includes some additional financial support for the family, as well some special benefits from the army. Kobi has worked tirelessly with the draft office, and once all the forms are in order, they are prepared to grant Noa a special status that will enable her to work part-time, in order to support herself and her family. "You have done such a great job," I tell Kobi. "I think that this is incredibly significant progress, and I can't see how the parents will say no."

"Thanks," says Kobi. "I remembered meeting someone a few months back who had a similar status. I wasn't sure that Noa would meet the criteria, but I thought that it was worth the shot."

"Absolutely," I say. "Well done! Now if only we can find her a job, that would be awesome."

"She can always be a waitress," says Kobi.

"She can. Nothing dishonorable about that, and I guess if it comes to that, it will not be a problem to find a job as a waitress. But perhaps we can find her something else that will contribute to her education, or, you know, anything else that she wants to do."

"Do we know what that is?"

"Not sure actually. We should definitely ask," I answer.

"There is still one thing that I think we need to do," says Kobi.

"What's that?"

"Well, you said that Noa's parents did talk about the other kids having an opportunity. I am handling the registration for next year. Should I look and see if this brother or sister is eligible to join the Nest?"

"That's a great idea. We would need to check that the kid is the right age, and that the school recommends it, but why not. Sounds excellent. Nice! Do you want to run with that?"

"Sure," says Kobi, "gladly." We both get up and stretch. It has been a long day and we have made excellent progress. "All right then," says Kobi. "I guess I better go."

"Any special plans?" I ask.

"Not really. I mean, nothing unusual. On Sundays, I usually meet with my sisters and they ride me about not having a girlfriend."

"Sounds like fun."

"Not sure about that. They also go on about me getting a proper job."

I roll my eyes. "You too?"

"Yes, accountancy or lawyering would have been preferable."

"Oh, for me it was medicine or engineering."

"Those are some high expectations!"

"The higher they are, the harder the parents fall," I say with a grimace.

"But seriously, what's wrong with us – doing these jobs, fixing the world one person at a time?" says Kobi.

"I ask myself that question every day." I tell him.

"Really? You seem so confident, so self-assured."

"Thanks. Managed to fool you, didn't I?" I say with a laugh.

"This job definitely isn't easy on the soul."

"You can say that again," says Kobi, and after a few seconds of contemplation, he asks: "So why do you do it? Why *are* you here?" His words are spoken softly, but land hard like a punch in the pit of my stomach.

"What do you mean?" I ask him. "You know why I am here. You know what I do. You know that I put my heart and soul into this place." I say defensively.

"That isn't what I meant," says Kobi.

"Then what *did* you mean?" I snap at him.

"I mean, why do a job that is so frustrating? Why not find something that has easier hours, and less emotional anguish?"

"Are you kidding me?" I snap at him. "You would love that, wouldn't you? You are always angling to oust me somehow. And it is getting really annoying." Kobi looks genuinely aghast. He exhales sharply.

"Relax, Tamara," he says. "I thought that for once we were having a genuine, open conversation. You are kind of hard to talk to, you know." It takes a few seconds for me to register the effect of my words on Kobi. He stands indignantly, but I recognize the hurt in his eyes. I really want to take it all back, every single word, maybe even to apologize, but I can't. I am frozen in the moment and still trying to digest how, within seconds, I have managed to kill all the good will and openness that have been garnered after hours of productive work. All I can manage to do is to cover my hand with my mouth. Kobi stands by the door for a few seconds, waiting for a response from me that doesn't come. Finally, he just shakes his head once or twice, turns around and walks out. *Well done,* I think to myself. *You are simply awful.*

That night, Elon catches me on the phone just as I get out of the shower. "Hey," he says. "I got a few minutes before I do rounds."

"Hi," I say back.

"Thursday breakfast?" he asks.

"Yup," I say with a sigh.

"What's up?" he asks. "I am not used to monosyllables from you."

"Sorry. Bad day."

"What happened?"

"Chewed out a colleague."

"Lucky guy. I am jealous."

"No, really. I snapped at him for no reason."

"I am sure you had a reason."

"Nope, it was all me. I overreacted."

"So did you apologize?"

"Not yet, but I am going to. "

"So what's the problem?"

"The problem is that I am trying to be a role model for these kids about restraint and doing the right thing, and yet I blow up over the stupidest thing."

"Listen, I don't know what happened or what was said exactly, but there's nothing wrong with working on yourself, if you think that you need to make some sort of change."

"Working on myself?" I say, and my skin prickles with irritation.

"Yes, it sounds like your over-reaction has upset you. So consider why that is."

"You make it sound like I have a chronic problem."

"Not at all, I really don't know you well enough to say."

"That's true, and yet you feel comfortable enough to tell me to work on myself."

"Tamara, I am just responding to what you said. I am not sure why you are getting so upset."

"How would you like it if I suggested that you 'work on yourself'?" I snap at him. "I am not sure what that even means? What exactly are you proposing? A course on etiquette, or perhaps something more extreme like anger management?" I say sarcastically. My harsh words are met with a stinging silence. Then Elon says: "How about just starting with curbing the cynicism?" The line goes silent again. My head suddenly feels very heavy. "Shit." I say. "I did it again."

"Listen," says Elon. "Obviously, we can still talk about this, and we must, but for now I have got to get back to work. Bye," he says and he hangs up. Once more I find myself with an unspoken apology.

After a restless night heavy with imagined re-enactments of how my conversations with Kobi and Elon could have finished in almost any other way, I wake up tired and drained with regret. I drag myself to the Nest, make myself a coffee so strong and so thick that with every stir of my spoon, I can see a cloudy swirl of grains. I don't even drink coffee, and this time is no exception. It sits on my desk giving off a strong coffee aroma, as if it were an incense stick and not a warm beverage to be consumed. At ten o'clock, Noa comes into my office.

"Hi," she says, peeking into the door.

"Hi Noa," I say. "How are you?"

"I am OK," she answers. "Two more tests to go and I am

done. Still stressing out about the army thing."

"Good luck on the tests," I say. You have worked so hard. I am sure that it will be OK." Noa nods and then says, "I spoke to Kobi yesterday and he suggested that we meet to talk. He said you might have a few updates."

"Yes, he's right," I say. "Did he tell you to come now?"

"Yes, but he said that he will not be able to join us. He will only be in later. When you won't be in."

"Yes," I say, thinking to myself that I would also avoid being in the same room with me if I were him. "I have a meeting in the afternoon," I tell Noa. "What's your schedule like? I mean, are you relatively flexible today? I really would prefer to meet with you and Kobi together. So maybe I will try to move my afternoon meeting around. But only if it is convenient for you."

"Sure," says Noa. "I can come back at around two in the afternoon. That's when Kobi said he will be back."

"That's perfect," I say.

"OK" says Noa, "then see you later," and she turns to go.

"Wait a second, before you go, what test do you have next?"

"My favorite: Biology."

"Really, you like Biology?"

"Yes," she says, "it just makes sense to me. It's not abstract. It doesn't require leaps of faith."

"Sounds like you have it in the bag."

"I wish. Liking something doesn't make it a sure thing."

"That's true." I say.

"OK, well good luck! Let me know how it goes."

"I will. Bye, see you later," says Noa, and she walks out. When she leaves, I immediately pick up the phone and give Joseph a call. "Hey," he says, "you aren't chickening out on me, are you?"

"No way. I wouldn't dare."

"Good!"

"But I would like to see if we can meet earlier."

"What's earlier?"

"I can leave the office now. That means that I could be at you in about fifteen minutes."

"Then *now* is perfect."

"OK, great, this is terrific. You are so helpful."

"Didn't you know, 'Helpful' is my middle name!"

I laugh, "I thought your middle name was 'Awesome'`"

"Who told you that?" asks Joseph in mock indignation.

"See you soon," I say, and hang up the phone.

"Got to run," I shout to whoever is in the Nest. "See you later." I hear a smattering of *byes* and *see you's* called out from the furthest corners of the apartment. I run down the stairs and out into the street and head towards Joseph's community center. *An impulsive decision*, I think to myself, *but a good one*. I am going to make things right by Kobi. I walk briskly through the streets of Tel Aviv. No one here walks at exactly the same pace; even now – at mid-morning – there are the slow walkers who seem to be moving aimlessly to nowhere, and the faster walkers moving with attitude and velocity towards a definitive destination. Finally, there are runners, running as far and as fast as they can in misshapen loops around the city. Joseph is sitting on the steps of the community center waiting for me. He has a tall glass of ice coffee in his hands and another one strategically placed below the banister so that no one will accidently kick it over. "I just made a fresh batch," he says. "I thought you would appreciate it."

"Thanks." I say, debating whether or not to tell him that I don't like coffee. Perhaps I can force some of it down. Just to be polite. "And also, thanks for the impromptu reschedule." I say. "Something came up at work."

"No problem. Whether something's up or something's down, we need to take care of it."

I sit next to him on the stairs. "You have a nice view here of the city."

"Yes, if you enjoy people-watching and urban landscapes."

"I do. I still feel new to the city, but I like the energy here."

"Do you miss living in suburbia?"

"Well, it didn't really feel like suburbia; it just felt like a smaller city and I was commuting anyway to work in Tel Aviv. But, you know, I was more in a hurry to get home . . . to David – my ex. Now, I am not in a hurry to get home to anything really. What about you?"

"Well, honestly, my work is my home. I am dating someone at the moment, and that makes a difference to my schedule. But I think that what I do here will always come first."

"I am sure you are right. You are so dedicated."

"And you aren't?"

"Well I am. I am good at what I do. I feel like I am making a difference."

"But..." says Joseph, pre-empting my doubts.

"Well, I guess that I just feel a bit like a fraud. You know, I am a professional do-gooder who goes through the motions. But I am on auto-pilot. I am an OK person who knows how to pass off as a good person. Essentially, I am not even that nice."

"You?"

"Yes, me. I lose my patience easily; I snap at my colleagues. The reason that I am here with you now instead of later is because I am trying to fix a mess that I made. I even snapped at this guy that I am supposed to be dating, who was only trying to talk me through the first mess that I made."

"Do you believe that you are a bad person?"

"Well, I don't want to believe it, but it does sort of feel that way. Not evil or anything. Just challenged and flawed, like I am no more than a kid going through an endless adolescence."

"Do you mind if I ask you a few questions? Perhaps we can work through this."

"Shoot," I say. "I guess that I was hoping that you would."

Joseph gives a knowing smile. "I did offer . . ." he says. "OK, so do you feel like your 'impatience' affects you personally or professionally?"

"A bit of both really. Not dramatically. It is more about my interactions with others."

"Does it hurt anyone in the long- or medium-term?"

"You mean besides me? No. I don't think so. Actually, maybe just a little." I say, thinking of the hurt in Kobi's eyes. That look was bound to have consequences. "It's hard to explain," I tell Joseph, "I feel myself getting caught up in a knot of emotion. I work myself up and then I usually say something that I land up regretting. By that point, I am too slow to apologize."

"*Usually* regret, not *always*?"

"Yes, like the other day, this guy started with me in the bar and I unleashed on him. In that situation, I have no regrets at all!" Joseph laughs and then asks: "Is this behavior of yours something new? Maybe since moving to Tel Aviv? Or since your divorce?"

I laugh. "Absolutely not, I have always been . . . I have *always* been—"

"Edgy, snappy, opinionated, determined?" asks Joseph, completing my unfinished sentence.

"I was going to say: moody, rough around the edges and direct."

"What would your friends say about you?"

"That I am all angles and edges. In fact, that *is* what they say about me, all the time."

"All angles and edges, hey? Do they say it with love, or with frustration?"

"I guess with love."

"So they aren't really trying to round you off, or to smooth out the edges."

"Not really. In fact, not at all."

"So really this is more about you."

"How do you figure?"

"Well, more specifically, it is about you being unable to accept yourself in the same manner that people who love you accept you."

I am silent for a few seconds and then ask, "but aren't I supposed to change? Aren't I supposed to iron out the edges?"

"Listen, there are some things that we can change. And some things we can't. Maybe we can make some slight tweaks or calibrations, you know. But the essence remains. What we do, you and I, is to read the essence of people, and to help them to calibrate. Our work is in that grey area – where people meet society. We move within that interactive space where personality meets socialization."

"You make it sound so black and white."

"Well it isn't. None of us are black and white and neither is the chemistry between us and our environment. It is dynamic, bubbling, volatile . . . Take Eran: your instincts told you that his essence is good, and you didn't give up on him. What you have been working on with him is the way in which he reacts to the people around him."

"I guess you are right."

"So the question is, do you accept that your essence is good?"

"My own essence? Are you asking me if I think that I am a good person? I don't think that I know how to answer that question. My ex divorced me because of the way I am. Maybe that says something."

"I am not a marriage counselor, but when people divorce, it is never just about one side. Both partners have accountability."

"I see your point. But still. Maybe if I had worked on myself then, we could have gotten past that."

"Do you have any regrets about the divorce?"

"Honestly, no. It was amicable, and I believe it was the right thing for both of us."

"So then, just for a minute, put whatever happened with your ex aside. What about your close friends, what would they say about your 'angles and edges?' "

"They'd fiercely defend me. They're always there for me."

"OK."

"OK, what? They are my friends. That's what friends are supposed to do. It's like a mother who thinks her child is the best looking kid, even if everyone else knows that he isn't."

"Your friends aren't obligated to defend you and to be blind to your flaws. You chose your friends and by sticking with you, they chose you back. You are not bound – not legally and not genetically."

"My friends are like family to me."

"So are you saying that they accept you unconditionally?"

"Yes."

"So, what's the conclusion?"

"I guess that my essence must be kind of OK."

"Kind of OK is a start."

"And I guess that Elon was right, I can also work on myself."

"Definitely . . .!"

"Definitely? Wow! That was emphatic. Sounds like more than simple encouragement . . ."

"Aaah, but wait . . . what kind of work should you do?"

I think for a few minutes and then answer: "I should work on my interactions, but accept myself for who I am." Joseph grins.

"Sounds like a piece of cake," I say with more than a hint of sarcasm.

"Oh you cynical creature."

"That's part of my problem!"

"That's part of your charm."

"Is that your personal opinion or professional?"

"Both!"

"But what about my job, oh wise one."

"What about it?"

"Am I in the right place?"

"How would I know that?" Joseph asks.

"I have a colleague who I think wants to oust me, a thousand self-doubts, and enough personal awareness to know that this job has kept me sane."

"So what's the question?"

"Should I stay or should I go?"

"What do you *want*?"

"I don't know."

"So, figure it out," says Joseph, "did you always want to do what you are doing now?"

"I guess not. I wanted to be a fireman, a policeman, a truck driver . . . you know, regular girl stuff..."

"Sounds like it . . ." say Joseph with grin. "Not that I expected anything less. But seriously, why do you do what you do? Because you love it? Because you know how to do it? Because that is the hand you have been dealt?"

"All of the above really. I also do believe in it, or I did anyway. Now it sometimes feels like I am going through the motions."

"So what are you missing?"

"I guess a challenge. I feel like I am missing a challenge."

"What kind of challenge?"

"I think it has to do with delving deeper into things. My job is high level. I am always looking at the bigger picture. Keeping the engine well-oiled and running. Making sure there are enough volunteers, building next year's agenda. Logistics. Admin. Calling the plumber. I have interactions with the Nesters, which are intense – often in crisis mode. These are the interactions that mean the most to me. I feel like I want to invest more in working though things on a one-on-one level. When I was talking Eran down from hurting Avi, I felt amazingly calm and exhilarated at the same time. Alive."

"So you want to be like a psychologist or a social worker?"

"I guess."

"So what's the problem?"

"Apart from me being underqualified?"

"Yes."

"It is not that simple"

"It isn't?"

"I have a job, financial considerations, and besides which, who says that this is even the right solution?"

"There are no guarantees. It all boils down to what you want."

"I don't know."

"So figure it out."

"That's the best that you can do? I thought you were going to set me straight."

"If you are all angles and edges, then why would I want to set you straight?" he grins.

"*Aaaah,*" I say, "back to self-acceptance. You are sneaky."

"I like to think of it as being consistent." We are sitting here in silence, his coffee long gone, mine untouched. The movement of the passersby is like a never-ending beat against the backdrop of the city. I hug my knees and think of all that has been said. I am not even sure at what stage so much self-doubt has crept into my life. Was I like this before the divorce? I can't recall. And when did my work at the Nest enter into the equation of doubts? My job has always been the one sure thing in my life. So much to think about . . .

"You know, I think that you are amazing, Joseph. It blows my mind how you are so sure of who you are and what you do."

"Don't make it more than it is. I am a tiny man in a city of normal-sized people who walk faster than I can run. I have my moments."

"I am sure. But, you don't project your moments, like others do."

"Everyone deals differently. Don't forget, I have come a long way from when you first met me."

"Also true. But I guess that was your rite of passage . . . your time of great personal growth."

"Figuratively speaking, of course." Joseph adds. I groan.

"Come on," he says, "I am allowed to make jokes like that . . ." I shake my head with a smile. "Anyway, listen, before you head off, let me just give you this," Joseph says. He hands me an unsealed white envelope. "You can look inside," he says. I pull out a pamphlet with a blue and yellow insignia and a program schedule in basic bullets points. "Wow, Joseph, what is this?" I asked.

"I spoke to one of our sponsors the other day. He is on the board of the Maccabi Tel Aviv basketball team. His name and number are also on the page. I told him a bit about you and the work that you do. He was very impressed and is prepared to sponsor your graduation event. It will include tickets for the Nest graduates, volunteers and staff to attend a game, meet up with the players, and shoot some hoops together. Also, the Nest graduates will each get signed shirts from the team members. What it doesn't include is whatever team building workshop, you may want to do beforehand, and if you want to have a bit of a spread before or after. All of the details and schedule are listed."

"Incredible!" I say, reading through the list. "This is amazing. I had some budget set aside for this, but this sponsorship takes me even further. This is absolutely amazing. You are amazing!"

"Didn't you know, 'Amazing' is my middle name."

I laugh. "One day, I am going to meet your mother, and confirm your names once and for all." Joseph laughs too.

"Seriously. This is wonderful. It is so much more than I had hoped for. Thanks!" I give him a hug. Joseph stands himself up.

"OK, I need to go. Got places to go and people to fix," he says.

"I wouldn't want to get in the way of that. Thanks for everything. Seriously."

"No worries. Really. Let me know what's going on with you, OK? Keep me posted."

"Will do. Hey Joseph . . . thanks for the coffee" I say and I sheepishly hand him my still-full glass of coffee. He laughs. "Sorry, coffee is not really my thing," I tell him.

"At least you know what you don't want," he says, and laughs again. "Bye, see you later." He turns around and walks back into the community center. I sit there for a few minutes more and then get up slowly, stretching my legs. I pull out my smartphone and send a text message to Elon:

    `Sorry about yesterday`

    `I was on edge after having that fight with Kobi`

    `Took it out on you`

See you Thursday?

I hit the Send button. I hope to see signs that Elon is on the receiving end and beginning to respond, but no such luck. *Oh well*, I think to myself, *I deserve that.*

I plug in a few quick lines to Aviva:
Hey…

Do you have any need for lab workers?

I may have someone for you - one of my Nesters

She needs to earn money while she's in the army

I get an almost instantaneous message back.
I always need help

Doesn't pay much, but more than dog walking!

Send me her transcripts

I send her a thumbs up and a smiley. *Good start*, I think to myself. I begin to walk, and as I walk, I dial Adam. He is going to be thrilled at all the new developments.
He picks up straight away. "Hey Tamara. What's up?"
"All's good," I say.
"Are you sure?" he asks.
"Yes. Why, what's going on?"
"Well, Kobi called and he was pretty upset."
"Oh, we had a bit of an argument."
"That's not quite what he said."
"Listen, Adam, I do owe Kobi an apology, and I plan to give it now. In fact, I am on my way to him as we speak. I just called to tell you — "
"Tamara," Adam says curtly, cutting me off before I can finish my sentence. "You know that I support you . . ."
"Yes."
"Kobi is a good person, and I support him too. The thing

is, he needs your support as well. Not many people want to do what you two chose to do. It takes a special kind of person. One with compassion and drive and belief in humanity."

"I know, Adam . . ."

"Wait, let me finish . . ." Adam continues. "And those who are driven need to be encouraged and motivated, not cut down or belittled."

"I know, Adam."

"Even if you have personal differences."

"It's not that . . ."

"Tamara, I know that things have not been easy since the divorce, and I am prepared to cut you a lot of slack, because I care for you and I think the world of you. But you are also a role model and more importantly, you are the face of this organization. So think very carefully about what you want to project to others."

"I am sorry; I will make things right."

"I know you will, but I do mean this sincerely: if you are unhappy or need a change, let's talk some more about how I can help you, OK?"

"OK," I say resignedly.

"Speak to you soon," says Adam. "Bye." And he hangs up.

This conversation did not go the way that I expected it to go. I didn't even manage to get a word in about the basketball event.

I have already reached the Nest, and I am too dejected and depleted to go upstairs. I sit down on the rugged old bench outside the building entrance. The stillness of the air is in stark contrast to the bustle of the city on the stairs of Joseph's community center. It is a suffocating stillness, a stifling stillness, and I plunge into a well of disappointment. What am I doing here in the Nest anyway? It was not motivation that brought me here, but opportunity – coincidental opportunity at that, *right-place-at-the-right-time* kind of opportunity. Do I need this kind of stress, this responsibility for young minds? Don't they need more sound role models than me?

Is this place just another way for me to avoid moving on with my life? Joseph's words resonate in my ears: *what do you want?* The only coherent answer that I can come up with grinds in my ear like a rusty crank – *how should I know?* The only thing that I do know is that I need to get out of this place. I send a text to Kobi:

    Not feeling well. Going home.

    Please tell Noa the good news

Kobi responds immediately:

    Didn't you meet with her already?

    No, I wanted to do it with you

I reply.

Kobi doesn't respond. I pick myself off the bench and head back to my apartment, every step feeling like a dead weight is pulling me down.

I spend the rest of the day with curtains drawn, lights off and smartphone on silent. It is indulgent, self-piteous, and I am unable to stop. By the end of the evening, I have convinced myself that I am a professional and personal failure. On top of that, my head aches with the dull pain of a stubborn headache. So in the dark house, in a dark mood, I go to bed.

Chapter 21

After having gone to sleep so early, I wake up at five in the morning. The city is still quiet except for the sound of birds and the occasional truck making its way tentatively through the city streets, trying to avoid the cars parked bumper to bumper along the side of the road. I slip into my bathing suit and go to the beach for a swim, taking only a towel and the key to my apartment, which I slip into a pocket in my bathing suit. When I get to the sea, I drop my towel and my flip-flops on the cool sand. In a few hours, the sand will be properly baked, and one will have to hop like a pigeon down to the water to avoid being burned. I wade in slowly, step by step.

The water is clear and cool. The tide is so low that to get thigh deep you have to walk into the water for over fifty meters. The sound of the sea breeze vibrating off the water fills my ears, and the salty smell from the sea spray fills my nose. I block out all thoughts. I take a deep breath, hold my nose, and go right under the water, where it is dark and cool. I hug my knees and sink until I am sitting on the bottom of the sea bed.

The pressure of the water pounds on my brain, as my thoughts come rushing in: What is wrong with me? Am I a bad person? Why do things feel like they are falling apart? Will Adam trust me again? How can I make things right with Kobi? Will Elon give me another chance? What do I want from him anyway? Where are my friends? Why aren't I letting them in? Why did my marriage fail? Is it me? Is it all because of me? What do I want? What do I want? What do I want? WHAT DO I WANT?

When I can breathe no more and it feels like my head is about to explode, I release my folded arms and kick off from the sandy bed of the sea and jet up towards the surface. I come to the top of the water gasping for air. In an instant, the pounding pressure is gone. The crashing questions are gone.

My lungs are filled with oxygen and my eyes are awash

with the sights of the Tel Aviv beachfront promenade: the hotels, the restaurants, the ice cream places and the fruit juice stands. My eyes take in the early morning stragglers, the athletes, the tourists, the pensioners and the party-goers still shaky-kneed after last night's clubbing; all of them coexist under an endless, light-blue sky pierced with a thousand rays of sun. I walk home, relieved to have sparred with all my questions – but empty and drained of any real answers.

I get to the Nest by eight o'clock. The apartment is quiet, which is unusual for this time of the morning. The study roster is up: by the end of the day, four volunteers will have done individual and group sessions, covering seven different topics for ten of the Nesters, ranging from Arabic to Trigonometry. Lunch will be prepared, eaten and cleared away, and quiet corners will be available for reading or listening to music or studying. My office door is open, as it always is – *sans* door. I step inside. Before I even get behind the desk, I see that there is a folded sheet of paper with my name on it. I recognize the handwriting immediately. My heart sinks even lower – as if that is even possible. I dump my bag on the table and unfold the paper.

To Tamara,
After a few years of working at the Nest, I have decided that it is time for me to move on. It is clear to me that there are no development opportunities available to me and I feel that it is better for the both of us that we no longer work together. Please accept my resignation and one month's notice.
Signed,
Kobi

The letter is short, clear and direct, with more than a casual hint of blame. Surprisingly, I feel nothing. I know that I have to call Adam, but before I do, the phone rings. It is Dana.

"Hey Dana, how did you know that I need a friendly voice?"

"What's going on? You haven't been answering your phone again."

"Had a bad day yesterday, so I locked myself at home, where I could do no more damage."

"Oh boy, what happened?"

"Hell is breaking loose and taking me down with it."

"Want to give me the short version?"

"The short version is that my life sucks."

"Elon?"

"Elon is mad at me and may not want to see me again. We had a fight. But that is not the main thing," I say, dismissing Elon without a second thought. "The bigger issue is work . . . "

"What about work? Is it the kids? Graduation?"

"No, those are fine."

"So what's the problem?"

"Kobi quit."

"So?"

"So Adam is going to blame me, and it *is* my fault."

"Kobi, the same guy who has been second-guessing you the whole time?"

"Yes, but that's not the point."

"Why isn't that the point?"

"I don't know, it just isn't."

"OK, so what is the point?"

"The point is," I say, lowering my voice, because I can hear movement in the house, "the point is that I don't know what I am doing anymore." The last sentence comes out half-whisper, half-whimper.

"Listen," says Dana, "I just called to remind you that it is Mattie's birthday next week, and we will be meeting at HaYarkon Park again. But, now I think I am just going to come to you; can I come now?"

"I completely forgot about his birthday."

"I've noticed that you are a bit off your game. That's why I called."

"But don't come to me now . . . I am at work and I need to speak to Kobi."

"Then I will come tonight."

"No, don't"

"Why not?"

"Because I am going to Karina and Josh. I promised I would come over. I have some dry cleaning that I need to return."

"Fine."

"OK, but I'll call you tomorrow morning."

"OK."

"Speak to you tomorrow."

Vaguely cheered by Dana, I pick up the phone and call Adam. "Hey," he says, "I was expecting your call."

"I just got into the office and I saw the letter. Can I assume that Kobi spoke to you before he made his decision?"

"He did share his deliberations, but I was hoping that you would speak to him before."

"I didn't get the opportunity."

"Yes, it does seem that he made his final decision really quickly."

"Do you think he will change his mind?"

"I don't know."

"Listen Adam, I am sorry about this. Yesterday you asked me to fix this, and I didn't. I went home, overwhelmed and stressed out, and I came in this morning thinking that I could make things right, only to find this letter. I have let you down."

"Yesterday, I was upset with you, Tamara. I still am. I am sorry to see Kobi go. But this is his decision. Speak to him. Let's see if he is determined to leave. If he isn't, maybe we can find a way for him to stay."

"OK, I will."

"Let's catch up later."

"OK, thanks Adam. Bye." I hang up the phone and the room reverberates with an empty silence. I fold my hands on the table and rest my head on them. Perhaps if I have a few minutes of quiet, I will be able to figure out what to do. I close my eyes and let the silence fill me up. After forty minutes, I am woken by the gentle buzzing vibration of my smartphone and the general hum of activity of volunteers and Nesters in the house. I pick up my phone. There are three new text messages.

From Kobi:

```
I guess you saw my letter

I know we need to speak

Am taking a few days off

Let's talk first thing Sunday
```

I send him a thumbs up icon. And I forward the message to Adam, with a brief comment.

```
Will update you on Sunday
```

From Elon, a response to my text from yesterday:

```
Not "breaking up" since we are not really a couple,

but thinking aloud…

Should we pursue "us"?

Can you meet tomorrow?

9:00 am at Joe's at the University
```

This day just keeps getting better and better. With a deep sigh, I send a quick reply to Elon.

```
Thanks for your candor. See you at Joe's
```

From Iris:

```
Is no news good news?

What's up with the doc?

If he's history, let's talk

Got some new prospects
```

I answer her, feeling my eyes get all hot and prickly.

    Not sure I am cut out for this

    It's easier to be single

Miriam comes to the door with a steaming cup of tea with lemon and ginger. "Did you have a good sleep?" she asks, and extends the tea to me. I look up at her with heavy eyes. I am not sure that I can hold back my tears anymore. I bite my lip out of instinct to keep it from quivering. I stare at the trail of steam as it winds and curls towards me, but keep my arms firmly folded. Miriam puts the tea down on my desk. "My child," she says, "what's so wrong that you are so sad?"

"Everything's wrong," I say and I burst into tears. Miriam comes around to where I am sitting and takes me in her arms and soothes me while I cry.

It is easier to retreat than to advance. Once I am all cried out, I spend the rest of the day on automatic pilot, blind to what is happening around me, oblivious to the noise and the people around me. The Nesters look at me with concern as I walk through the apartment, going through the motions of checking who's in attendance and what's going on. Their chatter drops to a hush as I walk by and then it rises again as I leave. I go pick up the dry cleaning. I wait in line, and don't even realize that it is my turn. Eventually, it registers that the old man behind the counter is asking me for my ticket, presumably for the umpteenth time. I put it on the counter, not remembering even fishing it out my bag. He huffs and walks off to the conveyor with the hanging clothes and fishes out my items. I pay him, and walk out.

On the street, a tourist asks me for directions, but I just stare back at her, unable to muster the energy to say anything back to her. She walks away, muttering under her breath. Burdened with the laundry, I hail a taxi. I open the door and get into the back seat. I give the driver Karina and Josh's address and close my eyes. Almost there. I hope someone will be there. I buzz the intercom, and I can hear the sound of kids.

Lots of them.

"Hi honey," says Karina when she sees me in the camera, "what a nice surprise. We were expecting you much later. Come on up," and she hits the buzzer.

I come to the elevator and hit the button to their apartment. When I reach the third floor, the door is open. There are balloons inside and a happy birthday sign. Josh comes out, "welcome to toddler hell," he says. "Get out while you can." I offer him a weak smile. "What's wrong with you, Tammy? You look like shit."

"I feel like it too. Can I come in lie down?"

"Of course. You won't get much quiet, but come in." We go in and he sneaks me past the raucous in the lounge area, filled with balloons, streamers, wild three-year-old tots and the smell of candy, and leads me to the bedroom. "Stay here," he says. "I will get you some water and Karina." I place the laundry on a hook by the closet and sit on the bed. Karina comes in a few minutes later with a glass of water and some aspirin.

"Happy Birthday to Nadav. Sorry I didn't remember . . . you can add it to the long list of black marks against my name," I say miserably.

"Honey, what's up?" Karina asks.

"I just wanted to bring you your laundry."

"It wasn't urgent."

"I know, but I just wanted to keep moving, you know what I mean?"

Karina hands me the water and the aspirin "Not really," she says. "What do you mean?"

"I just had a bad day, I mean a bad week." Karina heads over to the laundry to put it in the closet. "I guess I am a bit disoriented," I say.

"Well, I can see that. This isn't even my laundry," she says with a grin. She rips open the plastic, so that we can see the underlying clothes. "It's Orit's dress." I stare at the dress with disbelief. "I must have taken Mattie's ticket and he must have taken mine."

"Well, at least we know who to return these clothes to, and who's likely to have my things," says Karina. I lay back on the bed. "Just shoot me now," I say.

"Maybe later, honey," she says. "For now, just sleep." She closes the blinds of the windows. She turns off the light in the room, and then she shuts the door behind her. All of a sudden, the room is cool and dark. I welcome the darkness with relief and I shut my eyes.

I wake up with a start when a bright, glaring light pierces my sleep. The door of Karina and Josh's bedroom is open and in the doorway is a crowd of people staring anxiously in, shushing each other loudly. My eyelids are still heavy, but there is no mistaking who's there: Dana, Iris, Josh, Karina and Mattie. "Where are the last two dwarves?" I ask.

"You tell us, Sleeping Beauty," says Iris, and comes in loudly, switching on the light. I scrunch my eyes and sit up. The group seat themselves around me. Dana and Karina sit on either side. Dana puts her arm around me. Iris sits on Josh's side table. Josh and Mattie stand by the door. "God, I feel so stupid," I say. "I can't believe you are all here."

"We don't leave wounded soldiers behind," said Josh. "You know how it works in this country."

"Yeah, but there is nothing for you to do here. This is stuff that I need to sort out."

"Quit your stupid job if it makes you miserable," says Dana.

"It doesn't, it's just me: I am screwing up."

"Darling, you know what I think you need," says Iris.

"We all know what you think," says Dana, "but this is not about that."

"I am screwing up in the boyfriend department as well," I say.

"If you were just screwing in that department you would be in a better place," says Iris. Josh laughs and Karina gasps.

"You are being horrible Iris," says Dana. "She needs our support."

"You aren't screwing anything up," says Mattie thoughtfully. "You just are going through a bad patch. We all do." He speaks knowingly and with a strong conviction.

"My bad patches seem to be enough to fill an entire quilt at this point," I say. "And, I am sick of feeling sorry for myself. I hate it," I add vehemently. "I didn't even feel this bad after the divorce."

"Maybe it is just aftershocks. I had them after my divorce and I was the initiator. Just have your little breakdown and move on," says Iris. "What do you need? A girl's night out? Ice cream?"

"A bit of yoga by the beach?" adds Dana.

"A round of paintball?" interjects Josh.

"No one wants that, Josh," said Iris. "Not even when we say we do."

"Can't I just do this on my own?" I ask.

"You came here, honey," said Karina. "That's the universe telling you that you don't want to be alone."

"Wasn't it the universe telling me to return things that don't belong to me?"

"Unequivocally no," said Dana. "Karina's right."

"So what now?" I ask.

"Nadav's leftover birthday cake and coffee," says Karina.

"Then I drive you home," says Dana, "and I am sleeping over. Tomorrow you will go to work as scheduled."

"Shoot," I say, "I am supposed to meet Elon for coffee. He wants to break up with me face to face."

"What a man!" says Iris. "They don't make them like that anymore."

"Fine," says Dana. "I will wait for you outside and then I will drop you at work."

"Then I am coming to you at lunch time. We will go out together," says Karina.

"And, we are meeting in the evening at Bloom's, as scheduled," says Mattie.

"Bloom's? Really?" I object. "Please, just not Bloom's."

"None of that is negotiable," says Karina. "There are no

negotiations in my bedroom."

"There are *some* . . ." said Josh.

"But none for Tammy, sweetheart," says Karina.

"Cake time!" says Iris. "Why didn't you remind us it was Nadav's birthday? I would have brought a gift. What do three-year-old boys want anyway? Oh wait, don't answer that . . . three years old, thirty years old, sixty years old, they all want the same thing . . ." Iris's voice trails out of ear shot. Mattie and I are the last left in the room. He hugs me. It lingers more than a few seconds. "Are you OK?" I whisper in his ear.

"I am going through a bad patch of my own," he says back.

"Can we talk about it tomorrow?" I ask.

"I'd like that," he says, and we walk together into the kitchen.

That night, Dana and I lie together in my bed. "Doesn't this remind you of being back in school?" Dana asks. "Yes," I say, "only then, we would be whispering and giggling until our parents came in. It seems like so long ago."

"That's because it was", says Dana, "and we had so many plans, the four of us. Where we would be, what we would be doing . . ."

"At least you and Josh seem to be doing OK."

"You and Mattie are also doing OK. You may not be where you want to be, but sometimes the path is a bit more winding and convoluted." There are a few seconds of silence. Dana continues, "The fact that we are still here, together, in each other's lives . . . that is something."

"It sure is something," I say.

"I don't know what I would have done without you at school. You know that. I was like a moving red-haired target."

"A flag before a bull," I add. Dana turns to face me. "So now you need to let me be here for you. You need all of us to be here for you."

I frown. "It's not that easy. It's not like all of a sudden I have shut myself off. I have always been like this."

"I know, I know," says Dana. "All angles and edges. At least you are consistent," she sighs. The room is cool. Random shadows are cast by errant car lights that flicker through the bedroom window and disappear. "Remember that day on the playground?" asks Dana. "Do you remember when those kids started to bully me, and you came to help and they held you, and Josh and Mattie fought with them? And then, when they were gone, Mattie ran off. Remember?"

"Of course I do," I say.

"And then we all took off after him. But for some reason, at some point, you stopped running. We all looked back and saw that you were standing kind of frozen on the playground. So we ran back to you and Mattie said 'what's wrong, Tammy?'

You told us that you didn't feel like playing anymore. You said — "

". . . that I needed some space. That I needed to be alone. Then the bell rang. You guys started to run back to class, but I just stayed there," I interject.

"I called you to come, but you wouldn't. Josh called your name and said that we needed to get back to class, and that it wasn't a good time for you to be all angles and edges. And then Mattie . . ."

"Mattie brought you all back to me. He made us all hold hands. When our hands were interlocked and we stood facing one another, he asked, 'Do you know how many angles there are in a circle?' We didn't know the answer. So he told us: 'In a circle, there is only one angle.' I remember."

"And then we all ran back to class, holding hands," says Dana.

"I remember that," I say. I switch the light off by the side of my bed. *In a circle there is only one angle. I remember that*, I think to myself, and I also remember what I thought at the time: *There is only one angle in a circle – and I am it.*

Chapter 22

Dana jokes with me that this is like a drive-by break up. She pulls up to a bus stop outside of Joe's and tells me that she is circling the block and coming back for me. "The block" is about a ten-kilometer stretch that winds around Tel Aviv University, the Standards Institute of Israel and numerous other public structures. It is early in the morning. Students are flocking to class in the hundreds, jay-walking between the cars to make it on time. Taxis, buses and cars fill the lane with varying degrees of patience and impatience. Dana reckons that I have twenty minutes before she gets back.

Elon is sitting at the bar waiting for me, coffee and croissant in hand. "Hey," he says.

"Hi," I answer and I sit on the bar stool next to him.

"Can I get you anything?" he asks.

"I am not sure yet," I say. "I am still not fully awake."

"Had a bad night last night?"

"Had a bad few days. I have not been at my finest. As you know." Elon nods. "Listen," I say, "I am going to make this easy for you. I screwed up and I am not ready for a real relationship. I get it. It's OK. It's me, not you. You are absolved, and we can end this here and now." Elon looks at me, shakes his head and laughs under his breath. "Tamara, just because we had a fight it doesn't mean we can't work through it. Even if you were one hundred percent in the wrong, and I was one hundred percent the victim – which I am not saying was the case – grownups work through things; they don't run away."

"I am not running away. I just assumed that . . ."

"What did you assume?"

"That you thought I was a horrible person . . ."

"I have met horrible people. You are not one of them. Misguided, touchy, over-sensitive, temperamental – but not horrible."

"You said I should change."

"No I didn't. I said you could work on yourself. We all can. So can I. No one is perfect."

"But still."

"Still what, Tamara? If you want to break up with me, then do it. But don't pretend that it is about our fight or anything that you may think that I think about you. Because despite everything, I happen to like you." I turn to face Elon. He is a good person. He is genuine and honest and decent. Elon continues: "Say you are not interested, or not ready, or I am not right for you. We've gone on one amazing date, spoken on the phone a few times and sent some texts back and forth. We will both live if this is not meant to be."

"I don't know what to say," I tell him. "I was so sure that you wanted to break up with me. I came prepared for that."

"Yes, you even brought your own guillotine, but I won't be the executioner."

"So what now?" We sit for a few minutes, each one in his or her own thoughts.

Elon says: "What now? I guess that now we both walk away from here and continue on with our day. We get to think about whether there is potential here that is worth pursuing, or whether we want to walk away altogether. For me, that means asking myself whether I think you can work through whatever issues you are facing and whether I think there is a place for me in your life. For you, perhaps it is about trusting me, or liking yourself, or something completely different." I look at Elon closely; he looks back at me. Neither of us say a word. I look away.

We sit there in silence for another few minutes. The mad scurry of the morning has not yet subsided. Despite the frenetic pace of people rushing around the campus, I can't help feeling envious of all the students – their whole life still in front of them like a clean slate. The fast-paced music at Joe's, infused with radio bulletins, the caffeine-stained air, the impatient hooting of drivers desperate to steal through the quickly-changing traffic lights, all shake me back to reality. I look at Elon. He is staring out into the traffic, as if the answers to his questions will suddenly appear. He is a good guy. A really nice guy. Just like David . . . He has laid out all of his cards, and now it is my turn to be candid. "Elon," I say, "I am sorry. But I think we should both just move on."

He looks at me, staring right through me. "That's OK," he says. "At least you are being honest."

"Elon, I . . ."

"Really, you can spare me the 'it's not you; it's me' cliché. I think that we can both agree that in this instance you are correct - it is you." Elon gets up and stretches his legs. "Well Tamara, I hope that you find what you are looking for," he says and he walks away. I get up too and make my way to the bus stop where Dana dropped me off just fifteen minutes earlier. She pulls up within a few seconds. "Perfect timing," she says. "Are you OK?"

"I am OK," I said, getting into the car.

"What did he say?" she asks.

"That we should take some time to figure things out."

"Really?" said Dana, "So what now?"

"Now nothing, I guess." I answer her. "I just broke up with him." Dana stares back at me, at a loss for words. She pulls back into the traffic. "Are you sure you are OK?"

"I am positive," I say. "He is not right for me." Dana drives me to work. We sit in easy silence as she steers her way through the Tel Aviv traffic. As she pulls up to the side of the Nest so that I can get out, she says: "Don't forget that Karina is coming for lunch today."

"I won't," I say. "Thanks so much. For everything. For being there, for sleeping over. Thank Aviva for me as well. I am lucky to have a friend like you." I reach over and give her hug.

"So am I," she says. "The feeling is mutual."

"Dana," I say, "I did the right thing, breaking up with him."

"I know that honey," she says with a smile.

"How do you know that?" I ask.

"Because I know you. You might not always know what is right for you, but you always know what is wrong for you."

"So you don't think I am running away? Giving up too easily?"

"Quite the opposite. I think you are fighting for yourself. Fighting for what's right for you." My eyes fill up with spontaneous tears. "You are amazing," I say. "You know that, right?" I give her another hug. I wipe my eyes.

"We are both amazing." Dana says. "We always have been. Now go to work." I step out of the car and shut the door behind me. I turn around to wave good-bye. Dana has already pulled out and reentered the flow of traffic. I watch as her red hair fades out of sight.

I head up the stairs, reminding myself to put one foot in front of the other. There is a gentle hush as I come into the room. Volunteers and tutors look my way and nod briefly, so as not to break the flow of their sessions. I see Eran and Avi in the corner, working intensely on something. Miriam steps out of the kitchen. I know it is not her day to volunteer. I go up to her. "I am OK," I say quietly. "I am not happy; I am frustrated, I am upset. But I am OK. I would also rather not speak about it at the moment."

"Put your things down," she says to me, "and come into the kitchen. I have vegetables that need to be chopped and salads that need to be made."

"I have things to do."

"I know," says Miriam, "and you will do them, once you have cleared your mind." I dump my bag on my desk and head to the table. I wash my hands and say to Miriam, "I am ready." She leads me to a chopping board, hands me a knife and gives me a packet of onions to peel and chop. As the knife slices through the onions, my eyes begin to sting and burn. A steady flow of tears begins to fall. Miriam doesn't say a word. She continues to bustle about the tiny kitchen: tasting and spicing and stirring. I chop away, almost blinded by the steady flow of tears.

After peeling and chopping an entire bag of onions, I go to my office and sit down and begin to work. Like Miriam said, my mind is now ready and able to work uninterrupted. I settle the final details of the graduation party and send the agenda to Adam, Kobi and Joseph. I read Kobi's report from his meeting with Noa, and his notes about what needs to be done next. I review next year's candidates for the Nest, noting with mute satisfaction that Noa's younger brother is the newest candidate on the list. Before I know it, it is twelve thirty, and my phone is ringing. It is Karina.

"Hey Tammy, I am downstairs. Are you ready?"

"Sure," I say, "where are we going?"

"Anywhere, as long as it is fast food," says Karina. "I feel like something greasy and fatty."

"We can go to one of the places in the Ramat Aviv Mall," I say.

"Sure," says Karina. "Let's do it." I gather my things, shut down my computer for the day and head downstairs. Karina is double-parked outside, even though there are plenty of parking spaces. "Hi," she says, "how are you today?"

"Better than yesterday. Thanks. Sorry for the dramatics."

"Are you kidding, it was more entertaining than a house full of screaming toddlers."

"Gee thanks."

"Seriously, do you want to talk about what's going on with you?"

"I don't know. I just feel a bit lost."

"I thought things were going OK – with work, with Elon."

"Yes and no. I guess I am less motivated at work than I used to be, and as for Elon, we broke up this morning."

"You said that you he was going to break up with you."

"He was prepared to give it a chance. I broke it off."

"Why, honey? He sounded nice. It sounds like you . . . had fun."

"Yes, but it didn't feel right to me."

"You and Mattie. You are incorrigible. Like terrible twins."

"What about Mattie? He and Orit seem to be *on again, off again* all the time."

"He broke it off with her again last night. He said that was it. He said that if he gets back together with her again, he will have to marry her."

"I didn't know that. I guess I have been kind of self-involved lately. I haven't been a very good friend to him."

"You can talk to him tonight," Karina says. "I am sure that he can use a friend." It gets darker and more humid as we pull into the underground parking lot. Just like above the ground, parking down below is performed with minimal patience and maximum screeching and grinding. Karina parks half-on and half-off the pavement in a place that is not clearly marked for parking. "Don't look at me like that," she says. "It doesn't say that parking is forbidden." I shake my head at her and we head into the mall.

We move straight to the food court, past all the pricey and ostentatious fashion houses. "I am too hungry to even think about window shopping," Karina says. "Go sit there," she says, "and wait for me. I will order for us." Karina is formidable when she is not hungry. She is downright scary when she *is* hungry. I do as I am told, slightly comforted that someone else is making the decisions for me. A few minutes later, Karina comes back balancing two trays overladen with calories and grease. I laugh, I can't help it. There is something incongruous with the two of us slurping down this meal. But we both dig right in, attacking the food on all fronts: the fries, the soda, the burgers, the sauces. Karina is the first to finish. She sits back in her chair. "I can't believe I ate all of that, and so quickly. I feel sick." She grips her stomach with her hands and opens her mouth as if to say something, but instead, out comes a loud burp. The school kids at the table next to us begin to giggle.

"I can't believe that you are the elegant one," I tell her with a laugh.

"Me, the elegant one? Who says?"

"I do. Why do I come to you for clothes and makeovers

and that stuff?"

"Because Iris will turn you into a concubine and Dana will tell you that you should go as you are, because as far as she is concerned, you are already perfect."

"True, but no… I trust your opinion on this stuff. But that burp wasn't very ladylike."

"I don't want to be the elegant one. Thank you very much. Besides which, you have seen what is really going on in my closet."

"Yes, it's downright chaos in there."

"So you see, sometimes things are not what they seem."

"So if you are not the elegant one, who would you like to be?"

"For now, I would settle for other labels. Like the one who is back at work. Or the one who gets to sleep a full night. Or the one who does more than shopping, kids and the occasional yoga."

"So what's stopping you, from, say, going back to work?"

"For one thing, the fact that I am pregnant again."

"Oh my god, Karina that's such wonderful news."

"Is it? There are moments that I am happy, and times that I am miserable."

"I guess that I can understand that. But still. Josh must be so thrilled."

"He is. He is really supportive and I am so lucky to have him. But . . ."

"But what?"

"But, I am tired of this. Tired of being pregnant and being around little kids all the time. I admit that I am kind of envious of your life. Even if you are feeling a bit stuck."

"Envious of me? That's a laugh."

"You can do what you want. Go where you want. You can completely reinvent yourself."

"God, Karina, and here I am feeling sorry for myself."

"Strange isn't it. Things aren't quite what they seem," Karina says again. I look at her with new eyes and say, "My work doesn't feel like it is enough for me anymore. My life doesn't feel like it is enough for me anymore. Maybe this is just the way things are meant to be? The parts of us and our lives are divided across giant scales, and the division of happiness, satisfaction and meaning can never be evenly distributed . . ."

"Maybe, but within that there are some constants – like your ability to make changes to influence the scales, like the people who you allow to enter into your life."

"You are so right. I am only stuck because I think I am stuck. If I am not happy at work, I can move on. If I want more meaning in my life, I can keep looking for it . . ."

"And I can take better precautions so that this will be my last pregnancy, at least for a while, and then I won't have these crazy meat cravings."

"*Aaaah*, now I understand this insane meal . . ." I say.

"I think I need to vomit," moans Karina.

"Really or are you just saying it?" I ask.

"I don't know," says Karina, "but I will go to the ladies' room anyway. Just in case."

"Do you need help?"

"No thanks; you can wait here for me."

"OK, I will do that. Call me if you need anything."

"OK." Karina goes off in the direction of the bathrooms. I clear away our trays, throwing away all the empty packaging and my left-over burger and fries. I buy us two bottles of mineral water, sit back down to watch the passersby and wait for Karina.

As I sit and wait, I feel a gentle tap on my shoulder. I turn around. It is David. "Hey stranger," he says. "Hi David," I answer. I stand up and turn to face him. I fold my arms over my chest and without thinking, I look at the ring finger of my left hand, where my wedding band used to be. Under the glistening neon lights of the food court, that finger looks no different than any of the other fingers.

"Hey, Tamara, how are you?" he asks in that gentle manner of his.

"I am fine," I answer.

"I know," he says, "but are you OK?"

"David," I say with a sigh, "we are divorced; I don't really want to get into how I am feeling with you. Can't we just leave it with 'I'm fine'?"

"I thought that we were different from other people. We may not be married, but we can still understand each other. I can see that something is wrong," he replies.

I smile gently, "You will always be David 'the Good', won't you?"

"Only if you promise to remain Tamara 'the Bad'."

"David, I will be fine. We'll both be fine. But right now, this is too much for me." Karina comes up to us, a cautious look on her face.

"Hi, David," she says.

"Hi, Karina," he says.

"Are you ready to go?" Karina asks, turning to me.

"I am ready," I say. "Bye, David, see you."

"Bye," he says, "take care." Karina takes my hand and we walk away quickly.

"Are you going to cry?" asks Karina.

"I think so," I answer her.

She shrugs and picks up the pace. "I would too."

By the time we get to the car, I am bawling my eyes out. Second time today, although this time I have no onions to blame. "I can't get over how pathetic I have become," I tell Karina. "I am sick of myself."

"Look at the bright side," says Karina. "You just saw David. Did you miss him? I mean, did his presence fill any void for you?"

"No."

"Were you angry at him?"

"Not really."

"Were you regretful about anything?"

"No."

"Did you want to stay and talk with him? Chat about old times? Get all nostalgic?"

"No."

"So it is fair to say that you have moved on."

"Yes. I guess you are right. But it bothered me that he can still read me. It bothered me that he can see me sitting in a food court and tell that I am not OK just by looking."

"Anyone who knows you – really knows you – can tell. Honey, you don't exactly have a poker face. That's what we love about you. That's also what David loved about you. You can't be upset with him for something that is inherently a part of you."

"But what if I don't want it to be a part of me? David and I divorced because I couldn't change."

"You and David divorced because you were not right for each other. Period. But the traits you bring with you, honey, they've got to stay. It is so refreshing to know someone like you, where 'what you see is what you get': angles and edges and a soft, mushy inside." I smile at her.

"I have been told that I need to work on self-acceptance."

"That is very true," says Karina, "that is very sage advice. How did you get that nickname anyway – *angles and edges*?"

"Didn't Josh ever tell you? He is the one who made it up."

"I didn't know that. I never thought to ask him."

"We were in second grade at the time. It was a sports lesson and it was on one of those rare occasions that it was raining, so we were all stuck in the hall together. The boys wanted to play soccer and the girls wanted to play basketball, so our sadistic teachers put their heads together and decided to teach us how to waltz. They paired us off and I got Josh, or he got me. From the minute we were put together, we fought. I wanted to go left, and he wanted to go right. I would pick up the pace and he would slow it down. The teachers said that I should put my hands on his shoulders, and he should put his hands around my waist, but at that time, we were the same height, and I insisted that I lead." Karina laughs.

"Eventually, we were bickering so much that the teachers stopped the lesson and said, 'Tamara, Josh, what's going on here? You are spoiling the fun for everyone.' Josh said, 'It's not my fault; Tamara is always knocking into me.' To which I said, 'I am always knocking into you because you are a really bad dancer.' Everyone laughed, and Josh got really upset. 'I can't dance with you,' he said, "because it is like dancing with a block of wood. You are all angles and edges.'

'Well,' said the teacher, 'it is about time to switch partners anyway. Josh, you dance with Liza, and as for you *Miss Angles-and-Edges*, you can dance with . . .' and then Mattie chimed in 'Me. *Miss Angles-and-Edges* can dance with me.' The other kids all giggled, but Mattie – being Mattie – came up to me with a huge smile, and when the music started, we went off spinning around the room."

"That is the funniest story," said Karina, "and painfully true. Josh is a horrible dancer."

"I know, right! I wasn't trying to insult him . . ." Karina drops me off outside my flat. "Thanks so much for sharing – congratulations – I am so happy for you!" I tell her, "and thanks for being there for me."

"Are you kidding? You saw me wolf down that burger! That is punishment enough. And besides which – you really did me the favor," says Karina. "I also needed someone to talk to today."

"I am here for you, you know that," I say.

"I do," she answers, "and you know what – we will both be OK!"

"Yes, we will," I say. "Take care." I shut the door behind me and watch Karina as she drives off. I take out my phone. It is already three in the afternoon. I can't believe how the time has flown. I have a few hours to relax before I meet Mattie, and to think, think, think about what I want.

Chapter 23

It is past nine thirty and I am already at Bloom's. I can't believe that I am here. It is the last place I feel like being at. I should have told Mattie to meet anywhere else. But now it is too late. I am stationed at the bar, waiting for Mattie. He is late. I can't believe that he is late. I am not in the mood to be propositioned. Sasha is working the bar tonight. He has probably served a thousand people since I was last in, but he remembers my drink – "Non-alcoholic cocktail?" he asks with a smile. "No thanks," I tell him. "Tonight I would like something stronger."

"Shall I choose, sweetheart?" he asks me.

"Yes please, Sasha," I tell him. He turns away from me and with a dramatic display of bottle switching and flying ice cubes, he prepares me a cocktail with a pretty mix of fresh peach and cherries. "Thanks," I say as I take a sip. "Wow, this is delicious." I look at my watch for the thousandth time. Sasha laughs at me. "You know, the best punishment for latecomers is to arrive even later than them."

"In this country, that would mean that the bars would be empty," I quip.

"You are so right!" says Sasha with his accented Russian twang. "Maybe then it is best to come together?"

"Maybe we will – next time," I say.

The bar is quiet tonight. There is a group of friends – probably colleagues from work – enjoying a beer. There are a few couples dispersed around the room, probably regulars. Strange for a Friday night. Perhaps there is game on somewhere. Perhaps there has been an incident, accident or attack? Perhaps it is just a slow night. Sasha shifts off to another customer on the other end of the bar. I sit patiently and impatiently, staring at the upside-down glasses hanging from the rack over the bar. As I stare intently at the glass-filled rack, someone slides onto the bar stool next to me. I ignore him; there is enough room for everyone. "Hey," he says, "is it OK if I sit here?"

"Sure," I say, not looking in his direction at all. There is plenty of room. I shift my bar stool slightly away from him. I pick up my phone and try to decide how to distract myself while I wait for Mattie. Should I call someone? Check out the news? Play a game?

"Hey," says the voice to me, "I know this is cheesy, but I actually sat here for a reason – to talk to you." I shift the stool around. There's quite a bit of noise in the room, perhaps the voice isn't for me.

"Are you talking to me?" I ask.

"Are you impersonating de Niro?"

"No. That was a genuine question."

"Well, I *am* talking to you," the man continues. "I saw you were by yourself, and I thought you might like some company."

"Thanks," I say, "but I am waiting for a friend."

"Is it a *friend-friend* or a boyfriend?"

"It doesn't really make a difference, does it? Excuse me, I am not trying to playing hard to get. I simply have plans that don't involve you." I turn away. From the corner of my eye, I can see that Sasha is back at my end of the bar and trying to suppress a smile. "Well," the man persists, "while you wait, would you consider giving me your phone number?" I look at him. He looks normal, polite, and he doesn't seem particularly aggressive. Elon is officially history. Mattie is late. Perhaps I *should* go for it. But no, I simply don't have the energy for it. Another time maybe.

"Listen," I say, "you seem like a good guy, you know . . . *normal.*"

"Gee, thanks."

"That is a high compliment coming from me."

"OK then!"

"But I really am waiting for a friend. This is not some game that I am playing." The guy looks a bit crushed and defeated. I feel a bit bad, and briefly consider relenting. "It's OK, I understand," he says, but doesn't get up just yet. He takes a quick breath. "Will you then at least pretend to give me your number?" he says. "My friends at the table there said that you looked like a stuck up ice-princess and I said that I could melt your icy heart. They are betting against us." *Ouch!*

"Well, then," I say. "I wouldn't want to disappoint them." I swivel my chair all the way around back to the bar. "Is this enough ice for you?" I ask loudly.

"Bitch," the man mutters loud enough for me to hear. He gets up in a huff and walks off to the jeering of his friends. Sasha sidles up to the edge of the bar where I am sitting. He tops up my drink. "Ignore him, he's just an asshole," he says.

"Tell me about it. Thanks for the drink." I take a long sip. "He is an asshole and I am just an ice princess."

"More like a fire goddess with that flaming tongue of yours," says Sasha with a smile. I smile and continue to nurse my drink. Mattie comes in a few minutes later. He gives me a big hug and joins me at the bar. There is something about him that seems a bit pensive and quiet. "Is everything OK?" I ask.

"Sure," he says, "long day. Bit of a thing with Orit. But now it's over." I don't tell him that I already know about the breakup from Karina. He gives me a warm smile. There is something about him that is vulnerable and exposed. It makes me want to reach out and touch his face, just brush the side of his cheek with my fingers. But, I don't. Mattie orders a beer from Sasha and we sit there, the two of us, in comfortable silence, letting the day's grime and grit dissipate. When we are ready, we will talk. For now, we enjoy the silence. Old friends can do that.

We must give off the impression of being there alone, because a young woman comes right up to us, slides in between our bar stools, practically pushing me aside, and within seconds she is in Mattie's face. Her black cocktail dress is so short that she uses her one hand to keep it down. She brushes her chest against Mattie. "Oh sorry," she says, "didn't mean that," and giggles. I look at Mattie and roll my eyes.

"Hey, are you here alone?" she asks him.

"Well, no," Mattie answers. "I am with her, the girl sitting next to me, the one that you have your back to."

The girl doesn't miss a beat. "You are with *who*?" She turns around to me and looks at me, eyeing me as if I am the most insignificant speck of human waste.

"With *whom are you* – is probably the correct way to ask," I tell her.

"Her?" she says in disbelief as if Mattie were joking.

"Yes, I am with him," I say. This night just keeps on getting better and better.

"No," she says and turns back to Mattie, "I don't think you're together. You're just being polite, aren't you? But, she won't mind, will she, if you and I get to know one another." She turns to me and stares at me squarely in the eyes, daring me to object.

"Each other," I say.

"What?"

"She won't mind if you and I get to know *each other*, not 'one another'," I tell her.

"Whatever!" she tells me and turns once again to Mattie. She flings back her hair as if she were in the middle of a commercial for shampoo and conditioner, blocking me squarely with her back. The back of her dress has a large zipper from her neckline to just below her waist. Very indiscrete. I have kind of had enough of her. I can also be direct. "Hey, hey you," I say, tapping her on the shoulder. I could take this girl – knock her down in one fell swoop. Knock her out. "Hey, look at me for a second." Hair product girl swings around, rolls her eyes and says, "What do you want?"

I motion to her with two fingers to come closer. "Listen sweetheart, didn't your friends tell you? Come here," I beckon.

"Tell me what?" she asks.

I whisper loudly, "Come here. You have something between your teeth. It is green. There is something stuck there and there." I point to two random places in her jawline. "No wonder my friend isn't interested in you."

"Oh my god," she says, covering her mouth with both of her hands. "I am mortified. I am so embarrassed." And she scurries off.

Mattie starts laughing. "That was so mean."

"I know, I'm sorry, I couldn't help myself. It was either that or punch her. But it was the only way that I was going to get you to myself."

"Tamara," he says, "all you need to do is ask and I am here for you," and he puts his arm over my shoulder. His arm feels good there. Natural. I look up at him. Now he looks more like himself. I put my head briefly against his hand.

"Now where's that drink?" asks Mattie. He removes his arm from around me and waves his hand to get Sasha's attention. Sasha nods and brings a beer over. We begin to talk about his work and my work. I tell him about the pending graduation event. We are just about to launch into more personal stuff when Mattie's phone rings. He looks at the screen and pulls a face. I can just make out from the contact information that the caller is Orit. I give an audible sigh. "Just taking this. Won't be a second," says Mattie and he swings off the bar stool.

"Why don't you just tell him that you like him?" asks Sasha. I stare at him with a blank expression. "Come on," says Sasha. "This is not the first time that you are here with him. It is so obvious." I turn away from Sasha and set my gaze back on Mattie. He is talking in earnest, with a serious expression. And then he smiles, and then he laughs. It looks like whatever issues he and Orit had before he arrived are now resolved. I turn to Sasha. "I don't know what to say," I tell him. "I guess that I just didn't really realize it myself."

"But now you do?"

"Oh my god. I think I do," I say. "What the hell am I going to do?"

"Poor child," he says to me maternally. "I totally get what you see in him. He reminds me of my first boyfriend. He's totally delicious. If you don't go for him, you know, I might."

"Whoa there!" I tell Sasha. "This is a lot for me to process."

"Well process quickly, cherub," Sasha says. "He's coming back."

"I can't," I say. "I am his friend." I snap back.

"*Carpe diem*," Sasha counters in a sing-song voice.

Mattie comes back and takes his seat. "Sorry about that," he says. "Now, I am all yours."

I wish, I say to myself, and the words ricochet and echo inside me like a coin in an empty well. *I wish. I wish. I wish.* I can't believe that I am figuring this out only now.

"That was Orit," says Mattie. "She sends her love."

I seriously doubt that, but I manage a smile, and say "thanks."

"So Tammy, I was worried about you yesterday. We all were. What's going on?"

"I really don't want to talk about it. I am not ready yet," I say. "Do you mind?"

"Maybe tomorrow," he says. "You are coming, right?"

"Of course," I say in a shaky voice. "I wouldn't miss your birthday party." I can barely look at Mattie without thinking about my sudden realization. *I like Mattie.* I like him, and there is nothing that I can do about it.

Chapter 24

After an endless night of tossing and turning, I realize that there is no point in staying in bed any longer. The charade of sleeping is over. Today we are all meeting at nine o' clock in the morning at HaYarkon Park. It is an early morning wake-up for some. We are all going rowing on the river – Mattie's birthday, Mattie's choice. My head is heavy with thoughts about yesterday's revelation about my feelings for one of my best friends. Perhaps if I go for a walk, I will be able to clear the thoughts away. I grab a bottle of water, a hat, my handbag and I walk out. It is cool outside. There is a pleasant breeze and the air is fresh and clean. As I walk, instead of clearing my mind, I find myself fantasizing about scenarios in which I confess my love to Mattie. But in each and every vision, the fantasy goes horribly wrong. In every scenario, his eyes are wide with disbelief; his mouth gapes with horror and his legs turn him around and walk him away. I am the predator and he is the unwitting prey. Driven by tension and apprehensiveness, my brisk walk turns into a jog. By six thirty, I have reached the park and I am covered in sweat. There is no point in staying here for two and a half hours, so I make a slight detour, and decide to walk over to Iris's apartment.

Iris lives in the neighborhood that borders on the park. I have been here many times before, but never unannounced. Maybe she isn't even home. It is six forty in the morning. She is going to kill me, but maybe that is for the best. I am at the entrance of her building and I think to myself, *here goes nothing*. I press the buzzer once, then I wait for a few seconds, and then I press it again, a second time. For a few minutes nothing happens. I am about to buzz a third time when I hear a gruff familiar voice. "Tamara, one of us had better be dying, and honestly, I am hoping it is you. Come on up and make me coffee. You know how I like it." The door clicks open and I step inside. I walk up two flights of stairs and find Iris's door wide open. She is lying on the sofa in the lounge, barely covered by a silk robe. As I step inside, a young man with shaved hair and tattoos of different species of butterflies steps out. "Good morning," he says to me politely as he walks past. "Have a lovely day."

"Good morning to you too," I say, and watch him walk down the stairs. Iris's voice rings out from the depths of the sofa: "When I said that I would be there for you, I should have qualified that with opening hours." I step inside the lounge. "This establishment isn't awake at this ungodly hour. Now make me some coffee."

"Sorry," I say. "I got to the park earlier than expected and didn't know what to do with myself." I stick a coffee capsule into the machine and press the button.

"It seems like a familiar pattern with you."

"Sad, but true," I answer her. The espresso shoots angrily into a tiny little mug. "Karina and I covered that yesterday and we agree that I am pathetic." I throw in two cubes of sugar. Iris signals me to throw in another one. "And bring me some biscotti as well," she demands.

"So how can Auntie Iris help you if you refuse to help yourself?" I reach for the biscotti, take a couple for myself and hand the rest, as well as the espresso, over to the reclining Iris.

"What do you mean?"

"You never called that guy from Bloom's, did you?"

"No. How do you know that?"

"I saw his friend a few times. He spilled the beans."

"And you broke it off with Elon, the sexy doctor?" continues Iris.

"I did. How do you know that? Did Dana tell you?"

"No, Aviva."

"Same thing."

"So my dear, how can I help you?"

"It gets worse."

"How does it get worse?"

"Yesterday I realized what I want, or rather who I want. And I know that I can't have him."

"You did?"

"Yes I did."

"So go take him already."

"I told you I can't."

"There's no such thing as can't, only won't."

"He's involved with someone else."

"Are they married?"

"No. Not yet."

"So what are you waiting for?"

"But he's spoken for. He's taken."

"So go take him back."

"Iris, why are you doing this to me? I can't just take him."

"You can and you must. My darling, as glamorous, as all this seems," says Iris, making a generous sweep of the lounge with her hands, "as perfectly amazing and awesome as it is to live the life of hedonism and pleasure, don't you think I wouldn't trade it for the real thing?"

"You? You would trade your life for a life of commitment and monogamy? But you were in that relationship. You had that relationship. And you left it. You chose to leave it. Not like …" I let the sentence trail off.

"Not like you?" Iris smiles. "It's true. That is what I did. I left my marriage . . . both of them in fact, because it wasn't the right relationship, we were not right together. You may think that just because David instigated the divorce, and you didn't fight him, that makes your situation different, but it isn't. You went along with the decision, because you knew he was right. You are two good people who are not meant to be together. There is no shame in that."

"I saw David yesterday."

"And . . . do you want him back? Does he want you?" asks Iris.

"No and no," I say emphatically.

"Honey, it was just the wrong relationship. It doesn't make you a bad person, or a failure in relationships in general – it just means that you've got to try again."

"And is that what you are doing, trying again?"

"I, my dear, am trying again and again and again and again."

It is my turn to smile.

"It is no joking matter. While you are too scared to try, I am too scared to try *seriously*. I am too scared to be swept up, taken in, and committed and for it all to blow up in my face again. It is much easier to window-shop than to buy the actual goods. So, honey, if you know what you want to buy, if you are absolutely certain, then go into the damn shop and make it yours."

"But Iris. How can I?" Iris gets up and stands with me face to face. She takes both my hands in hers.

"How *can't* you darling? You are meant to be together. It is so clear."

"But I haven't even told you who he is." She loosens her grip slightly.

"My darling, didn't I tell you I would help you both? Haven't I been trying for months now to get you together?"

I stare straight into her eyes. "Oh my god, Iris. I like Mattie." She puts her hand on my shoulder. "I know my darling, I know."

I have been in the vicinity of the park for over two hours and yet, Iris and I are still the last to arrive. Karina and Josh are already at the boats. Karina gives me a smile and blows me a kiss. "Hey, Tammy," says Josh, and picks up the baby's hand, and waves it. "Hey Ben," I say and blow him a kiss. Nadav comes running up to me. "Tammy, give me a monster hug," he says. I scoop him up and hug him so that his legs are flailing about in the air. "Monster hug!" I say, squeezing him. "Where's Roni, Iris?" asks Josh.

"She's with her father today," says Iris. "What about me, Nadav," she says. "No hug for your Auntie Iris?" Nadav runs away and hides behind his father and his little brother, Ben. I understand him. Iris can be a little intimidating. While Aviva is at the counter paying for a family-sized pedal boat, Dana is with the kids, who are being fitted with life jackets. Orit and Mattie are also nearby, but they are whispering at a bit of a distance from the rest.

"Trouble in Paradise?" Iris asks Karina and Josh.

"No, just that Orit doesn't like boating," says Karina. "But Mattie set this up ages ago and he didn't want to cancel. Orit can sit with me. I'm also not going to sail. I will sit here with this adorable little creature." she says, taking Ben from Josh.

"You can sail with him," says Iris. "He is so little that you can hold him the whole time."

"True," says Karina, "but I am feeling a bit under the weather myself today, so I prefer to sit it out this time."

"*Aaaah,*" says Iris. "Poor Karina. Damned time of the month."

"Don't worry about me. I will be fine," says Karina, and gives me a wink once Iris is looking away.

Orit and Mattie come up. "Mattie my boy, happy birthday. Come here and give me a hug." Mattie steps forward obediently and gives Iris a hug. "Hey Orit," says Iris.

"Hi," she answers sullenly.

"Hi . . . uuuh, hi, Mattie," I say clearing my throat. "Happy birthday," I say, keeping a good distance between me and him.

"That's not how you say happy birthday to a good friend," says Iris and she pushes me into him. I go flying and Mattie catches me, dropping Orit's hand in the process.

"Iris," Mattie and I say in unison. She looks at us with a grin. I shake my head at her angrily. "Sorry," I say, looking up to him, my eyes ablaze with irritation at Iris.

"Don't worry about it," he says.

"Happy birthday," I say and give him a small kiss on the cheek. He is freshly shaven and the feel of his taut skin along with the subtle smell of aftershave are a bit intoxicating. I step back. "Hey Orit," I say, "how are you?"

"Fine, I guess," she says. "Can't believe we will actually be getting on a boat. They look like leaky barrels. I bet they haven't been inspected for ages."

"We can ask, if it will make you feel better," says Mattie.

"You don't have to get on the boat if you don't want to," says Iris. "Karina isn't"

"You aren't?" asks Orit.

"No, got the baby here, and a bit of a tummy ache. I think I will stay on *terra firma*. Why don't you stay with me?"

"What about Mattie?"

"I just want you to be happy and smile," says Mattie. "If that means you don't sail, that would also be OK with me. Next time, we will choose another activity."

"I am going to need help with Nadav," says Josh. "Preferably someone who can look after him while I let the engine rip," he says, looking at me with pleading eyes. Before I can respond, Iris says, "You don't need to ask me twice Josh; I am your woman. It is about time that Nadav and I spent some quality time together." I shake my head at Iris for a second time. What a transparent ploy. "Are you sure?" asks Josh, "maybe Tammy would be . . . *better suited* to keep him distracted?"

"I have actually raised a daughter of my own, as you know," says Iris indignantly, "and besides which I am very good with men."

"Fine, fine, fine," says Josh, unwilling to turn this into an argument.

"I guess that leaves us," says Mattie turning to me. "Awesome. It will be fun."

"It better be," says Iris giving me the eye. Josh and Mattie go up to the counter to pay, and Iris, Nadav and I go hand-in hand to fit him for a life jacket. Aviva and Dana and the kids wave to us as they get into the boat and then speed off.

"You have an opportunity," hisses Iris," just take it."

"Under Orit's nose?"

"Is that who you want your friend to land up with? I am not Karina, who sees roses and sunshine in everyone. Is that who Mattie deserves?" I look at Orit – she is using baby wipes to wipe down the bench where Karina is sitting with Ben.

"She isn't that bad. We all have our issues. So do I," I say, "I haven't really given her a chance."

"Now is not the time for you to smooth out those angles and edges, darling. Look at him, look at Mattie; isn't that what you want?"

I look over at him and I know that Iris is right. His eyes catch mine, and he keeps them there for a few second and smiles. "I'll see," I say. "This just isn't a good time. It is his birthday, and she's here."

"There will never be a good time," Iris says to me. "So just do it now!" Josh and Mattie beckon us over to our respective boats. "Come on, you guys," shouts Aviva, sailing perilously close to the pier. "Catch up already!"

"Come on in!" shouts Dana. The speed and angle of their speedboat send a huge wave of spray over us. "We're winning! You are losers," shout Aviva and Dana's kids.

"Come on Josh, this means war," says Iris, wiping the spray off her sunglasses. She sits up front with Josh and buckles Nadav in between them. "Let's go get the bastards. Nadav," she says.

"Iris, watch your language," says Josh.

"Nonsense," says Iris, "Nadav can handle it. Right Nadav?"

"Yes!" shouts Nadav.

"Now," continues Iris, "do you want Daddy to go fast? Do you want to go so fast that your head spins?"

"Yes, please, Daddy, please." says Nadav.

"Do you want to spray Auntie Aviva and Auntie Dana?"

"YES!" shouts Nadav.

"OK", says Josh, and dropping two tones, he declares in a manly voice, "This is war. Let's do it!" With a rev of the engine, he speeds off.

Mattie and I get into the front of the speedboat. Mattie offers me the captain's spot, but I decline. "Let me get my water legs first," I tell him. He stretches his legs and pulls down the throttle. With a jerk, the boat goes forward. I am thrown forward by the force. Mattie catches me with his hand.

"Sorry about that," he says. "Turns out I am not a natural born captain either. I'll get the hang of it soon." He tries again, gently this time, and we make our way slowly, cruising down the water. This man-made "lake" is fed by the waters of the Yarkon River. The water is green and murky. The banks of the lake are lush and fertile, but there are foreboding signs advising boaters to stay away from the edges so that the boat does not get stuck. The lake is tiny – it is the dead end of the Yarkon – and it gives off the feeling of sailing about in a rusty old bath tub. The water goers, all amateur would-be sailors and would-be kayakers, are a happy bunch They take what they can get because of the closeness to home. They speed around the lake, bumping happily into one another, family against family, friends against friends. Mattie and I laugh as we see Josh and Iris pursuing Aviva and Dana. Dana is leading now, and she is surprisingly adept at staying out of the way. Force of habit, I guess. The kids are enjoying the water wars and are egging their parents on. "Why aren't you charging as well?" I ask Mattie. "Isn't that what you came for?"

"*Naah*," says Mattie, "I came to be out and about, and with my friends. I am happy to float quietly by with you."

"I like this too," I say. "Boating was a great idea. To get us all out like this. Together. Inspired."

"I thought you'd like it."

"What's not to like? Outdoors, open air, and each one can go in whatever direction and pace they want. That's my kind of activity."

"Mine too. Apparently not Orit's . . ."

I look away from him. "I don't know what to say." I tell him.

"Why not?" he asks quietly. "Don't I always encourage you? Don't I always support you?"

"Mattie, of course you do. But, I feel like here I need to stay quiet."

"Because you don't like her? You don't need to tell me; you have made that quite clear."

"It's not that. I don't really know her . . ."

"Then what is it?"

"I just feel like there is a conflict of interest here . . ."

"How so?" asks Mattie. He stops steering the boat all together. We drift to a slow, but complete stop. The water bobs gently up and down all around us. Other boats speed past. They spin around us, but they are nothing more than an idle background buzz. All I can see is Mattie. "Where's the conflict of interest?" he asks. I look away from him, and focus on a bird on the top of a tree at the furthest part of the shore and think for a few seconds. The bird flaps her wings suddenly and flies off. I turn back to Mattie and say: "The conflict of interest is more like a personal dilemma. A dilemma that is a bit difficult for me to share."

"But you will anyway, right?" he responds.

"Sure. It is just a bit difficult . . . never mind. Well, you know that recently I have been kind of miserable for a number of reasons." Mattie nods. "And at the same time," I continue, "I have been trying to get back out there. To sort out my life. To meet people."

"OK."

"Well, I have recently understood that one of the reasons that I am having a hard time in my personal life is because I am with the wrong people."

"So what? What does that even mean? You continue on until you find the right person."

"You see, that's the thing. I would like to be with the right person, to know that we fit together."

"Everyone wants that."

"Yes, but I think that not everyone has what they want right in front of them. I mean, literally right in front of them." I look straight at Mattie. "We've been friends forever, and I understand now what I haven't understood before. I understand that you and I, together, can have more than just a friendship. I want more. I want us. I want you . . ." The world around us has gone completely silent. I can feel Mattie's breath, I can hear him inhale and exhale. My eyes trace the outline of his lips and then try to search in his eyes for a response, for any response. But none comes. After a few seconds, he looks back at me, his eyes lowered, and he says quietly. "I think I should get back to Orit." He revs up the boat and we head back to the shore.

Oh my god, I think to myself as we head back. *What have I done? What have I done?* My head is spinning and I can feel prickles behind my eyes. *Just don't cry. I mustn't cry. No crying, not now.* We get back to the rickety wood jetty, and I get out first. I don't look back at Mattie. Dana is sitting with the kids, Orit, Karina and the baby. I don't go over. Josh and Iris and Nadav are still in the water. They are making their way back to the jetty. I yell, as evenly as I can, that I am going to help Aviva at the kiosk. I head over to where Aviva is buying ice – cream and drinks for everyone. By the time I get over there, I have managed to control my impulse to cry. "Are you OK?" asks Aviva. "You look a little seasick."

"I am," I say. "Maybe also a little dehydrated."

"Well then," she says, "you have come to the right place." She hands me a bottle of mineral water. I struggle with the bottle and she opens it with an elegant twist of the wrist. "I think you need some sugar as well," she says. She orders another popsicle – pineapple flavor – and opens it for me. "Thanks," I say, and indeed, I begin to feel my energy slowly being restored. Iris comes up to us. "Aviva dear, did you happen to order me a strong, hot black, black coffee?" she asks.

"Nope," says Aviva. "I figured because you like it hot, I should wait until you are back on land."

"Aviva, you take the ice creams and drinks to everyone," I say. "I will order for you, Iris."

"Thanks," says Aviva. "Iris, just stick around with this one. She is a bit dehydrated and seasick." Iris nods and Aviva heads back to the group. Iris orders her own coffee, flirting with the man behind the espresso machine, as she usually does. I wait for her, forcing myself to take constant sips of water, and to eat my popsicle as normally as possible. "OK, what happened, babe?" asks Iris.

"I told him that I liked him, and he rejected me."

"What did he say?"

"Nothing."

"So he didn't reject you."

"Nothing *is* a rejection."

"No, it isn't. It is a pause to digest."

"He said nothing, except that he wanted to get back to Orit."

"Honey, it isn't over. You need to gather yourself together and try again."

"No way. I am done. It is over."

"No you aren't. You have to do this."

"Humiliate myself?"

"No, state your case."

"I don't think I can."

"You must. You have no other option. Now take a deep breath, and come on. Let's head back to the others." She threads her arm through mine and we head back to the group. There is no need to worry about awkwardness. As soon as I get back to the group, Roy, Amit and Yael jump on me, and soon I am roped into kicking the ball between them. I can feel Mattie's eyes settle occasionally upon me, but as soon as I look up, he looks away. Josh, Nadav, Dana and Aviva soon join us, and the game turns from random passes into a rowdy round of football.

After about an hour, kids and adults alike are getting antsy for food. We do a quick round of who wants what. The group is divided between those who want hotdogs and those who prefer pizza. Only Orit remains obstinately undecided. Mattie runs through a few additional options: "There is also falafel, a plate of hummus, schnitzel, pretzels . . ." To each suggestion, Orit remains adamantly opposed. Mattie goes back to the kiosk to see what other options he can offer her. "I tell you what," I say to Iris, anxious to restore a bit of quiet.

"There is a Greenhouse Café on the corner. Why don't I go and get you a salad?" I give her my phone so that she can browse the online menu and make an order. When she has made her selection, I say to her, "You stay here. The place isn't far. I will go and get it."

"Are you sure?" she asks.

"Yes, absolutely. I feel like the walk…" I tell her.

"I'll go" says Dana.

"Don't be silly. You should be here with the kids," I answer her.

"I'll go," says Iris. I really think that you should stay. Let Orit go." Orit glowers at Iris.

"I need some alone time," I say. "I am going."

"Fine," shouts Iris at me as I walk away. I make my way swiftly to the Greenhouse Café. Most of the clientele are sipping ice teas and eating cheese or carrot cake. The kids are running around happily and several families are there with their dogs at their feet, enjoying a lazy nap. I sit at the indoor bar and drink a lemon tea while I wait for Orit's order to be ready. As they are packing up the salad, the phone rings at the counter. The maître d' picks it up and says, "Yes, yes, she's still here," and then he adds, "Sure, absolutely," and hangs up. "Your friends have added to your order," he tells me.

"OK." I say. "What else do I need to bring?"

"An assortment of cakes and four ice teas."

"OK," I say, wondering to myself how I am going to get it all back to the group.

"How much do I owe you?" I ask.

"Nothing. It is already paid for."

"OK," I say.

"Give me five more minutes and it will all be ready."

About ten minutes later, he comes back with a cake box and two cardboard cup holders. I put the bag with the salad in one hand, along with a cup holder with two ice teas. I put the bag with the cake box in the other hand along with the other cup holder and the two additional ice teas. *This is going to be a tedious balancing act,* I think to myself, and I start to slowly walk back to the group. After about twenty meters, I take a few minutes to sit down and relax the tension in my hands. Then I begin again, until I reach the next bench. At the third bench, just as I am getting ready to stand up and start again, Mattie appears out of nowhere. "I came to help," he says quietly.

"It's OK," I say, standing up. "You can go. I will manage."

"I came to help," he repeats. He reaches his hand out for one of the parcels.

"Mattie, let's not make this harder than it already is."

"You made it harder."

"I was just being honest with you."

"Well, your timing sucks," he says, and sits down on the bench. "It always has." He places his head between his hands in exasperation.

"When was the last time it sucked?" I ask.

"When you divorced, and I called off my engagement. I thought we could try then. But you went *AWOL,* and have been missing practically ever since."

"Mattie, you never said anything."

"I thought you would understand. I thought that you would catch up with me."

"But I didn't know . . ."

". . . And now . . . when things are getting serious with Orit, now you choose to speak up?"

"I am sorry," I say. "But, does that have to mean that now it is too late? Doesn't it mean that we should at least try?" I put my hand on his shoulder. He lifts up his head, so that we are eye to eye.

"Honestly, I don't know." he says. "I don't even know, right now, while you are here in front of me, whether this is something that you really want. Or is it part of the current crisis that you are in? I mean, how deeply do you want this? How long until you run away or disappear from me again? I have been waiting for you for so long. I have been waiting patiently, picking up after you. Picking you up and hoping that you will see me."

"I am here now," I tell him. "I see you now," I say. I stroke his cheek, and move his hair off his forehead. "I see you now and this is what I want. I want you. I want us." I lean in and kiss him. He reaches for me, puts his arms around my waist and pulls me closer. I melt into him, feel myself soft and warm against his taut body. In that moment, absolutely everything feels like it was meant to be just so. After a few endless seconds, Mattie pulls away gently. "Tamara," he says. "Tammy, we need to get back. I . . . I . . . don't know what to think. I need some time." He takes the cake and the salad bags, and I take the two cup holders. We walk quietly and briskly back, he, a few steps ahead of me all the way.

When we get back to the group, Mattie hands Orit the salad. He gives the cake box to Josh, who opens it. Karina pulls out a few candles and Iris contributes matches, and they light the candles and initiate a rowdy chorus of Happy Birthday. Everyone joins in, even random passersby. Everyone, except for Orit, who is eating her salad quietly on a bench. When they are done, I ask Dana, "Who are the ice teas for?" I am still holding onto the two cup holders. "I don't know," says Dana. "Iris ordered them; you should ask her." *Of course it was Iris,* I think to myself. *Of course.*

"Never mind," I say to Dana.

"We haven't really spoken today," says Dana. "Why don't you come to us this Friday for supper?"

"Sure," I say quickly. "Sounds good. I am going to offer this to Orit." The less I talk, the better. I can't trust myself at the moment. I put the drinks on the bench next to Orit, offering her one in the process. "Is it sweetened?" she asks.

"Yes," I say.

"With sweetener, or sugar?"

"I think sugar water."

"Oh, I don't like sugar water," says Orit. I shrug, not really wanting to continue the conversation, especially considering what has transpired between me and Mattie only minutes earlier. I walk off and go up to Iris. "I need to get out of here," I tell her.

"What happened?" she asks.

"I kissed him," I say, reaching out and touching my lips absently. Iris's eyes open wide and bright. "And . . .?"

"And nothing. He said that he needs time. He said that he is confused. And then he walked away."

"Did he kiss you back?"

"Yes, I think so. Yes. He didn't stop me. Listen, I need to go. I really need to go." Iris gives me a quick hug. "OK, honey, speak later."

"Tell the others that I said goodbye."

"Will do." I turn around and start walking in the direction of home. *I kissed him.* I think to myself. *I kissed him. I kissed him.* My walk turns into a skip, and then into a run. *I kissed him and it felt like home.*

Chapter 25

The feeling of elation lasts the whole of Sunday. I come into the Nest with a smile. Kobi is waiting for me in my office. Not even his presence can dampen my spirits.

"Hey," I say genially, "how are you doing?"

"I am OK," he says stiffly, "I assume that now is as good a time as any to speak."

"It is," I say, laying down my bag and settling into my chair. "I have been waiting to speak to you, but wanted to respect your request for space." Kobi nods. I continue, "Your letter wasn't exactly a shock, especially not after I was so difficult with you a few days before. So I want to start with an apology and say that I am very sorry that I was so defensive and accusatory. I know that I am not always easy to get along with."

"That is an understatement," says Kobi with a grim smile. "You know; you really make it hard to like you. I know that your temperament is part of what makes you good at your job – your hardness, your determination . . ." he trails off. "And, actually, I can look beyond all that. That is not why I am quitting, although I would be lying if I denied that it *is* a part of my decision." I nod, reminding myself to keep quiet and to allow him to continue.

"I think the bad chemistry between us may be because I guess I am a little similar to you: obstinate, forceful. I know it isn't easy working with me either. I guess that I feel that two people like that in this place . . . well perhaps there isn't enough oxygen for the both of us."

"Are you saying that this is about ego?"

"Maybe a bit, but I don't think completely. I think my decision to leave is less about ego and more about personal challenges. I feel ready to do more, and even if you wanted to give me more, there isn't much more for you – or Adam – to give me. There really isn't a need for a number two, especially when the number one is so strong."

"So are you saying that if there was more of a challenge, more responsibility, you would consider staying?" I ask.

"I don't think so. Honestly, there is still the chemistry thing. I don't think that this is working for us." He points from himself to me and back again. "I am not trying to be difficult and definitely don't have any alternatives to propose. You see, I really do believe that I need to take on more responsibility, more challenges. I feel underutilized. I feel like I am not applying my full potential. But even if that could be done here, I don't think that our working relationship is healthy."

"I see," I say. "I appreciate your honesty. Let me think about this a bit. I understand that you are looking for something else." Kobi nods and I continue: "But maybe we can figure something out."

"I don't see how," says Kobi, "but go ahead, knock yourself out." I look at him closely to see whether he is speaking with sarcasm, but he looks back at me with an expression clear of any guile. "Anyway," he says, "next week is the graduation ceremony, so we have enough on our plate to keep us both busy." And as if to signify the end of our personal discussion, he fishes his smartphone out of his pocket and begins to delve into some work-related activities. "I am going by the basketball stadium today and will talk to the team coach and sponsor about the pre-match event, based on our discussions with Adam."

"Great," I say. "You have my comments and feedback. I think that the session with the pros will be fantastic." Kobi nods. I continue from where he left off: "On my end, I have closed the refreshments, invitations have been sent, and the order of the speakers has been set. I have also gone over Joseph's activity, and I think it will be fun. His plan is to incorporate all the participants, not just the Nesters."

"Sounds good," says Kobi, "I am glad that he has agreed to lead the activity."

"Me too," I say. "Additionally, a movie clip is already in the making. One of the Nesters is working on it. I have also been in touch with the schools to ensure that a representative will be there to hand out the graduation certificates."

"We have done very well this year. It is our first year with a 100% pass rate." says Kobi.

"Yes, it is an amazing achievement. And it looks like all but two will go into the army."

"Are you counting Noa?"

"Yes, we still haven't heard from her parents. Even after the financial issues have been sorted out, it is still not a *fait accompli*."

Kobi sighs. "Let's hope that it goes OK," he says.

I continue: "Adam also needs to review the presentations, but I will send them to you first to go through them. "Will that be OK?"

"Sure," says Kobi. "While I am still here, I am completely in it."

"OK then," I say, "we have our work cut out for us!" Kobi nods, gets up, turns around and walks out. I sit at my desk for a few minutes, deep in thought about the situation at hand. What is the solution to this issue? How hard should I be fighting to keep Kobi? Like he says, it has never been smooth sailing between us anyway. If I fight to keep him here, would it be because I want to, or because I feel obliged to? If I fight for him to stay, what can I give him? Maybe there really isn't a need for the both of us? My thoughts are disrupted by the ringing of my phone. I answer quickly. "Hey Iris."

"Hi babe, how are you feeling? Still floating?"

"Practically," I say. "Did he say anything after I left?"

"No, we all basically went off in our own directions. It was a long morning. Has he called?"

"Not yet. Should I call him?"

"He said he needed time, right?"

"Yes,"

"So maybe wait a bit longer."

"How long?"

"I don't know, till the end of the week."

"That long?"

"Maybe."

"But, if he doesn't call by the end of the week, then maybe I shouldn't call at all."

"Don't speak like that, darling. It's Mattie, it's you; of course he'll call."

"You are right, I say. "He'll call." We hang up the phone, and the sudden silence leaves me with an uneasy emptiness in the pit of my stomach. I brush it aside and throw myself into administration, logistics and planning for the graduation ceremony.

Monday and Tuesday come quickly and without any fanfare. Regrettably so: still no word from Mattie. I throw myself into the graduation ceremony with verve and determination. The question of what to do with Kobi still remains like a flashing light in the background. We work together quietly and efficiently, keeping our interactions to the bare minimum. In my updates with Adam about the graduation ceremony – which suddenly become more often and more intense – we also discuss the issue of Kobi more than once, and both of us consider the options from all directions. These conversations invariably end with a question hanging in the air like a helium balloon floating frustratingly out of reach – a question that seems to be at the core of all of my recent frustrations: *What do I want? At this point,* I think to myself with Mattie flashing in my mind's eye, *I am not sure that I even care.*

On Tuesday afternoon, there is a gentle knock on my office door. I look up, and standing timidly, waiting for permission to enter, are Noa's parents. I try to read their minds, to get a hint of what lies ahead, but find myself unable to read their expressions.

"Hello," I say. "This is an unexpected pleasure. Why don't we get a cup of tea or coffee in the kitchen?" This is always the fallback plan, because my office isn't big enough for three adults sitting on normal-sized chairs. Thankfully, the kitchen is empty. There is no way to make the space private. It is also not meant to be, so I do what we always do under these circumstances, and I call out in a loud voice to anyone in the house: "Hi guys, I am in the kitchen with visitors, so please put off coming in for now." I get back different signs and sounds of acquiescence from all corners of the Nest. I turn back to my visitors. "What will you have: tea, coffee or something cold?"

"Turkish coffee for me, please," says Nava, Noa's mom.

"Nothing for me thanks," says Eli, Noa's dad.

I put some grapes and some sesame-seed biscuits in front of us. Eli absently reaches for a biscuit, muttering under his breath the prayer that is said when partaking of this kind of food. I pour three glasses of water, prepare Nava's coffee and sit down and wait patiently for them to tell me why they are here. I know that I need to bide my time.

"You must be so proud of Noa for graduating high school," I say.

"We are," says Nava. "She has always been so smart. Even when she was little. Even when she was so difficult a few years ago."

"She will go far," I say. "We are all very proud of her." Eli just nods. "And I am so happy that Noa's brother will be joining us next year – provided that you agree, of course. We have just received the approval letter from his school this week."

"We are very happy to allow Maor to join the Nest. We know how much you have helped Noa. We are happy to give him the same opportunity," says Eli. I remain silent, hoping that he will continue, but he doesn't say another word. After a few seconds, Nava begins to talk.

"Noa told us what you have done for us. We were contacted by the municipality about giving us extra financial support. She also told us that the army recruiter has confirmed that she has been granted a special status so that she can help us out by working part time, if she decides to serve." I can feel that I am holding my breath. I consciously force myself to exhale as noiselessly as possible. "Then yesterday," continues Nava, "Noa'leh got a call from some lab, a few roads down from us, saying they had seen her high school transcript, and would like to see whether she can work for them part time." *Aviva!* I think to myself. She came through for me, for Noa. I smile and close my eyes. This is terrific news.

Nava seems to be spent, exhausted from the effort of talking. Or maybe she is just waiting for her husband to respond. My smile disappears quickly. I turn to look at him. His face is full of tension. His eyes are scrunched closed and his mouth is pursed shut. I feel nervous about what is coming next. He clears his throat, but says nothing. He takes a sip of water. He coughs and takes another sip of water. I look at Nava, but she just looks away. Eli covers his mouth with his hand, and says something that I cannot quite make out. I look at Nava, and she puts her hand gently on his. "Say it again," she says to him softly. He coughs, clears his throat and tries again. This time, I can make his words out quite clearly. "Thank you!" he says. He rubs his eyes and a single tear slides down the side of his cheek. "Thank you for everything," he says more strongly. "Noa can go to the army." My eyes widen with excitement. "That is wonderful news. That is fantastic!" I say, overwhelmed with happiness. Nava sits quietly with closed eyes and a wide smile, which lights up her whole face. She holds her hand over her husband's with a gentle but firm grip. "Thank you for everything," she says to me. "You have changed our lives."

"It is for Noa," I say, "it is all for Noa. She's worth it."

Nava and Eli stand up proudly and, holding hands, they leave the kitchen and exit the Nest as quietly and modestly as they had appeared. I remain in the kitchen: stunned, happy, and with a certain degree of disbelief. *We did it,* I think to myself. *I did it. I can't believe it!* I send off an elated text to Kobi, telling him and thanking him for his role. He responds immediately with slew of icons expressing the absolute magnitude of the moment – balloons, flowers, smiley faces and blaring trumpets. This is a very unexpected and welcome outcome.

I dial Adam's number. "Hi," I say. "I have some exciting news to share. I would like to come over; is that OK?"

"Fantastic timing," says Adam. "Come on over." I grab my bag and head out, yelling goodbye to the Nesters and volunteers as I shut the door behind me.

On Wednesday morning, I come into the Nest with a sense of restlessness. The graduation is ready. The Nesters and volunteers are excited. The activities are all aligned and prepared. There is nothing left to do, nothing more to organize, or manage, or arrange.

My discussion with Adam the afternoon before went really well. I told him with excitement about Noa and my meeting with her parents. We spoke about the pending graduation ceremony. I told him openly and candidly about my decision to leave the Nest along with the graduating class. For the first time in a very long while, I had absolute clarity about where I want to be and what I want to be doing.

On the other hand, still no sign of Mattie. Without a hint of elation lingering from our kiss, I feel deflated and depressed. "Don't worry, honey," says Iris when we catch up that morning. "I know he has been busy," she encourages me. "You focus on the graduation ceremony and all the work-related stuff, and in a few weeks' time we will all have a bang-up birthday celebration for you."

"What terrible creatures of habit we are," I tell her. But even I am looking forward to the annual barbecue at Dana and Aviva's, celebrating my birthday.

Just before noon, Dana calls me. "Hi Tammy," she says. "You haven't forgotten about Friday night, right? We are expecting you."

"Of course," I say. "Can I bring anything? How about some of the dried fruit that Aviva likes, and some nuts?"

"That would be perfect," says Dana. "Is everything sorted out now?"

"What do you mean? With whom?" I ask her nervously, thinking to myself that I have so much to tell her.

"Is everything OK with Kobi and with the graduation?" she asks, and then, as if she is reading, my mind she continues: "Why? Is there something else that I should know about?"

I smile. "We'll talk tonight. See you soon."

An hour later, I call Karina to find out how she is feeling. "Pretty exhausted," she says, "but everything is looking good, and the doctors are happy. So I am happy. What about you?" she asks. "How are you doing?"

"OK," I say.

"You seemed happy on Saturday, cheered up."

"I was," I say, "I guess . . ." my voice trails off.

"And now, you aren't anymore?"

"Just busy," I say. "You know; graduation is next week."

"Of course! Fantastic. I can't believe it is that time of year again. It seems like just yesterday that you were planning the graduation ceremony in the Old City of Jerusalem."

"Actually, that was two years ago," I say with a smile.

"I can't keep up with you," says Karina. "Listen, do you want to come over on Friday night? We've also invited Mattie and Orit." I register her words quietly, and say as evenly as I can, "No thanks. I promised to go over to Dana and Aviva's. Listen, I've got to go. Something has just come up."

"OK," says Karina cheerily. "See you," and she hangs up. I close my eyes and wring my head between my hands. *So that's that. He has chosen her. Now it's definitely over.*

Two hours pass with unproductive sitting and shifting papers around. Suddenly I feel the urgent buzz of my phone. I pick it up. It's a text message from Mattie.

    Can we meet?

I consider not replying. What's the point? I know the bottom line already. But my fingers act faster than my brain.

    OK

I reply.

    Tonight - 10:00 @Blooms?

Mattie writes.

    Not Blooms, @Terry's

I respond. I can't handle a meat market tonight, especially not in anticipation of what's coming. I need a place that settles me.

Mattie sends me a thumbs up icon.

I send Iris a text message:
    It's over. He wants Orit

Then I shut my phone off altogether, for the first time in months and slip it into my bag. I gather my things and walk home in a daze.

Later that night, I head out to Terry's. The warm, aged red leather interiors and the brass fixtures are a soothing sight. In the room, there is a low hum of people enjoying the quiet of a late Wednesday evening. I look for a free booth, and am surprised to see Mattie already waiting for me in the booth nearest the bar. I walk over and sit opposite him.

"I ordered you some red wine," he says.

"Thanks," I say.

"If that's not OK, we can order something else."

"It's fine," I say. "It's what I would have ordered myself." *Of course he would know what I like*, I think to myself. I sit in the booth, considering my own position and Mattie's obvious discomfort. *Perhaps I should put him out of his misery*, I think, as we both sip our drinks in silence. *He looks like he is about to cry.* The silence feels awkward and miserable. I push my wine aside.

"Remember when we could sit together quietly and it didn't feel like hell?" I blurt out. Mattie makes a feeble smile.

"I am sorry," he says, "I don't know where to begin."

"They say it is always best to start at the very beginning," I answer him.

"I can't start at the beginning," he says. "We have known each other for so long, and I have had feelings for you for almost as long as that."

"Then begin at the end," I say. "You know where I stand. You know what I want. I was the first to say it aloud. You may have wanted it, but you never told me."

"I was stupid," he says. "I don't know why I was so stupid. I kept on thinking that you would wake up and realize."

"I did," I interrupt him. "It has taken me time, but I have finally woken up and realized what I want." I put my hand on his. "Mattie, perhaps we have wasted time. Perhaps we could have figured it out earlier, perhaps it is late in the day, but it is not too late."

"Tammy," he says in a low gentle voice, looking at me straight in the eyes with a look that bespeaks a thousand emotions and leaves me with a sliver of hope and expectation. "Tammy," he says and his expression suddenly changes, "It is too late. I have waited for too long. We both need to move on and put this behind us." He gently withdraws his hand from beneath mine.

In that instant I have a mental flash forward of the dissent and strife associated with breakups of deep-rooted couples: awkward social gatherings with mutual friends, social circles split right down the middle, if we are lucky. Mattie was the one who helped me get through all of that when I divorced David. Who will be there for me now? So many mistakes have been made by both of us. So many feelings have been denied the right to be actualized. So much wasted time. I get up slowly. "Good bye, Mattie," I say, and walk quietly out of Terry's without so much as looking back. I know that I will never come back to this place again.

Chapter 26

Thursday and Friday pass in a quiet blur of work. I dismiss all phone calls from my friends with some text message or other:

```
-in a meeting

-can't talk now

-speak later
```

But I never call them back. I spend most of my time tying up loose ends. Between the basketball stadium and Joseph's community center, I catch up with Joseph, telling him the latest developments and discussing my decision to leave the Nest. We talk about his role in the graduation event both as honored guest, and as the newly appointed leader of our warm-up activity.

Back at the Nest, Kobi and I confer over the graduation activities. We also review the plans for the new group that will be joining the Nest in less than a month's time, at the start of the new school year. As needed, Adam joins us for our calls. This is our crunch time. I work through everything like an automaton, denying any place for thoughts about Mattie and our failed conversation at Terry's.

Without even comprehending the passing of time, it is already Friday evening. On my way out, I go into the market by my apartment and buy some dried fruit and nuts. I then hail a cab, and make my way to Dana and Aviva's.

Dinner is a relaxed family affair. If Dana and Aviva notice that I am more quiet than usual, they never say anything, or maybe they attribute it to my hard work for the graduation. After the meal is done and the kids have gone off to their respective activities and repose, the three of us go to sit in the Zen garden outside with some wine, dried fruits and nuts. We sit there quietly for a while, Dana and Aviva relaxing after a long week, and me summoning up the courage to share with my friends all that has been going on.

Aviva is the first to break the silence. "So I am hiring one of your Nesters," she says.

"Oh, my goodness," I say. "Of course, I heard. Her parents told me. Thanks so much. She is really such a terrific kid. Definitely one of our success stories this year."

"Is she the one whose parents were reluctant for her to go into the army?"

"Yes," I say, "but now everything is aligned, and she will be able to enlist in a few months' time. Thanks so much, Aviva."

"Are you kidding? It is getting harder and harder to find lab workers in this country. No one is learning vocational skills anymore. Everyone wants to be a doctor and no one wants to be a technician. To have her for the next two years gives me some quiet. I have decided to pilot this, and if it is successful, I may continue to do this kind of hiring. It is worth the training that we will invest. And she will get an education out of it, a career."

"Win-win" I say.

"That's fantastic," said Dana. "You must be thrilled at the way things have turned out this year. What are your plans for next year? Are you still having second thoughts about work or are you over it?"

"Actually, I have come to some major conclusions about my role in the Nest," I say, "and I want to tell you about it, but I guess that I would like to share something else first. Something that is harder for me to talk about."

"What's wrong?" asks Dana, with an alarmed tone. "Are you OK?"

"*Shhhh,*" says Aviva, putting her arm around Dana. "Let her tell us when she is ready." I take a deep breath and think to myself: *Start at the beginning.*

"You know that my friends are like family to me: you, Josh and Karina, Iris and Mattie." Dana and Aviva nod. Dana begins to say something, but Aviva stops her. "You have always been there for me, and it all began with the four of us – Josh, Mattie, me and you. Like you said, who knew that after all these years, we would still be in each other's lives." I stop talking and take a deep breath.

"We have been through schools, youth movements, army service, engagements, marriages, childbirth and divorces. In all this time, I have always felt loved, protected and supported." I stop talking and take another pause. "Over the past few months, I have gone through a crisis. I have felt down, depressed, and unable to pull myself out of the rut. Yet throughout this time, you have all been there for me. I have felt like it was raining on all sides: professionally, I was dissatisfied and personally, I felt stuck. The divorce affected me more than I had imagined it would. It made me feel worthless and unworthy of love, partnership and affection." Dana comes over and sits next to me and puts her arm around me without saying a word. "And then something quite amazing happened. Apart from the support that you all gave me, I began to see clearly what I wanted. I began to realize that all this time, the person who I want to be with is right in front of me. The person who understands me, and loves me for who I am and has always been there."

"Mattie," says Dana quietly. I nod miserably, tears streaming down my face.

"So I told him, and I kissed him, and he said he needed time," I say, crying for real now. "And, and then, he, he . . ."

"He turned you down," says Aviva. "Idiot."

"Shhhh," says Dana. "It will be OK."

"How will it be OK?" I ask. "I have lost him and his friendship, and now, none of us will ever be the same again."

"Shhhh," says Dana, stroking my arm. "You will be OK. We will all be OK." We stay there in the garden, under the starless black sky, until my crying subsides and the sound of the crickets takes over.

Chapter 27

Sunday comes sooner that I thought it would – the day of the graduation. I get up extra early, and go for a run on the beach, and then come home to shower. When I get out of the shower, I check my phone for the first time, and see that I have been inundated with messages:

From Dana:
```
Good luck today Tammy

We know it will be a huge success

Big hugs. We are so proud
```

From Karina:
```
Graduation!!!!

Have some fun and enjoy
```
and then like a sober afterthought, she adds:
```
When you are ready, let's talk
```

From Josh:
```
Tell us how it goes

We are rooting for you!
```

Then comes a bunch of icons: trophies and flowers and medals. *It is unusual for Josh to send a message;* I think to myself. Usually, Karina does the talking for both of them. *So they must know.* I wonder whether they have heard it from Iris, or Dana, or even from Mattie himself.

From Iris:
```
Darling, babe, sweetheart - good luck.

Call me soon. Onwards and upwards

CALL!!!! You hear me?!

Enough with this delicate flower crap
```

Nothing from Mattie, no surprise there. I don't allow myself to feel anything.

The graduation ceremony event is to begin at four thirty at Joseph's community center. Kobi and I and several volunteers get there at two o'clock to help set everything up. The sound system is already in order and one of our volunteers has already put some music on in the background. We work steadily and quickly to the sound of Middle Eastern pop music. The catering arrives at the same time we do. I take it upon myself to organize the food. One table has just drinks: hot and cold, as well as cinnamon sticks, mint leaves and lemon grass for flavor. Another table has basic finger foods. There is a plate of *burekas*, pastry pockets filled with savory delicacies: spinach, mushroom, cheese and potatoes. There are cut vegetables of all types, and various dips: hummus, tahini, pesto made from coriander and parsley, as well as *pilpelchumo*, a spicy Libyan dip made from sun-dried tomatoes, chilies and garlic – not for the fainthearted.

The last table holds the desserts. There are all sorts of fruits: cherries, watermelon, star fruit, prickly pear, dragon fruit and pitango, as well as an assortment of cakes and sweets, including a passionfruit mousse, cheese cake, brownies, lemon squares, almond biscuits and poppy seed muffins. Except for the tables of food located at the entrance to the hall, the rest of the space is divided between the bleachers and the court. All the guests will sit in the stands, with the Nesters and the sponsors in the first row. A parallel line of chairs has been set up in front, next to a wooden podium and a large screen, from which the presentations can be viewed.

I make my way to the podium to ensure that my presentation is up and working. I deposit all the graduation certificates onto the shelf of the podium, so that they will be easily accessible when the graduation ceremony begins. We work tirelessly and consistently. On the court, Joseph is getting ready for the warm-up activity, with his two dedicated helpers, Eran and Avi.

Adam arrives a few minutes after four. He, Kobi and I step aside and go to sit in Joseph's office to review the agenda, and to make last-minute changes to the presentation. As our discussion begins to draw to an end, Adam says: "I want to thank you both. This has been a challenging year and our results are phenomenal. I know that you have worked hard, and with great dedication. And I know it hasn't always been easy." Kobi and I look at each other and nod. "But the results speak for themselves and I know that you both have put all of your energy into helping each and every one of the graduating Nesters. In a few minutes, I will thank you both publically, but for now, I want to thank you personally and from the bottom of my heart."

"Thanks, Adam," I say.

"Thanks so much," says Kobi.

"I just want to add," I say, "that I really appreciate your guidance and support." I take a deep breath and continue. "On a personal level, this has been a difficult year for me, and I want to say that I do not take it for granted that you have had my back every step of the way. Both of you. Even with our differences in opinion. And I look forward to a new year with new challenges for us all." I look at Kobi, who nods and smiles.

"OK," says Adam, "time to begin, let's go!" I turn to walk away, but Adam catches me by the arm. "Wait a second," he says to me. "We'll catch up in a second," he calls out to Kobi, who continues walking out of the office and back into the hall.

"Are you sure that you are ready to leave us?" he asks.

"This is it, the point of no return!" I nod my head.

"I am not sure about many things," I say, "but of this I am sure. I am ready." Adam gives me a hug. "Good luck," he says. "Let's do it." We walk together back into the hall.

At five o' clock, after everyone has had a chance to inter-mingle and eat, I finally open the event, a half an hour later than scheduled. After welcoming and introducing all of our special guests and thanking each one of our sponsors by name, I call Joseph up to introduce the warm-up activity. The idea of the activity is to showcase the teamwork of the Nesters and to give them an opportunity to take center stage. In graduation events of the past, the activity was the lion's share of the event, but this year, the most significant activity will be to shoot hoops in the stadium with the professional basketball players.

Joseph begins the warm-up activities by calling the Nesters to the court. After they come up, excited and full of energy, he begins to shout instructions to the group. As he starts the activity, I notice a familiar flash of red from the corner of my eye. I turn around to look, and in comes Dana, blowing kisses in my direction. I smile and gesture to her to join the crowd on the bleachers. She takes her place in the second row with a lot of the parents . . . those who could make it. I see Eli and Nava, Noa's parents. I see Rita, Eran's mom. Behind them sit many of the volunteers and tutors, Miriam and Avi among them. Miriam catches my eye and waves. I wave back.

Joseph begins to work the group of Nesters: "If you love vanilla ice cream, go to the left. If you prefer chocolate ice cream, go to the right. If you just *like* ice cream, come to the middle ..." The groups sort themselves out in a frenzy of action.

"Next question," Joseph continues: "If you love television, go to the left. If you prefer movies, go the right. If you prefer to read, come to the middle . . ." The groups unscramble and reassemble according to their preferences.

"Next scenario," says Joseph: "Favorite pastime: A day at the beach, to the left. Doing something active, like sport, to the right. Going to a restaurant, to the middle . . ." Once more, the Nesters realign themselves.

"Now," says Joseph, "in your groups, left, right and center, I am going to give you all special instructions. Are you ready?"

The groups yell in affirmation. "Group on the right, bring people with grey hair from the audience to your group. Group on the left, find people with jewelry and bring them to your group. Group in the center, find people who were born in the first half of the year, and bring them to your group." A mad scramble begins as the groups begin to vie for audience members who will join them. Slowly the floor begins to fill with parents, tutors, volunteers and sponsors.

"Now," says Joseph, "gather the remaining audience members and bring them to the floor. Group on the right, find someone who can name three current members of the Knesset. On the left, find someone who can name three authors. And finally, in the middle, find someone who can name three chefs." By the time this round is complete, no one is left in the bleachers. There also aren't really three groups anymore, just a buzzing hive of action and activity.

"Now," says Joseph, "we are about to get very specific, so listen carefully. All Nesters: introduce yourselves to at least two people whom you didn't know previously and tell them why you are here today and what you hope to do in the future." After about eight minutes or so, Joseph continues, "All volunteers, introduce yourselves to at least two people whom you didn't know previously and tell them what you do at the Nest and why." And, finally, Joseph says: "All parents and family members, find at least two Nesters – one of them can be your child – and tell them why you are so proud of them."

By the time the activity is over, the floor is awash with emotion, pride and more than a tear or too. Joseph reaches one last time for the microphone and says, simply, "Thanks everyone, thanks for allowing me to be a special part of this day." A round of applause follows. "Thanks to all the Nest management and volunteers and a special thanks to Tamara, who has made this all possible with her love." The people on the floor cheer and slowly begin making their way back to their seats. As they shuffle back, I head to the microphone to thank Joseph, but am cut short by Eran and Avi. "Before you continue, Tamara," Avi says, taking the microphone, "Eran and I would like to say a few words on behalf of the Nesters and the volunteers." I take my seat and let them continue.

"My name is Avi and I am a volunteer at the Nest. I came to the Nest at the beginning of the year because I wanted to help. Volunteering work is good for the curriculum and something that I have been educated by my parents to do." He looks out into the audience to a couple whom I have never met. I guess they are his parents. He smiles and continues. "I came in week-by-week, pouring knowledge like a water jug, and when I was done pouring, I left. And then, one day, after an incident that shook me, I almost left, gave up, went home. I almost decided that too much was expected of me – little old me, just a jug of knowledge." He takes a breath and continues. "With Tamara's encouragement, I decided to stay, and little by little, I learned that the Nesters here can teach me too: real lessons, life lessons. They can water me with their experiences, their pains, their passions. And now, I can say for sure that I am the one who has grown the most. So a big thanks from me on behalf of all the volunteers." The audience claps. Avi and Eran hug and then Avi hands the microphone to his friend.

Eran begins slowly and nervously. "My name is Eran and I am a graduating Nester. I never imagined that I would be up here, holding this thing," he says, gesturing to the microphone. "But the Nest has been a place for me that has defied my imagination. In the past year alone, I have needed to face many challenges and also to learn so much about myself: my limitations and my strengths, my fears and my wishes for myself." He pauses for a few seconds and then continues. "I almost screwed it all up, threw it all away. If it weren't for the support of the Nest – Tamara and the other staff members, volunteers like Avi and special people like Joseph – I probably would have quit." He laughs a gentle laugh. "But no one would let me. No one would let me fall.

And if I did fall, no one would let me stay down. I came here an angry and frustrated boy. But I am leaving with a clear mind, a conscience and a capacity for friendship. Who knew? Thank you so much, from the bottom of my heart."

I get up, tears in my eyes, and hug both boys, who have come so far and who have meant so much to me. I can see Rita, Eran's mother, sitting next to the couple that I now can identify as Avi's parents. It briefly occurs to me how the circles of influence of the Nest are like outstretched arms embracing all those in its reach. I thank the boys and Joseph, and begin to deliver the presentation of *The Nest – a Year in Review,* which includes a brief glimpse into the year ahead. After it is done, I call Adam to speak. He gets up slowly and comes to the podium with quiet confidence. He looks at me, and says quietly, "This is it Tamara, time for the big announcement. Are you ready?" and I nod and smile at him.

Adam takes the microphone and begins to talk: "I was brought up in the streets of Southern Tel Aviv. My father died at an early age. My mother did what she could to keep me out of trouble. It wasn't easy. I was a restless, uninspired youth. The temptations of the street were great. My mother, like most single moms, worked very hard and was often absent from home. Because I loved my mother, I did my best to stay out of trouble – not always succeeding, mind you. I did what I could to support the family, including doing all kinds of odd jobs. One such job brought me to the door of an elderly lady. She had trouble getting around, and would call down to the corner store for some basic supplies: butter, flour, oil, and I would be given a few shekels to deliver the goods to her door.

One day, I came up to her apartment and the door was slightly ajar. I knocked and went in. She was sitting at a little table in the kitchen waiting for me. "I left the door open for you," she said. "I opened it this morning when I heard the newspaper being delivered and I left it open, so that I wouldn't need to get up twice. My legs are ailing me today."

I wondered to myself for how many hours the door had

been left open and to what extent she must be in pain in order to have to avoid getting up more than once. Out of nowhere, I asked her, "Is there something that I can do to help you before I go?" To which she answered, "Will you read to me a bit?" I nodded, and picked up the morning newspaper. In the end, I read that paper to her from start to finish. We would stop reading occasionally in order to discuss the general state of affairs in the country and the world.

After I left in the early evening, I told her that I would be back the next day. And I was. I came back the next day, and the next, and the next. The following week, we began to read Dostoevsky and – like anyone who has read Dostoevsky knows – by then I knew I was in it for the long haul." The audience laughs generously. "As it turns out, that lady used to be a teacher, and before I knew it, we would divide our time between newspapers, literature and my homework. She helped me throughout the rest of my schooling. I would continue to do odd jobs for her and for others, but when they were done, I would come to her, and we would work and read together. Her home became my home away from home – my nest – for the hours in which my own mother was absent and couldn't take care of me. From that moment, I decided that if I could, one day, I would build a Nest for children like me and that is what I have done."

The audience applauds. "I am so proud and happy to be here today. Thanks to Tamara's leadership, we have had an excellent year with terrific results. Tamara, Kobi and all the other staff members and volunteers have made me proud and the Nest continues to grow and strive towards bigger and better things.

I want to thank all of our donors and sponsors, who believe in us. Hopefully, you have seen today how important your investment has been. As for the parents, I have no words to express my gratitude for entrusting us with your most precious children, and for allowing us to grow with them and learn with them. There is a Talmudic saying that says "To help someone in need, you should not give them a fish, but teach them how to fish." Teach them to do things themselves, to be independent, strong, mindful. That is what we try to do here in the Nest."

The audience applauds even more strongly. Adam continues: "In order to achieve what we have achieved, we have not compromised on our leadership and this brings me to the last order of the day before we hand out the certificates to our graduates. Just one minute before we all get on the buses and go to play basketball, I would like to ask Tamara to please come up." I get up and walk over to Adam. "Tamara has been with me from the very beginning of the Nest. She has grown it from a conceptual inkling in my imagination to the well-oiled machine it is today. She has handpicked every new Nester group, the staff and the volunteers, at times by herself, and more recently with the strong support of Kobi. She runs a tight ship, including logistics, inventory, fund raising, as well as being available 24:7 to me, to the staff, volunteers, and it goes without saying, to all of the Nesters. So believe me when I say that she has been an indispensable part of the Nest and its success." The audience claps generously, and the Nesters whistle and whoop in support. Adam continues: "Therefore, it is with some sorrow and immense pride that today, we have decided to share the news that Tamara will be leaving us, finally leaving the Nest."

There is a gasp of disbelief in the room. I catch Dana's eyes, which are wide open and filled with astonishment. "Tamara has decided that in order to create an even greater impact on society, she would like to take some time to do a master's degree in psychology, with the hope that she can open a practice geared to working with individuals who need her.

We are so proud of her, and we wish her luck on her way. The Nest is so lucky to have had her with us up till now, and we are also lucky to have a wonderful replacement - Kobi - who brings with him much experience and a real passion for the job. We feel that this transition will be smooth and easy. So Tamara, we thank you so much and love you very much. And I would like to ask you to please close this wonderful event."

Kobi comes up to me and hands me a bouquet of flowers, and gives me a peck on the cheek. "Thanks Tamara," he says, "I really mean it." Adam gives me a big hug and whispers

"I am so proud of you . . ." and they both step back and hand me the microphone.

I begin: "Over the years, I have learned that most of us simply want to belong. We want to feel understood, and to feel like someone knows us, is thinking of us, loves us. We all have moments in which we feel alone, feel different, feel misunderstood. We all have times in which we don't know what to do, or don't know how to move forward, and the feeling of being stuck seems to be eternal. For me, the Nest was about creating a place where loneliness wasn't checked at the door; it was accepted and understood and worked upon. Where frustration wasn't banned or scoffed; it was accepted, understood and resolved. Where your background obstacles – financial, personal, or other – were not held against you, but were accepted, understood and leveraged as a milestone to growth. It is OK to be lonely. It is OK to be frustrated. It is OK to have real obstacles. In the Nest, we don't deny them; we work through them together. It has been a great privilege for me to work with all of you. I too have loneliness, frustration and obstacles, and each one of you – Adam, Kobi, volunteers, parents and dear Nesters – have contributed to helping me work through my issues. My decision to leave has not been an easy one, because for me, like for you, – the Nest has been my home and my comfort zone. And mostly, I believe in what we are doing. And so, to all of you – but especially to you, Kobi – I would like to place my name on the list of volunteers. I cannot teach Dostoevsky, like Adam here, but I am sure that there are some other things that I can do to contribute." The audience claps and laughs. "And now . . . without further ado . . . the time has come to graduate and to get on those buses. The basketball game will not wait for us . . ." The audience breaks into a rowdy applause. The Nesters cheer.

Adam comes up and together we call the names of each of

the volunteers who will receive certificates of honor. Then we call upon the Nesters, who come up to proudly accept their graduation certificates. There is lots of hugging and mutual congratulations. As each Nester gets his or her certificate, they leave the hall in excitement and board the bus to the game. Adam leaves with the sponsors. Kobi follows soon after with some of the parents and volunteers. The room has emptied out significantly, and some of the community center workers began to come in to clean up and to get things out of the way.

"How are you feeling?" asks Joseph.

"I feel exhausted, but relieved," I tell him.

"I think you are amazing," he says. "You made a decision. Not an easy one, but you did it." "Thanks to you," I say. "Your mother was right to give you the middle name Awesome. I couldn't have done it without you. Not reaching a decision, maybe not even getting through all the issues that I have faced this year, particularly with Eran and Avi."

"Actually, my middle name is Edward."

"Edward . . . I must admit, that I am a little disappointed."

"Tell me about it." Joseph laughs. "I was happy to help wherever I could, but your understanding of what the boys needed, your sensitivity to them . . . that was all you. You did it."

"I suppose I did." I say.

"Anyway, I am getting on the bus now; are you coming?"

"Yes, I will be there soon. I just need a minute."

"OK. I will save you a seat."

"Please!" Joseph walks away, and I walk towards Dana, who is sitting and waiting for me in the front row. She gets up when she sees me coming. "I am so proud of you," she says, "I could cry. I was already crying. But I will cry again."

I laugh. "You don't have to cry for me," I say. "Thanks so much for coming. It means so much to me."

"Are you kidding, I didn't want to miss this. And I had no idea that it would be your last appearance here."

"Yes, we were so busy talking about other things that I

didn't get to telling you. But I am happy with the decision and I have already enrolled in studies."

"I can't believe that you are going back to school. How awesome is that?"

"I know, and who knows – maybe the other parts of my life will also just sort themselves out. I can hope, can't I?" We hug and then I say, "I've got to go. The buses are leaving soon. Do you want to come with us?"

"No," Dana says, "I am going to go home. Tell me all about it . . . I can't wait to hear."

"OK," I say, "wait – keep these for me please." I hand her the bouquet of flowers that Kobi gave me. "I love you," I say. "I've got to go." We walk out of the hall together, she goes to her car, and I board the bus as it is about to leave the community center.

Chapter 28

The next few weeks pass by in a blurry haze of busy-ness and detachment. Between studying for the academic units that I need to complete before my Masters can begin, and doing handovers with Kobi and the other staff members at the Nest, my days are extremely full. I am up and about from the very early hours of the morning: jogging or swimming on the beach, and I am still burning the midnight oil in the very late hours of the night. It is during this time that I revisit the student's life and cram for hour after hour, trying to digest the material of entire semesters in preparation for the four examinations that I need to pass. My days are both long and short at the same time, with little opportunity to think too much about personal failures and regrets.

When I am not doing all of that, I spend time with some of the others: Dana, Aviva and the kids look after me, making sure that I eat and drink and have some company, particularly on Friday night, when my energy is spent and all I need is the gentle buzz of family sounds.

Joseph and I meet periodically to discuss my academic plans. He helps me study and introduces me to the theory and research of some of the more influential and modern psychologists and thought leaders in the field. I spend many hours cramming with him, in his and his girlfriend's little apartment in the Florentine neighborhood of Tel Aviv.

Karina and I meet at the shopping mall, our new *go to* place. We walk around: she shops and I window shop . . . such is the life of an unemployed student.

Iris and I occasionally meet at some bar. Every time I meet her, she has a new proposition, a new excellent man for me to meet. Sometimes, I agree to meet him and sometimes I don't. My decision-making is purely random. Trivialization is my only defense mechanism. When the bartender gives me my drink and if there are two olives in it, I allow Iris to give out my number. However, if the next person to come into the bar is a man, I do not. Iris – because it is Iris – is more amused than frustrated with me. Maybe, because even with all my shenanigans, she does manage sometimes to set me up. I go out with an accountant with too many cats. I go out with a software executive with too many gadgets. I go out with a fitness instructor who smells of coconut oil. I go out with an Arabic teacher, who is *nice*. We even go out more than once. But I call it off. I don't have the energy to invest in turning *"nice"* into *"the one for me"*. Besides which – if I am being honest – he isn't Mattie. Not that I am pining for him – far from it. I have basically accepted the situation for what it is: another issue to work through and resolve. But not now. I can only think about that later. I will begin to heal later. For now, I am focusing on my studies. I avoid all talk about Mattie with the others. I do not ask about him and do not dwell on what might have been had he chosen me instead of Orit. Frankly, I am so busy studying that I am too busy to attend any mutual gatherings that arise. My friends sometimes try to drop his name casually into the conversation, to dangle it like bait, but I always turn away. It is simply too painful.

By the time September rolls around, I have completed all of my pre-Masters requirements and I am enrolled as a student, two and a half days a week. I have completed all of my responsibilities and handovers in the Nest. Now, I will only be there once a week to volunteer. I have given myself the rest of September to settle into studies and a regular routine. In October, I will look for some freelance work for the remaining days.

Like every year, my birthday falls around the time of *Rosh Hashana* – the Jewish New Year. For the Orthodox among us, this is a time of contemplation and prayer; for me and my friends, this means a birthday barbecue at Dana and Aviva's.

At ten o'clock in the morning, the taxi drops me off outside Aviva and Dana's beautiful home. The front door is slightly ajar so I let myself in. From the lounge, I can see out into the garden. There are six kids of all ages romping around. Even Iris's daughter, Roni, has come this time. She is the spitting image of her mom and just as loud. Karina is sitting with Dana and Iris on a soft blanket that has been spread out on the grass of their home underneath a massive oak tree. Her pregnant stomach is now sticking out boldly for all to see. Ben, the baby, is speed crawling on the blanket, grabbing for the colorful soft toys that have been left lying about.

Aviva and Josh are at the grill, flipping burgers, kebabs and steaks, as well as tofu burgers and grilled mushrooms for Dana. I can hear them marveling over some gadget or sauce or condiment. It is, objectively, such a beautiful day. The sky is clear blue and there isn't a cloud to be seen. But I am unsettled and uneasy. I feel reluctant to join the familiar crowd of revelers. I don't feel like stretching out on the blanket. I don't feel like standing over the grill. I don't feel like joining the messy train of kids running around with boundless energy.

Mattie is nowhere to be seen. At least that. One less thing to feel nervous about. I drop my bag on the couch and let myself back out the front door. I begin to make my way down the small path that leads to the secluded Zen garden. I need just a few minutes to recharge. *That's all I need*, I think to myself. *And then I will join the others*. I get to the garden and lay myself down on the swing chair, and rock myself backwards and forwards and forwards and backwards, over and over again.

I am woken up by the sound of voices. Many of them.
"I told you she was here," says Dana.
"No, you told me you saw her bag," says Aviva.
"Is she sleeping?" asks Josh.
"Not anymore," says Karina.
"All work and no play, makes Tamara a dull girl," says Iris, as she gently places her hand on my shoulder. I move and

stretch. "Sorry you guys, I just needed a few minutes for myself and then I guess I must have dozed off."

"Dozed off? More like a drug-induced coma. I wanted to check to see if you were breathing," says Dana.

"Well, I am fine," I say. "Too much studying is all. You see, I am OK," and I sit up.

"Well, if you are fine," continues Iris, "I have found quite a man for you. Actually, it's my nephew, Oren."

"Your nephew? Of Superman fame? How old is he now anyway Iris, nineteen?"

"Actually he's twenty-one."

"Oh Iris, come on. He's a baby."

"Yes, he is. I think he can benefit from a woman of the world like yourself. And besides which, if it all works out, then you will have to call me Auntie Iris." I laugh despite myself.

"Leave me alone, Iris." I groan.

"Yes," says Karina, "that's really too much. It is practically cradle snatching. Besides which, Tamara can find someone herself, and if she really wants, there's this guy from Josh's work. Just last week we were thinking that we should set them up."

"He's a really nice guy," says Josh. "I am sure you would like him."

I can feel the panic begin to rise in my chest. You must be kidding me. Is this what my birthday barbecue is going to be like? "Really, you guys," I say, "this is too much for me. I think I will just go home."

"No, don't go, don't go," says Dana. "Of course those are all bad ideas. Tamara is more than capable of getting what she wants by herself. These imbeciles are all kidding of course. Enough with the matchmaking jokes," Dana says in a scolding voice. "Take a few minutes for yourself and then come and join us. We have to go and make sure that the kids haven't burned down the house."

"Good idea," says Karina.

"So what if they do?" asks Iris. "You will just build another one."

"Thanks very much, Iris", says Aviva.

"What's insurance like on this place anyway?" asks Josh.

Dammit – I think to myself – *Why can't it be like when we were kids?* I know the answer to that of course: because we are not kids and things don't just work out like they did way back then.

"Tamara." I hear my name. I turn around. The others also turn to see. It's Mattie. He comes up from behind the others. "Sorry I am late," he says to Dana and gives her a peck on the cheek. She catches his hand and squeezes it. The others gather back around us.

"Tamara, I have a really nice guy for you," says Mattie taking a step forward.

"Please Mattie, just *don't* . . ." I say, holding my hand out like a stop sign.

"Just hear me out, OK?" he asks. "True, this guy is a bit of an idiot, but that's not his fault. It turns out that he has momentously bad timing and has unrealistic expectations of people around him being able to read minds." He takes another step forward.

"Mattie . . . I . . ." I begin to say.

"Let me continue. He has loved you from third grade and has never once asked you out. He watched you get married and never tried to stop you. He watched you get a divorce and thought it better to wait. He watched you go out with other men and sat idly by, even though inside, he was so jealous that he wanted to scream. He loves that you drink tea with ginger and lemon, and that you rarely touch coffee. He loves that you are direct with people. He loves that you need your space and your privacy. He loves that you love your friends and that you care for them so much. He let you kiss him and it was the greatest kiss ever, and then he let you go. Tamara, I am so sorry. I have really messed this up." He sits himself down on his knees opposite the swing chair. "I am sorry that I am such an idiot, but, if you let me, I want to be the man you belong with, the one who belongs with you. I am the one who loves you – all your angles and edges. I am the one who has always loved you. If you will have me, we can build the place where we belong, together.

I lean forward in the swing chair, tears slowly begin to fall down my cheeks. I stretch out my hand and gently move his hair away from his eyes. His beautiful eyes. He looks at me, not daring to move or to touch me, just waiting. I move in closely towards him and kiss him gently on the lips. He pulls me towards him and we both stand up, wrapped in each other's arms, tightly bound together, all angles and edges enveloped in a never-ending circle.

Epilogue

It would be remiss of me not to tell you where I am, what I am doing, and who I am doing it with. But I am not going to. Some things change, but my angles and edges have stayed sharply and resolutely in place. It's not that I don't want to share. It is just that I don't want finality: I don't want to close this chapter of my life and declare that all is said and done, because that is never the case. I don't really believe in endings. Things are never really through, done, finished, and hermetically sealed.

I believe that whatever we do, whoever we meet, whomever we touch stays with us, like an invisible fingerprint on the soul. Sometimes that fingerprint triggers a memory, a reaction, an instinct. Sometimes that fingerprint unlocks a door of endless beginnings:

A fingerprint of being bullied becomes a source of comfort.

A fingerprint of injustice turns into a lifetime of doing what's right.

A fingerprint of brokenness turns into a need to fix things.

A fingerprint of alienation turns into an intricate tapestry of belonging.

A fingerprint of a childhood friend evolves into a story of love, passion and acceptance.

So I leave you with my hands wide open: ready to receive, ready to be welcomed, ready to leave a fingerprint on your soul.

Acknowledgements

Many thanks to my family who are my first readers, biggest critics and greatest source of support: my husband Alessandro, my parents, Solly and Arleen, my sisters, Tali and Carmi and my brothers-in-law, Daniel and Jeremy. I appreciate your partnership in my journey.

To Merav Shelkowitz, who rightfully challenged the authenticity of my voice, and questioned the ending that I envisioned. It is to you that I owe the epiphany that there are no endings unless you want there to be.

To Martine Maron Alperstein, who became an early reader quite by chance, your response to my manuscript was like a gift greater than gold.

To Judy Kestecher, my friend and editor, for keeping me honest to myself.

Not least of all a big thanks to Liron Shapira, who introduced me to the association: *'Gesher El HaNoar'* (**www.gehserelhanoar.org.il**) and the wonderful work they do helping youth who are at high risk of dropping

out to find their place in the Israeli society. 'The Nest' in this story is inspired by this association and the wonderful work that the staff and volunteers do. I wish you all much continued success.

A Personal Message

Dear Reader,

Thanks so much for taking the time to read this book. I am very appreciative of your support. Please consider writing a review and keeping in touch. You can find me at:

Amazon – amazon.com/author/rkmayer
goodreads – https://www.goodreads.com/RKMayer
My website – https://www.rkmayer.com

Yours,
R. K. Mayer